DARKEST BEFORE THE DAWN

THE SECOND DARK AGES, BOOK 3

ELL LEIGH CLARKE
MICHAEL ANDERLE

DARKEST BEFORE THE DAWN (this book) is a work of fiction.

All of the characters, organizations, and events portrayed in this novel are either products of the author's imagination or are used fictitiously. Sometimes both.

Copyright © 2017 Michael T. Anderle and Ell Leigh Clarke
Cover copyright © LMBPN Publishing

LMBPN Publishing supports the right to free expression and the value of copyright. The purpose of copyright is to encourage writers and artists to produce the creative works that enrich our culture.

The distribution of this book without permission is a theft of the author's intellectual property. If you would like permission to use material from the book (other than for review purposes), please contact info@kurtherianbooks.com. Thank you for your support of the author's rights.

LMBPN Publishing
PMB 196, 2540 South Maryland Pkwy
Las Vegas, NV 89109

First US edition, October 2017
Version 1.02, October 2017

The Kurtherian Gambit (and what happens within / characters / situations / worlds) are copyright © 2017 by Michael T. Anderle.

DARKEST BEFORE THE DAWN TEAM

Beta Editor / Readers
Bree Buras (Aussie Awesomeness)
Tom Dickerson (The man)
S Forbes (oh yeah!)
Dorene Johnson (US Navy (Ret) & DD)
Dorothy Lloyd (Teach you to ask...Teacher!)
Diane Velasquez (Chinchilla lady & DD)

JIT Beta Readers
Erika Daly
James Caplan
Joshua Ahles
Keith Verret
Kelly ODonnell
Kimberly Boyer
Micky Cocker
Mike Pendergrass
Paul Westman
Peter Manis
Sherry Foster

*If we missed anyone, **please** let us know!*

Editors
Stephen Russell
Lynn Stiegler

*To Family, Friends and
Those Who Love
To Read.
May We All Enjoy Grace
To Live The Life We Are
Called.*

PROLOGUE

The dream was quick, it flitted through his conscious as he slept in a new bed. His mind wandered through a mist, a gray mist seeking his love.

What he had instead was pain.

He survived the pain to leave the mist, falling from nothing to a mountain in the middle of the old United States of America.

He traveled through the states, picking up Jacqueline, the daughter of an old acquaintance and a young male vampire he saved in the City-State of New York.

Traveling across the Atlantic in a blimp, the trio survived attacks by Pirates. There, they met Sabine who had been running from cannibalistic Were's through the night. Finally, they and other friends fought off massive packs of Were's in the old country of France.

Yuko, Eve, Mark and Jacqueline went back to Japan – helping the local police fend off an attack while Michael and Akio escaped an effort by the Duke to kill them under the remains of Notre Dame.

Now, Michael is focused on finding and killing William hopefully in the most painful way possible.

1

Frankfurt, Germany

Captain Miles O'Banion nodded to the agent and accepted the documents that allowed him to moor his ship to the large tower. The Antigrav Ship *Michael the ArchAngel Returns* was a solid vessel, and he was damned pleased to be able to keep her.

Looking around the offices, he had to admit the Germans had pulled together after the WWDE. They had worked to restore their city, and now they had moved it into the future as well.

He was a bit jealous.

Captain O'Banion left the large stone building which had been built hundreds of years before WWDE, and he squinted when the sunlight hit his eyes. The last few rays slowly disappeared as the sun sank below the buildings across the square.

He turned right and started walking. His crew was enjoying a bit of a night on the town. They had made it through the weather, a day-walking vampire, a vampire that had been a legend before the real legend had shown up, and now they knew there was a job for them in a couple of days. He had been able to procure cargo to take with them to England.

Life, he thought to himself, *was finally looking up.* There were no Nosferatu in his hold, no Forsaken around his ship, and—so far—no Duke around the corner ready to rip his entrails out of his body and shove them into his mouth.

Those rather grim thoughts kept his mind occupied until he spied the name of the bar that had been suggested to him earlier.

The two old oak doors were stained so dark a brown that they looked black. He grasped the copper handle and pulled the right door open, then stepped into the decently lit bar. There were at least fifteen tables in the middle of the floor, about eight obligatory personal booths for more private conversations on the wall to his left, and the holiest of holies—the fifteen-foot-long bar with its ten stools. Only two were occupied.

Captain O'Banion walked over to it, nodding to the barkeep as he grabbed a stool and sat. "Rye, if you have it."

The tall barkeeper nodded and turned to the shelves to take down a bottle of liquid whose unique brown color came from aging in wooden casks. He grabbed a clean drinking glass, walked over to Captain O'Banion, and set the glass down. Placing the neck of the bottle on the edge, he asked "Half or full?"

"Better give me half." Captain O'Banion sighed, then chuckled as he reached for the glass. "I don't have to be anywhere, but if a call comes in, I can't be worrying about slurring my orders." He lifted the half-filled glass to the barkeeper, who grabbed the change the captain had laid on the bar. "To living beyond our wildest hopes."

The barkeeper raised an eyebrow, taking in the man in front of him. The captain certainly wasn't well dressed, so he wasn't speaking about money. "Rough time?" he asked. The captain sipped his rye and nodded. "Weather or pirates?"

The captain put out the pinky on the hand holding the glass. "*Very* bad weather," he told the barkeeper, and then put out the finger next to his pinky, holding the glass with his thumb and first two fingers. "Pirates," he added a finger, and the barkeeper frowned. "And vampires."

He took a sip of the rye, then realized he couldn't release any more fingers without dropping his glass as he completed enumerating his challenges. "Oh, and Weres. It was damned scary."

The barkeeper looked down the bar to the two guys drinking and talking before throwing a rag on the bar in front of Captain O'Banion. "Vampires?"

The captain nodded.

"You from the *Michael the ArchAngel Returns*?" he asked, his voice low—damned near a whisper. The captain nodded once more. "I heard someone in here last night with the latest news of what ships were arriving. Said your ship was one of those that went west across the Atlantic for the Duke?"

Captain O'Banion grimaced. He hadn't chosen to be a captain for the Duke, but life was like that. One minute you were minding your own business, the next they shanghaied your ass, placed Nosferatu in your hold, added some vampires to keep them in line, threatened to kill you if you disobey orders, and shipped you to America. "I am the *captain* of the *Michael the ArchAngel Returns*."

"You interested in making some money?" the barman asked. O'Banion eyed him, and the bartender shook his head and put up two hands. "It isn't illegal. Some people wanted confirmation on the name of your ship." He looked around the bar, keeping his voice low. "There is a lot of speculation. The people," he pointed to the captain and then back to himself, "who can confirm the information without any doubt will get a nice payday."

"Oh." The captain tossed his drink back and then lowered the glass, dropping it on the bar. It made a solid *whump* when it hit. "I can do that."

"Word is out that there are some people who want to know if that ship belongs to a vampire."

"It did, and it still does, sort of." Captain O'Banion temporized, "Truth is, it belonged to the Duke. Another vampire named Michael took it over, had me change the name, and gave it to me so long as I stopped here first."

The barkeeper's eyes gleamed in delight. "Michael? He said his name was *Michael?*"

The captain nodded. "Since we are sharing information, what is the amount?" he asked the barkeep.

"Over three hundred for quality information, four hundred if you can give them assurance, and a thousand for solid proof." He picked up the glass and placed it on a tray under the bar. The glass clinked against some other dirty glasses down there. "That's why I'm willing to share. Half of a thousand is more than the full amount for just assurance."

"You'd likely just get the three hundred for quality information. They would give me the thousand for proof."

Captain O'Banion considered Michael's last words before giving a mental shrug and saying, "I'll go for the thousand, but we have to talk about your cut before I do this."

"How are you going to confirm?"

The captain reached up and scratched his forehead above his left eyebrow. "I've got the images to prove it," he replied.

"Pictures?"

He nodded and smiled. "We captured footage those first few hours." He looked at the barman. "With permission, of course."

"When can they see them?"

"How about noon tomorrow?" he replied. "That will give us time to make the ship ready for visitors. If they give me until the day after, I'll have better video they can take with them."

"You going to charge them for the extra video?"

"Nah, they can just take it raw if they want. I'm not going to piss anyone off. They made offers, so I'm taking them up on what they want and not trying to jerk them around."

Captain O'Banion pushed against the bar, slid off the bar stool, and eyed the barkeeper, hoping his warning was getting through the man's avarice. "Greed never works. Take the big score that just walked into your hands and be happy."

With that, he gave the man a nod and walked back to his ship. He hoped Amanda and Arnold were still on the ship, then at least he wouldn't be lonely when he locked the doors and made sure no one tried to climb aboard without permission.

It seemed like Michael had gotten what he was looking for, which was attention when Miles got to port.

Unfortunately, the captain wasn't sure it was the kind of attention the old vampire had been looking for.

Three Days Later

Michael took a sip of the drink in his hand as he and Akio sat in the old café looking at the city's skyline in the evening light. He made a face. "Gahh!" He put down the small cup. "This is making me wish for Starbucks, and that is saying something," he admitted as he looked around the city block.

Akio just smirked and took a sip of his tea. He had plenty of leaves from Japan with him and had purchased some hot water to steep it in.

Both men flitted their minds from person to person, trying to catch anyone thinking about the Duke. Unfortunately, those thoughts had been pretty sparse. Their best plan wasn't working worth a damn.

"You would think," Michael continued, leaving the cup of burnt-bean-flavored water on the table, "that a scary bloodsucking man would have more than absolutely no one worried about him."

"He has been," Akio answered, sipping his tea and bringing his thoughts back to Michael, "annoyingly intelligent about his proclivities."

Michael turned back to Akio. "Damn large words, Akio."

"*Hai*, Michael-san. Need me to provide a few words with less syllables?"

Michael pursed his lips. "Good test. I didn't even consider hurting you at all." He shrugged. "Since he's a genocidal megalomaniacal bastard, I thought for sure we would have an easy time finding a hint of where he is."

Akio stayed quiet.

Michael reached for the cup as he thought and brought it toward his mouth. Stopping mid-lift, his eyes opened in alarm, and he leaned forward to set it down on the far side of the table. "That was too close," he mumbled. "Thank God for alien-enhanced olfactory senses." Michael resumed his previous commentary. "Seven syllables, one word. Beat *that*."

Akio's lips pressed together, then he slowly grinned as he shook his head. When he noticed Michael smirking like a mischievous boy across the table from him, he started chuckling. "Can I use Japanese?"

"Hell, no," Michael responded. "I never learned your language, so you could say something, and I'd never know it wasn't seven words all strung together."

"You're suggesting I would cheat?" Akio raised an eyebrow.

"Don't get your honor in a twist, Akio," Michael responded, waving his hand. "I've been down that path, and it doesn't end up in a good place. You need to allow the simple comments to float over you."

Akio took a sip of his tea. "You happened to find a good woman at the end."

Michael grunted. "Took a thousand years," he whispered. His head started tracking to his left and Akio's head turned to the right as they both caught the thoughts of an older man. He was well dressed and had just roughly pushed another person out of his way as he mumbled under his breath. His mind was a jumble of anger, hostility, and fear.

Both men caught the face that caused the man's emotions.

Michael stood up and threw a small tip on the table for those who would clean it, and the two stepped out of the café into the darkness.

One second they were in the dark, the next second neither men could be seen at all.

2

Nagoya, Japan

"I just have a few errands to run," Yuko explained to Jacqueline and Mark as they finished breakfast in a local greasy spoon.

Jacqueline shrugged. "Ok. Suits me fine. I'd be happy to have a look around."

Mark peered over his coffee cup as Yuko looked to him for his agreement. "Yeah. I'm in," he confirmed.

"Ok," Yuko said. "Eve will be with you. And in fact, she has a number of places in mind that she thinks you'll enjoy."

Eve grinned cheekily across the little breakfast table. "I'll show you some of my favorite places in Nagoya. I'm sure you'll like them too."

Jacqueline was warming to the idea. "It will certainly be nice to do some things for fun, not for training or survival." She placed her teacup in its saucer. "I can't remember a time when I could just have fun," she said, her voice distant as if reliving her traumatic history. "Maybe when I was little."

She felt Mark's hand land gently on her leg under the table. It was comforting. Even though he still didn't know the half of what she had been through, he did know that Michael had rescued her from a pretty abusive situation in the wilderness. Now it was Mark's job to keep her safe.

She placed her hand over his and their fingers magically interlocked.

"Ok, so it's settled then," Yuko said brightly, a strange excitement laced into her voice. Eve picked up on the difference in tone, but said nothing.

When they were finished eating, and Jacqueline had cleared up any meat products remaining on Yuko's and Mark's plates, they paid their check and headed back to the container.

Within half an hour Yuko was depositing them in a side street in the downtown area.

"Keep your wits about you," she warned as the three stepped into the street. "It's relatively safe here, but this area gets a lot of tourists, and with tourists come opportunists." She glanced at Mark. "We don't want anyone Were-ing out on some unsuspecting pickpocket because that would alert people to our presence here. Right?"

Mark nodded seriously, only to have his interaction with Yuko interrupted by a sharp slap across his body as Jacqueline swiped at him. "Hey!" she called indignantly. "Standing right here!"

Yuko smiled at her and shrugged as if to say, "Case in point."

Jacqueline pulled her jacket around her tighter and

crossed her arms. "I can control myself," she grumbled, a little less convincingly than she had hoped.

"Ok," Yuko called as she headed back into the box. "You have fun! I'll let Eve know when I'm heading back to get you."

Mark, Jacqueline, and Eve waved as Yuko disappeared and the door closed.

"This way," Eve directed, excited to show someone around one of her favorite cities. She strode off at a brisk walk, causing Jacqueline and Mark to trot after her.

Nagoya, Japan, Hirano Residence

Yuko stepped out of the black box and stared at the apartment building. Though she would never admit it to Eve, there had been many a night over the last weeks when she had thought about coming back here. She'd resisted looking up his communication details for fear of Eve pressuring her into something. But she remembered exactly where she had dropped him after their last encounter in the park.

The encounter that had led to her sharing the details of her mission here on Earth with him, and her charge to unite Michael with Bethany Anne.

She closed the black container's door behind her and started walking toward the apartment building. At a guess, at this time of the morning on the weekend, he was home.

She hoped he wouldn't be so she could spare herself the anxiety of explaining why she was there.

She took a deep breath and kept walking.

At the building she scanned the door buzzers, searching for his name.

Hirano.

She ran her finger down the list of scrawled names and Japanese characters, reminding herself that it was unlikely he would have used his police title on the label.

Hirano.

She found it.

Her heart beat hard in her chest, but this sensation was so different from when she exerted herself in physical training. Or fighting.

She pressed the button, scrambling in her mind for the right words to say.

There was a long moment of silence.

She heard a hovercar stream past behind her. The birds were singing in the trees. Everything was perfect for a Saturday morning. She was even aware of the sun beating warmly on her back.

She wondered if she should ring the buzzer again. Her finger hesitated over the button.

"*Hai?*" A male voice responded.

"Hello? Inspector Hirano?" she clarified, her heart still in her throat.

The voice hesitated. "Yes?" he confirmed suspiciously.

"This is Yuko," she explained. "We met a few weeks ago when…" Her voice trailed off.

There was a silence. Yuko imagined she could hear the cogs turning in his brain as he scrambled to remember who she was.

"I'm not here to wipe your memory," she added hurriedly, suddenly thinking he might be assuming the worst. "I... I just thought we could talk," she admitted, not wanting to overwhelm him by being too forward.

There was another pause.

"Hello?" she called again.

Just then the door buzzed open.

"Second floor," he called through the intercom.

Yuko pushed the door open, feeling adrenaline pulse through her insides.

She stepped into the building.

Yuko arrived at the second floor via the stairs. Hirano had come out of his apartment in bare feet and was walking down the carpeted corridor to meet her.

"Yuko," he said, shaking her hand. "It's very good to see you!" He ushered her along the corridor and into his apartment.

Yuko allowed herself to be led, relieved he was receptive to her visit.

She stepped into the apartment ahead of him. It was light and airy, with pale laminate wooden floors and lots of open space. She was pleasantly surprised at how he managed to retain a very traditional look and feel despite how Western Japanese trends had been changing since the war.

Hirano flitted around, moving discarded clothing, towels and other items to make the place more presentable.

"Please don't tidy up on my account. I apologize for showing up unannounced," she told him politely, now embarrassed by her rash decision to come here.

"No, no. It's good that you're here. I had no way to reach you, so I'm...glad." He seemed to settle down as he became accustomed to the situation. "May I offer you some tea?"

Yuko bowed. "That would be lovely."

Hirano disappeared into the kitchen. "Please make yourself at home," he said, waving to the sofa area. The low sofa simulated the old-style futon seating arrangements she had grown up with.

Yuko made herself comfortable, amused at the mixture of customs they were abiding by. After all, she would never have shown up at a man's apartment a hundred and fifty years ago, especially not unannounced.

She sighed to herself, her eyes wandering all over the apartment and appraising his trinkets and decor.

Shortly he returned with a tea tray and set about preparing the drinks. He sat cross-legged at ninety degrees to her around the central low table, and their meeting took on a formal air.

The pair made small talk and took tea together. Yuko couldn't remember a time when she had ever been quite so happy.

Saint-Genis-Pouilly, France

William "Duke" Renaud's eyes flashed red once. He needed this intelligent bore, and he needed to understand exactly what he was trying to say.

He'd also need a lobotomy to allow him to sleep at night, he feared, after he absorbed all of these new technology and science concepts.

Physicists could be damned scary. Why he hadn't considered using them before to help kill those he didn't like, he would ruminate on later.

For now, he just needed to try to find the patience to not kill the doctor as he worked through his many—and painful—talking points.

"So you see, your Grace," Scientist Evan Vaulcott completely missed the Duke's flashing red eyes, "it was all a sham! A lie to keep us—"

"Wait." The Duke put up a hand. Sitting behind a desk in an old building at CERN, which was still in remarkable condition, he refocused his attention away from ways to kill himself to avoid the self-inflicted pain of listening to all the dry information. "Are you saying that there was an effort to hide the truth?"

"Oh, absolutely!" Evan nodded his head vigorously as he waved a hand toward the window. "All this damage we see? Completely fake." He shook his head. "Sorry, I don't mean the damage isn't there; we can both see there are destroyed buildings. However, it was all a *ruse*. They blew up unnecessary facilities to give the impression that the war we were told about really happened. With your people helping, we should get access to the main shafts soon. I'm willing to bet dinner on it."

The bet caused the Duke to smile. William had learned that Evan absolutely loved good food. This man was all scientist and didn't worry about any potential *ethical* issues—another reason he should work with more scientists if Evan was representative of even ten percent of his type of people.

Evan continued, "And I will bet my dessert that we will find everything down below in pristine condition."

William leaned forward in the chair and laid a hand on the desk. It was past sunset, so he didn't need to worry about the sun finding him. However, he felt very unprotected up here in these aboveground buildings. "The collider, it is *how* far underground?"

"The rings?" Evan asked, and the Duke nodded. "Anywhere from about fifty to a hundred and seventy-five meters. Pretty damn deep. Plus, it is over twenty-seven kilometers in circumference. Well, the big ring is." He paused a moment before looking up at the ceiling.

The Duke understood that physical mannerism to mean that Evan's brain was off on some sort of tangent to their conversation. However, the tangents could occasionally be interesting.

"We ran across some early discussions and notes about the project." He looked at his boss. "Did you know they hypothesized that the Hadron Collider would open doors to additional dimensions?"

William blinked a couple of times. "And this would do what?"

Evan shrugged. "I've no idea, but I read a post by Sergio Bertolucci, former Director for Research and Scientific Computing of this facility, that it would produce tiny doors and they would shut down quickly. There isn't any predicted risk, so I just find it interesting."

"Yes." William leaned forward and stood up. He fixed the cuffs on his coat. "Something we can discuss over dinner after our major project is completed." He stepped out from behind the desk. "Let's go look at the challenge that is blocking the teams from getting below," he told the scientist as he headed for the office exit. "I feel a need to have a few hundred meters of Earth above me."

It wasn't lost on him that just a few decades before he had been trying to get out of the ground. Here, however, there were multiple exits, and he intended to figure out how to build a few more.

This might be the best location for him to settle down and found his new royal city.

Who knew? He wondered as the door shut behind Evan, who was jogging to catch up. He was going to rule Earth and pretend he was giving them the future, all because a bunch of dead scientists made sure he finally had a way to kill that bastard, Michael.

He supposed that the brouhaha Evan had told him about regarding the old CERN logo and the religious people saying it had the mark of the Beast in it because they supported the devil was going to come true.

Downtown Nagoya, Japan

"So what exactly is this?" Jacqueline asked Eve, trying to understand the little bits of English on the tickets.

Eve led them into an old theater that was more of an enclosure in a castle than a modern Japanese building. Her expression was one of girlish glee. "Come on," she cajoled them, not answering the question.

There was a round arena in the center of the stone-walled shelter, circled by tiny fires built into the ground. In fact, the place was mostly illuminated by fires burning on torches on the walls, the shadows dancing providing an atmospheric feel. Only a moment before the group had left the bright pleasant sunshine behind behind, and now they were in the cool darkness of what felt like a place of magic.

"This place is giving me chills," Jacqueline remarked quietly to Mark.

Mark put his arm around her shoulder. "It's ok, baby, I'll protect you," he said, his voice tinged with a hint of irony. Jacqueline jabbed him in the ribs. "I'll protect myself, thank you very much, Geek-boy!"

Mark chuckled and rubbed his body where she had poked him. "I've no doubt you will," he agreed, shaking his head and looking around.

A crowd was already assembling around the arena. Not a huge crowd, maybe a few dozen people. Mark imagined they were probably mostly out-of-towners, judging by the different clothes they wore.

"So now what?" Jacqueline whispered to Eve.

Eve turned and looked at them both, the fires reflecting off her face. "Now…we wait," she told them theatrically.

They didn't wait long before half-dressed acrobats and performers started prancing around the arena, dancing, flipping, and generally wowing the crowd.

As the show wore on, the acts became more involved and intense. Music filled the arena and reverberated off the stone walls, captivating all who were present with the sound and the vibrations. Acrobats suspended by invisible wires swung in the air throwing fire between themselves—and water balloons onto unsuspecting audience members.

Volunteers were taken into the inner circle for various displays of shooting skills and illusions. Jacqueline, Mark, and Eve deliberately kept themselves from being chosen for such feats.

That was, of course, until one acrobat dropped down directly above Jacqueline, causing her to move quickly.

He came face to face with her for a brief moment before his harness pulled him away again, but in the instant it would have taken to merely give a human a fright Jacqueline had already started to change, her eyes flaring yellow and teeth growing out of her mouth.

The performer panicked and lost his flow, twisting back in mid-air to see that the monster had been replaced by a mere girl with her hand clapped over her mouth and a concerned boyfriend consoling her.

"You ok?" Mark asked her, standing directly in front of her so no one could see her as her face returned to normal.

She nodded, her hands still over her mouth. "I think so, but what the fuck? And that guy was a Were. I could smell him," she exclaimed, the anger still blazing beneath her shock.

Mark wrapped his arms around her as Eve watched them. Eve mouthed, "Is she ok?"

Mark nodded, whispering to Jacqueline to calm her down.

"Do we need to go?" Eve asked quietly.

Mark conferred with the hidden Jacqueline, then shook his head. "Less conspicuous if we stay," he relayed.

Soon the three were enjoying the show again, the fright and near exposure almost forgotten, if not forgiven.

Finally, the show started wrapping up. The performers took their bows and accolades from the crowd. Applause rang through the little courtyard.

Jacqueline looked around the appreciative crowd. "Time to go?" she ventured, aware they wanted to keep as low a profile as possible—especially now.

Eve nodded and started leading the way.

Mark leaned down and teased Jacqueline as they made their way through the loosely packed crowd. "Can't take you anywhere!"

"Not my fault," Jacqueline hissed back at him, careful not to let anyone overhear their conversation. "I thought that Were was going to land on me!"

Jacqueline's protest turned into a giggle. "It's a good reaction to have when *your* ass needs saving!"

Mark chuckled. "Can't disagree with that. I'm still thrilled I have the badassiest girlfriend on the planet."

With Eve acting as their beacon, they wove through the crowd and the passageway back out to the street.

No sooner had they hit the street beyond the modern foyer than Jacqueline felt someone pulling her from behind.

She spun around, ready to end whoever it was.

"Excuse me?" A young man still dressed in full costume and makeup from the performance released her and bowed shallowly, moving to get out of the way of passersby.

Jacqueline frowned, no longer feeling threatened. Mark had moved on a step or two but still held her hand. She released him to allow people to pass between them on the busy street.

"Yes?"

The young man moved a little closer, dodging an elderly couple. "You're one of us," he whispered. "What are you doing here? In this city? I've never seen you before."

Jacqueline glanced at Mark, who had seen that she had stopped. She couldn't see Eve. "Yes" she admitted to the performer. "I'm here with my boyfriend," she said pointedly.

The youth waved his hand in dismissal. "I was just curious," he explained, "because you're Were, but you seem... different. Even for a Were."

Jacqueline felt her barriers go up. She didn't like discussing herself with a complete stranger. "Well, yeah," she said cagily. "I get that a lot."

She glanced at Mark and Eve, who had reappeared and was watching the interaction. "Look, I've got to go. Nice to meet you," she added politely before heading down the street again.

The youth looked disappointed as she left him standing in the busy cobbled street.

Mark put his arm around her shoulder, still watching the youth she had left standing there. "What was all that about?"

"I'm not sure," she confessed. "He recognized that I was Were, but different. Just curious, I guess. I hope he keeps it to himself," she added grimly.

They caught up with Eve, who seemed to have heard the whole thing. She nodded. "He was the one who scared you inside. And yes, you made a good decision to keep your secret to yourself," she confirmed. "Come on, let's get you off the streets. We should probably be a little more discreet, just in case. These are strange times in the dark ages, even here."

Within a matter of minutes, Eve led them into another grandiose building.

Mark looked around in awe. "It's a palace!" he gawped. "A technology palace!"

Jacqueline was less impressed, mostly because she had lost Mark's attention. Even so, she had to admit the place was amazing.

She ran her eyes over the array of advanced computer consoles, each displaying holograms and games. Every thirty yards there were doors, entrances to what she suspected were some version of immersion reality. Holodecks...at least that was how they were labeled. Not that she knew what these things were. Her mind boggled, trying to comprehend what was really going on in each room.

Eve stopped in front of the pair of them. "Welcome to one of my little creations," she said, waving her arms around more like a hostess than someone bragging.

Mark could barely speak, so Jacqueline did it for him. "What *is* this place?"

"Entertainment Centrale," Eve told them. "All these rooms have different types of games and experiences you can undergo. I'll talk you through them, but first there's something very important I want you to try."

Jacqueline waved her hand in surrender, indicating that Eve should lead the way.

Eve turned on her heel and stomped her little AI body through the grand walkways of probably the plushest and extravagant building Jacqueline and Mark had ever seen.

After a few turns into similar corridors with differing decors, she stopped in front of a stand and spoke to the person running it.

A delightful smell came from the machine atop the stand, and there were wisps of some kind of substance within it. The man put a stick into the windowed box and waved it around, and moments later he produced a cloud-like fluffy substance on the stick.

Jacqueline couldn't take her eyes off it, her Were sense of smell going bananas over its delightful scent. "What is it?"

Eve smiled, taking it from the man and handing it to Jacqueline. *"Wata kashi!"* she told her, delight tinting her normally even voice.

Mark took a sniff too, his eyes softening in bliss. "But what *is* it?"

Eve sighed, unable to experience it herself. "You eat it. Pull a bit off and put it in your mouth."

Mark tried it first as Jacqueline watched him with narrowed eyes. His face lit up as the sugar melted in his mouth. "That. Is. Amazing!" he declared, reaching for another piece. "Try it."

Jacqueline didn't move, obviously tempted by the smell but unsure of this strange new substance. Mark stopped with his second piece almost at his mouth and instead held it toward her. She opened hesitantly, and he popped it onto her tongue. Almost instantly her expression relaxed and her eyes widened. "Om nom nom…" was the sound she made, trying to express the sensation in words.

Eve laughed. "I'm glad you approve." She thanked the man and paid for it with the swipe card she used as currency everywhere in this country, then ushered them down one of the wide halls, talking them through the different game options.

Mark and Jacqueline followed, filled with the scent of *Wata kashi* and awe, wooed by the lights, and of course, the technology.

3

Frankfurt, Germany

"I swear," Jan Freholt mumbled as he stepped around the older lady, accidentally bumping her shoulder. She spat a muffled curse and he ignored it. "If that bastard says anything to me about my company after he missed a meeting that was six months in the making…"

He glanced nervously down the lamplit street and saw an alleyway on his right half a block further down. A tiny ribbon of sweat started to trickle down his forehead, and he reached up to wipe it away with the back of his shirtsleeve.

Better to not mention anything out loud.

He heard footsteps following him. He surreptitiously glanced around, taking a second to peek behind him.

There was an Asian man back there with his eyes trained on Jan.

Shit.

Jan started walking a little faster, glanced back once more, and took a shallow breath—the man behind him didn't seem to have sped up. When he turned back around, there was a bald man with his arms crossed waiting for Jan on the sidewalk.

Jan stopped and turned back. The other man was now standing right behind him.

"Hello, Jan," the bald man said. "My name is Michael, and the person you are angry with and afraid of is someone I wish to speak with."

Michael and Akio watched Jan continue down the street. His memory had been fuzzed so he would not remember anything the two men had questioned him about.

Directions?

"He had a meeting set up with William, but William has been missing for a couple of weeks." Michael considered what the two men had learned. "Using a different name—that is a level of sophistication I don't remember William having."

"Perhaps all those years underground allowed him time to think." Akio looked back into the alleyway, his eyes flitting from shadow to shadow but not finding anything.

Michael frowned. "Well, I didn't provide him any toys to occupy his time. That'll teach *me* to do something half-assed. I should have just killed him."

Akio turned back to Michael. "I believe that has been the common complaint from characters in movies and books for centuries."

Michael's eyes turned and he looked at his companion. "Did you just associate me with the likes of the James Bond villains?"

Akio pursed his lips. "If the truth fits…"

Michael shook his head and then pointed back in the direction the man had come from. "Club was that way?" Akio nodded. "Fine. But in my defense," Michael went back to the previous conversation as he started walking down the street with Akio next to him, "I was more into punishment fitting the crime at the time."

"When did that change to 'just kill them?'" Akio's voice traveled on the wind.

"I think about seventy years later," Michael answered, slipping his hands into his pockets as the two traveled in and out of the light from the streetlamps. "I got into a major disagreement with a pack leader and his core leadership team. They wanted to take over a portion of a forest and kill anyone who came inside. I disagreed."

Michael stepped around a large hole in the walkway. "It got to the point where I was extremely annoyed, and my patience was wearing thin, so I decided to institute the 'No Disrespect Protocol.'"

"Is that the one that basically says—" Akio started.

Michael finished it for him. "'Do what I say or die.' Then, I followed up quickly with the corollary, 'Give me any lip and die,' and occasionally, 'Look at me wrong and die.'"

"Lots of dying there," Akio commented.

"Well," Michael admitted as the two men took a left and saw the club just two streets down, "I had zero patience left, it was so easy to just kill them and be done with it. I rarely dealt with any repercussions, except for the occasional effort to smoke me out and kill me."

"Practice."

"It was a bit of a game, true."

"So, you implemented the policy and instances of trouble went down."

"Not always down," Michael answered as they stepped across a street to step back up the curb on the other side. "But it did bypass any annoying issues with negotiations, or someone whining about it not being their fault. If I was around, they ran or fought. If they fought, I killed them. If they ran, they were guilty."

Akio looked at him and Michael touched his temple. "Bethany Anne wasn't there; I was always in their mind."

There were two large men in front of the club, whose name was rendered in red fluorescent script above the dark wood doors.

"'Don't Make Me Angry.'" Akio read the name, then added, "You won't like me when I'm angry."

"Why is that familiar?" Michael asked as the two nodded to the guys watching the front and stepped inside. The sound level was pretty normal, which was to say quite low for a club that wasn't full of Weres.

"Lots and lots of sensitive ears," Michael mused quietly. The inside had twelve circular booths, each of which could fit three comfortably or five if they sat really close together. There were plenty of metal tables in the middle, all looking pretty banged up.

"Weres!" Akio grunted. "I think I know what is on the agenda for tonight."

"Someone has an answer for me," Michael told him,

then nodded to the huge man sitting at one of the round tables in the back, "and I pick him."

"Of course you do," Akio smirked. "Why start at the bottom?"

"Akio, I'm trying to be civil here," Michael whispered. "It would be easier to just lock the doors and beat the shit out of everyone. I'm sure they have all done something that deserves a knockdown. However, I'm giving them the benefit of the doubt."

"Because that is what Bethany Anne would want."

"And don't forget to let her know how hard I tried," Michael answered, and popped his knuckles. "I bet I can have him mad in just three sentences."

"I'll do it in two," Akio retorted, a gleam in his eye.

Michael looked at him sideways. "Oh?" He looked back at the large man. "I'll bet you one run-on sentence."

"Fine, but I get to anger the next one."

Michael snickered. "I'm not sure which of us is going to upset Bethany Anne more in the end," he told Akio. Three guys stood up from nearby tables when they saw the two newcomers heading toward the rear of the club.

The three guys stepped between the vampires and the man in the back, who was eyeing them. All three crossed their arms. The middle one, who had black hair and a tear in his t-shirt, spoke first. "You guys in the wrong place?"

Michael glanced around at the twenty or so pairs of eyes watching them. They didn't look very welcoming. "Akio, didn't that man say to go five blocks before we take a left. Then two blocks before we smell the stupid that comes out the door?"

Akio shook his head. "That was two sentences."

"I'm not speaking to the Alpha yet."

The middle guy's eyes flashed yellow. "How about I stuff your two sentences down your throat?"

Michael lifted his chin at the Alpha in the back as he kept his eyes on the man who was speaking. "You couldn't stuff your tiny little wiener inside his—"

That was all Michael got out before the three men jumped at him and Akio. The Alpha in the back started moving his huge girth out of the booth, his eyes flashing yellow as he roared his challenge.

Akio ducked the first punch and smashed his elbow into the left-hand Were's chin, slamming his head back. "I cannot believe this," he said, his voice calm as he kicked the legs out from under the one he was fighting, who threw his head and torso forward as his legs were pushed off the floor.

Akio's left fist met the Were's forehead and cracked it open before he pivoted out of the way. The head continued downward to slam into the floor.

Turning, he saw that one Were already had a broken arm and the other was trying to get over the fact that Michael had caught his fist in mid-punch. "The problem is, your form is terrible," Michael was telling the man. He rotated the guy's hand to the left. "If you would start from this position and twist it as you yell *Keayah!*, you'd do better."

Michael ignored the scream from the guy; apparently

he had twisted the arm so quickly he broke his lower wrist. "Well, they don't make Weres like they used to." Michael slammed the back of his hand against the man's forehead, he went down, out cold. "You were hurting my ears," he commented as he stepped across the comatose guy. The Alpha took one look at his three guards.

"You come into my place and expect to get out alive?" Big and Large asked.

"Really?" Michael looked around. "I thought this was the Duke's place." He heard Akio take out two more behind him. They must have thought he was fair game.

Akio was going to owe him for starting this fight.

The big man's eyes narrowed. "Well, now you have sealed your death. No one talks about the Duke that we don't know." He nodded to Michael. "It's a rule. You got a name?"

"To tell the Duke?"

"No, for your headstone," he answered, and where there had been a large man, there was now a bear that was six feet tall at the shoulders.

"Well," Michael whispered, wincing when the bear roared his challenge. "I take back what I said about them not making Weres like they used to."

Akio called from behind him, "You had to pick a fight with someone that big?"

Michael turned toward Akio. "I never—" he started to say as the Werebear dropped to the floor and leapt across the few feet between them. Michael frowned, then disappeared.

"Oh shit!" someone yelled when he dematerialized.

Akio turned to see that the bear had missed Michael and was now heading in his direction.

The bear's momentum was halted just five feet from Akio, but the bear's paws, the size of large dinner plates, continued to take swipes at him while Michael held onto his back leg. Seconds later, a sudden *crack* sounded when Michael broke the bone in the back leg. "Have I got your attention yet?" Michael asked conversationally.

Akio turned around. Three other Weres had stopped getting up from their seats when they saw this man start tearing their Alpha apart.

One guy off to the left reached under his jacket and flung something in Akio's direction. Akio dodged as his hand snaked out and caught the throwing star. Akio looked back at the Were, who was starting to reach around to the back of his jeans. "Yours?" Akio asked and threw it back, the star embedding itself in the man's stomach. "If you pull out a weapon, I will blow your *Gott Verdammt* head off," Akio told him as he pulled out his pistol.

"The Shadow," someone whispered. Akio turned in their direction and bowed his head slightly.

"What the hell?" Michael grunted as the bear, whose leg was healing for the third time from Michael breaking it, peered around the massive beast at Akio. "You have a reputation?"

Akio replied over his shoulder, "I have lived here for over a hundred and fifty years. I have tried to solve problems through the judicious use of fear and intimidation rather than killing."

"Is he lying?" a woman to their right whispered. "The Shadow has killed a lot of times."

"But not *lately*," Akio countered. "The Shadow has not killed in the last two decades, I believe." He chose that moment to try out his latest smile. From the looks in the audience, he needed to work on it looking welcoming.

"Oh, *shut* the hell up!" Akio turned to see Michael dancing with the bear, pulling the bear's leg out and moving in a circle as he tried to turn around and slice through Michael's guts with four-inch-long claws. "Change back, or I'll break every one of your legs and rip off your testicles," Michael told the Were.

Half the men in the room winced.

Michael broke the back leg a fourth time, then jumped onto the bear's back, clamped his legs around the bear's sides, and started punching the back of the bear's head.

"I *said*..."

PUNCH

"Shut."

PUNCH

"The."

PUNCH

"Hell—"

Michael stopped punching when he realized he was sitting on top of a barely conscious male whose clothes had been destroyed during his change.

Akio came over and watched as the man's head started healing. He looked at Michael, who had grabbed a towel and was cleaning the blood off his hand. "See?" Michael pointed to the man on the floor. "I'm being *civil*."

The two men stood there for a couple of moments before Michael started for the door. Akio followed, but his eyes narrowed. "We aren't going to question him?"

Michael turned around and winked, then touched his forehead. "I already got what we need."

Akio shook his head and stepped over one of the first guys he had knocked out. "And when did you get this information?"

Michael stopped walking to speak to a short haired waitress who was standing by the door. "Do you want to go tell your friends we are coming out and to get out of our way, or shall I just shoot them now?"

Her eyes flitted toward the door and back to Michael, who nodded. She stepped over to it and knocked. "Tim? Henry?" she called. "I'd make sure you don't piss off anyone coming out. I don't think these two vampires would appreciate it."

"No, we wouldn't," Michael agreed and spoke over his shoulder. "See? *Civil*."

A moment later the two men left the club and nodded to Tim and Henry. Halfway down the block, Michael finally answered Akio's question.

"It was when we were negotiating how many sentences we would need to start the fight."

Akio shook his head. "What did we learn?"

"We learned that William hasn't been in for two weeks, but he called two nights ago. Said he was going to be away for business reasons, and our friend back there was to kill anyone who came looking for him if they didn't know the password."

"What was the password?"

"'The Duke expects,'" Michael replied.

"And why," Akio asked as the two men turned left into an alley, "did we not just use the password?"

"Because the rest of the password was 'our loyalty and our respect.'"

There was a bit of silence as Akio thought about it. "You couldn't…"

"No fucking way," Michael answered. "Not in this or any other lifetime."

4

Undisclosed location, Tokyo, Japan

The sun streamed over the dusty floorboards in an abandoned building Kuro had bought eighteen months ago for the sole purpose of remaining off the radar.

He stood in a dignified stance with his hands behind his back, watching the passersby on the street below.

Orochi, his most recent business associate and ally, sat leafing through reports on the sofa he'd brought to the apartment to make their visits a little more civilized. After all, it wasn't as if they could be seen meeting in public or at any of their offices.

The third member of their alliance, Raiden, sat at an old desktop computer, still frustrated with trying to recreate the hardware they very much needed for the next part of their plan.

"It's no use. These chips are still working too fast for them to sync with the old processors," he declared finally, sitting back in his chair in frustration. He dropped the two electrical pins he'd been trying to connect into the open hard drive onto the desktop.

Kuro turned from his position at the window. "Well, then we will try something else. What other options do we have?" he asked, unemotionally switching into problem-solving mode. He hadn't amassed his wealth by giving up at the first, the second, or even the third hurdle.

The tech genius stood up from the computer and pulled his hair as he started pacing.

Thinking.

Orochi casually looked up from his papers as he sat on the sofa. "We may not have to figure this piece out."

Kuro glanced at him. "What do you mean?"

Orochi normally had a slightly arrogant manner, but Kuro suspected there was a good reason for it on this occasion. His eyes narrowed. "What do you know that you're not telling us?"

Orochi shuffled his papers together and closed the folder on his lap. "I've heard rumors that they are looking again."

Raiden frowned, catching up to the conversation. "They? You mean the Diplomat is back in town?"

Orochi nodded. "It seems that way."

Kuro remained skeptical. "Have we had any confirmation, though?"

Orochi shifted his crossed legs and picked at imaginary lint on his pant leg. "Not yet," he replied, "but my people are working on it. It's very difficult to get confirmation on them. They have earned much loyalty among people here, and much fear around their names abroad. But I have put something in place, just to make sure it's her."

Kuro looked concerned. "Please don't tell me you've found someone dumb enough to try and take her out."

Orochi waved his hand. "Don't worry. If it really *is* her, they won't have a hope."

Kuro pursed his lips disapprovingly. "You plan to send someone to their death?"

Orochi shrugged. "It's the only way we'll know for sure. Remember, we don't have any photographic reference or DNA. All we know about her is that she is female, goes by the name of 'the Diplomat,' and is lethal when she needs to be. Other than that, she's a ghost."

Raiden had turned around, his hands now resting on the back of his head, fingers interlocked. "So this means…"

Kuro translated. "If it *is* her, it means the rumors of the ArchAngel are correct. And that means they're going to start assembling the ship. Which," he said, his smugness elevating by the second, "also means we don't necessarily have to solve these problems ourselves. We can simply wait until they solve the puzzles with their advanced resources and then let them lead us straight to the pieces."

"Finally!" Raiden exclaimed in relief, dropping his hands from his head and sitting back down again.

Kuro turned back to look out of the window again, contemplating their next move. "Well, if this is true, it's only a matter of time before she returns to Kashikoi's little faction. In which case—"

"In which case we're perfectly ready," Orochi agreed, a knowing smile spreading over his lips.

Kuro faced the room. "And this time we just need to hope that she doesn't catch on to what we're planning. We don't want a repeat of last time."

Orochi bowed his head. "At least we managed to avoid them thinking there was anything untoward going on."

Kuro frowned in annoyance and turned his body slightly, keeping his face hidden from Orochi. "Yes, but we missed our opportunity," he reminded him. "We don't know how many opportunities we have left in this lifetime."

Orochi still sounded overly confident for Kuro's liking. "But with our forces now combined, we will defeat her," Orochi insisted. "And her little friend."

Kuro sighed, trying not to get too annoyed by Orochi's attitude. "I agree," he conceded. "Plus, she doesn't have the temperament for winning," he mused out loud.

Raiden injected himself into the conversation from across the room. "I wouldn't be too sure about that," he called from his computer terminal. "I heard rumors on the message boards that she's been quite different since the ArchAngel is back in play."

Kuro turned to face him. "I thought that was just a sensationalized rumor to shake things up a bit." He frowned quizzically. "Could he really be back from the dead?"

Raiden shrugged. "My contacts in America seem to think so. One reported getting up close and personal, and living to tell the tale."

Kuro's frown deepened. "Where is he, then?"

Raiden checked his handheld. "Last reported sighting was in London, I understand," he reported, shrugging. "That's all I have."

Orochi uncrossed his legs and sat forward, his papers forgotten on the sofa next to him. "He's in London, and his

Diplomat is out here? Makes you wonder what is important enough to pull him away from finding the ship."

"Yes," Kuro mused, rubbing his chin with his thumb and forefinger. "It appears there may be something we're missing."

He paused thoughtfully, his eyes glazing over for a moment. "But no matter," he said, his chirpy confidence returning. "As long as he is out of the way, we have an increased chance of tackling this one." He turned to Orochi. "Even so," Kuro added instructionally, "best not to underestimate her. Or her little friend."

Frankfurt, Germany

"That," Michael said as he pointed to a building with three gabled roofs, "is the Römer. I helped lay a few of the bricks when I was passing through after it was sold to the city. Just some minor work, when it became the city hall."

Akio nodded. The two of them were walking through a spacious open square with a large statue in the middle. "Over there was the old Saint Nicholas Church." He looked closer. "Not sure what they have done with it now."

The two men continued through the square, heading toward another unique place. This time it was supposed to be a nice bar and restaurant. Overhead, the antigrav cars slid through the night. Their engines produced an annoying whine that Akio wasn't terribly pleased with.

Three blocks later they found the sign, which had a small moon in the lower left-hand corner. Michael grimaced. "Not terribly subtle, are they?" he asked as he pulled open the door and waved Akio through. "You get the first shot, remember?"

"*Hai.*" Akio nodded and entered, his hesitancy at showing Michael too little honor becoming less of a problem.

The number of people in the restaurant was surprising. At least fifteen tables occupied the middle of the large open floor, and twenty secluded booths ran along the side and back walls. On the right was a long bar with another five patrons chatting about half-way down.

Maybe two tables were empty.

"Can I help you gentleman?" the hostess, a blond woman, asked. Her hair was pulled into a bun on the back of her head.

"Please," Michael answered. "We would like to speak with *Fraulein* Hilga Overstead if we could?"

The hostess pursed her lips. "If you will take a seat and order, I will have someone inform the *fraulein* you are requesting an audience."

"Certainly," Michael waved his hand toward the tables. "If you would seat us?"

The two men followed the woman to a booth and slid in. She placed a menu in front of each of them. "What would you like to drink?"

Akio turned to her. "Do you serve blood?"

The lady smiled at the joke, but then lost her calm when she saw Akio's two fangs slide a little way out of his mouth.

She shook her head. "No."

"Pity," he answered.

"I'll have a steak." Michael handed the menu back. "Rare, of course."

"I'll have the same." Akio passed his menu to the hostess. "Don't bother cooking it."

When the lady had disappeared into the back, Michael raised an eyebrow. "'Don't bother cooking it?'"

Akio leaned forward. "Are we expecting to eat here, then?"

Michael looked around, trying to scan through the minds and see if he could locate the lady they were looking for, but then grimaced. "I suppose not."

Akio leaned back. "I was trying to be more theatrical." He tried his smile again.

"Keep working on that," Michael told him. "I think the muscles in your face are having to regenerate after all these centuries."

"*Hai*," Akio agreed, then his eyes flitted toward the front of the restaurant behind Michael.

"Trouble?" Michael asked.

"Only if a red-haired lady in a drop-dead-sexy black velvet dress is a problem." Akio paused. "Accompanied by two guys holding semi-automatic weapons trained on us."

"I guess your version of intimidation went a bit far?"

Akio shrugged. "They didn't shoot us out of hand."

"That," the redhead interjected, her tone severe, "is still open for negotiation. If either of you so much as flinch, either Edgar or Chris will fill you full of holes as quickly as the guns can shoot. Since they fire at eleven hundred rounds a minute, that is a lot."

"We came here to speak with you, not to kill you," Michael replied, as he noticed Akio wincing.

"We would like some answers related to—" Akio was shut down by the lady.

"I do not care what your questions are," she turned to Michael, "and I don't kill easily."

Akio wanted to roll his eyes. This lady was going to make the project difficult. Michael had probably already pulled the information he wanted from her brain.

"Well," Michael temporized, moving his hands together on top of the table and clasping them, "I can tell you that you do it poorly." Both men pointed their weapons at him.

The lady's eyes flashed yellow a moment before she calmed down. "Do what poorly, exactly?"

"Not get killed easily, of course," Michael explained. "If I had wanted you dead, I would have just killed you earlier."

The man on her right, the one next to Akio, spoke up. "If it wasn't going to hurt business, I'd just end you now."

Michael turned to him and smiled. "Try."

"*Kichigai*." Akio sighed when Michael disappeared, the bullets from the two submachine guns tore up the booth where he had been sitting.

Michael appeared behind the men and lashed out, punching them both in the back of their skulls.

They dropped like rocks. "I don't think they were Weres, Michael," Akio commented as the Archangel grabbed the lady by the neck. His nails grew, stabbing her skin and puncturing it. "If you change, I will kill you," he whispered.

Akio had his pistol out and pointed at someone behind Michael. "You will pull your hand out…" The silent rounds from his Jean Dukes pistol caused massive carnage behind Michael, which he couldn't see. The man started screaming in pain, and Akio finished his instructions. "The idea was to pull your hand back out without a pistol. Now you get to heal your shoulders, and for good measure, your kneecap. Pray that I don't hear about any plans to shoot us another time."

Michael pushed the woman forward. She used her Were reflexes to twist into the seat, turning to stare at Michael as her neck healed. "If you say another word I find distasteful," Michael told her calmly, "or use a tone I don't like, I will cause more pain. Eventually, I will just kill you."

"Who are you? Are you from the Duke?" she hissed.

"God, no." Michael motioned to her and she moved back, allowing him to slide in.

She glanced at Akio, who still had the pistol out and pointing at the others in the room, then back at Michael. "May I issue orders?"

He nodded. "Be my guest." He waited patiently for her to calmly command the others to get someone to help everyone that was hurt and clean up the carnage.

She turned back to Michael. "The Duke is going to come back to Frankfurt, and he is not going to be happy with anyone horning in on his territory."

"Color me unconcerned," Michael answered. When he noticed she looked puzzled, he tried again. "I do not care."

At that moment Michael saw the door to the kitchen open. Two waiters came out and headed in their direction. He withheld a smirk as they approached. Akio glanced at the men as they came into his view.

They set Michael's rare steak in front of him, then a completely raw steak on the table for Akio, who made a face.

"What?" Michael asked, amused. "Too rare?"

"I had expected," Akio answered, staying aware of those around them, "that we would have already killed everyone and the steak would be superfluous. Now, I have meat and no desire to…"

Michael pulled up the sleeve of his shirt, then reached across the table and placed his hand above the steak. Soon Akio could feel heat coming at him in waves, and his steak started to brown. "You might want to turn that over," Michael told him.

Michael pulled his hand back, and Akio reached over to turn his steak. Then Michael returned his hand to over the plate and finished browning the top. "All better?" He smirked.

Akio grabbed his jacket and slid his pistol back into its holster. "I think it might be fine, Dark Messiah."

The woman in the booth gasped.

Michael turned back to her and smiled maliciously, his eyes glowing red as her head slowly turned back and forth. Her mouth was silently saying, "No no no no" over and over again.

"Did you see a ghost?" Michael asked her.

5

The two men left the restaurant and turned right, and the building itself seemed to breathe a sigh of relief. They headed down a dark alley.

Both stayed quiet, their mouths set. The last few days had been a bit of an enjoyable time as they had worked to find one asshole, but now both were blaming themselves for something they hadn't known.

Seconds later they had both disappeared into the Myst, streaking across town to a hotel whose name and location the woman had shared with the two of them.

Quite willingly, once she understood who he was.

Even Michael had been surprised to find out that rumors of him had crossed the Pond and made it here to Frankfurt. He assumed they were from the ship's captain, but he wasn't sure just yet.

Either way, while they had been puttering around looking for the Duke, there had been someone who needed them.

The woman kept pulling the little boy, who had almost given up as she dragged him along.

"You aren't my momma!" Little Michael tried once again to yank his arm back from the lady, but she was stronger than his own mom was, or at least had been.

She stopped and bent down, flashing her eyes at the little kid. "Listen, you little brat. I may not be your momma, but I'm the only one you need to worry about. Those people in the hotel were going to throw you out with all your stuff since your Mom never showed up. You have nothing."

Little Michael noticed her face seemed to twist, her eyes flashing in the night. He wanted to obey her, but...

But...

She wasn't his mom!

She let go of Michael's arm and reached up to fix her jacket, still staring down at the kid. "I paid off the hotel, explained I was your aunt and that your Mom was down with a strange form of madness. If you shut your mouth, you will at least have table scraps, you miserable little PITA." She huffed. "If my last little slave hadn't died I wouldn't need you, so be grateful he mouthed off one too many times."

She leaned over, putting her eyes just inches from little Michael's. "Don't make me eat you too."

The little boy stared at her in fear, believing every word the woman told him. She oozed something that made him want to curl up in a little ball and cry, not allowing himself to look up so that hopefully she was gone when the sun came back up.

His mom had told him to run back to their hotel weeks ago, and had never shown back up. Now he was with some woman claiming she was his aunt.

His eyes narrowed at her. His mom hadn't feared the horrible man in the alley the night she disappeared. And if this lady ate him, he hoped she choked on one of his bones.

Her cry of surprise when he lashed out and kicked her was satisfying, and he turned to run. He made it two feet before something slammed the back of his head and he went flying.

Little Michael hit the ground, skinning his knees as his hands reached out to stop his head from bouncing off the concrete.

The lady hissed, "Little bastard, you will learn or die. I really don't care which." Her voice dripped with anger. "And you will learn no one kicks Analine without penalty."

"Oh, I think there is one who can." The voice of the male who spoke from behind her was dark, malevolent, and deadly.

Analine whipped around to find a man in a dark coat just two feet away. His vampiric eyes flashed red and his face was contorted in absolute hatred.

Behind her, another man was picking up the young boy. "Don't look," he told him. "She isn't going to hurt you anymore."

Blood dripped out of Analine's mouth; her shock was wearing off and she looked down. The first man's hand, its fingernails looking like daggers, had opened her chest and grabbed her heart. "I don't think this was working anyway," he told her before his hand crushed the heart. His hand continued upward, cutting through her rib cage and slashing through her head from chin to brow. Her eyes lost focus as her body dropped to the concrete.

Michael made the sign of the cross over the dead Were. "Go to hell," he told the woman as he stepped across her dead body. "Call the Pod, Akio. We are going back to Paris."

Akio subvocalized his request to Eve and turned to follow Michael to a twelve-story building across the street.

"We will go to the roof," Michael told him, his paces resolute. "We will walk, so we don't scare the boy."

"*Hai*," Akio agreed.

Minutes later the three came out of the door that exited onto the roof. Little Michael held Akio's hand and stared in wonder as a black ship descended from the night sky. "Who are you?" he asked, looking from the ship to the men and back.

"Some call him," the bald man said, pointing at Akio, "the Shadow." He pointed to himself. "My name is Michael. I've been called 'the Archangel' in ages past, and now?" He smiled. "Now I am the Dark Messiah."

Akio jumped into the front seat. Michael reached under little Michael's arms and picked him up, placing him in Akio's lap. "You will have to ride up here until we get back to Paris and find your people."

"Paris?" little Michael whispered, choking back a sob.

"We cannot do anything for your mother," Michael admitted. "She is gone. But boys need to be with their family so they can grow up into the men they were meant to be. We will take you back to your people, your tribe."

The sleek black craft rose into the sky, then turned and headed toward what was left of the great city of Paris.

Nagoya, Japan

Jacqueline squeezed her lower legs around her horse's barrel to go faster. Mark was just behind her, but hell if she was going to give him the satisfaction of getting ahead of her. She knew that if he did, he would be on top of that ball and returning it to the other end of the field in an instant.

And that would make the score a tie.

And that just would not do.

She had also realized in the last twenty minutes of playing polo—despite the simulated nature of the game—that he had an agility and balance that matched her own.

And he had spent far less time training tirelessly with Michael.

Not that she resented it. In fact, she found it kind of hot that he could hold his own. But she couldn't let him win this point.

She squeezed harder, and her horse's gait changed. She felt it suddenly go bumpy, like something uncontrolled was happening. She looked back over her shoulder just in time to see Mark come up beside her in only two strides and then overtake her. As he did, her horse swerved into him and then away, kicking as it went as if also resenting the other horse overtaking it.

Figures, she thought briefly as she swerved with it, falling to the side and then forward, grabbing a handful of mane for balance.

Then the horse swung the other way, and one stirrup

had already been lost. She was completely off-balance, and a second later she felt herself slipping. She tried to put her weight on a stirrup that simply wasn't there.

She fell forward over the horse's shoulder.

In slow motion she slipped off, reins providing no help or balance. She flinched, tucking and trying to avoid the trampling motion of the hooves she was falling on top of.

Soon she would be beneath them.

She looked upward, seeing horse and sky, and then she was aware of the wind being knocked out of her as she hit the deck.

She couldn't cry. Her body was in shock, even though it was a simulation and her Were capabilities should be able to take it.

She could only lie there waiting for her visual display to return something that wasn't quite so scrambled. She turned her head toward the sky, noticing that her steed was now patiently standing a good few feet to one side of her, as if on reset. Mark had already hit the ball down the field and was turning his horse around to head over to her.

She inspected herself, feeling with her gloved hands to make sure her body was ok. She felt normal one moment and the next was not quite herself, as the sensory stimulation of the program flicked between her brain's reality and the reality the program was feeding her. It was the most bizarre sensation she had ever experienced.

Within a few moments, she was fully back in the virtual reality of the scene on the churned muddy playing field. She rolled over and picked herself up as Mark arrived.

"You ok?" he asked her.

She looked down at her muddy polo shirt and jodhpurs

and her muddy gloved hands. "I'm fine, I think," she said cautiously, making sure she really was ok.

Mark grinned at her. "You stayed on well. Until you didn't."

He was too high up to swipe at. Best she could do was thump his horse, which wouldn't be fair to the horse even if it was a simulated entity.

"You want to keep playing for this point?" he said, looking in the direction of the ball.

Jacqueline narrowed her eyes. "One condition," she said sternly. "You wait until I'm back on before we continue."

Mark thought about it and then agreed. "I'll even hold your horse while you mount if you like," he offered with a flourishing bow.

"Chivalry?" she commented, bobbing her head with her bottom lip pushed out, impressed. She picked up her polo mallet, which was also caked in mud at this point. She flicked as much off the handle as she could and wiped the rest on her boot.

Mark grinned as he trotted past her to the horse that was standing quietly, a few strides over. Jacqueline arrived at its side and hauled herself back up as Mark held the reins for her. "Good thing they're programmed to reset," he commented. "If this were real you would have ended up black and blue, the way you went down. And trampled."

Jacqueline grunted as she put one foot in the nearest stirrup, heaved her other leg over the horse's back, and sat down on the saddle.

Without waiting, Mark had already transitioned his horse into a canter from almost a standing start. Jacqueline flicked her reins and urged hers on too, trying to reach the ball first. Her mallet was tucked in at the horse's side, ready to swipe into action when she was a few strides out.

Just then the field deteriorated into a pixelated wash, leaving them chasing through blackness. A split second later the horses, mud, and polo wear disappeared, leaving a dull view of the room they had started in.

"Heeeeey!" Jacqueline called, looking down at the metal horse torso she was straddling. Her gloved hands held onto nothing since the reins and everything else she had touched were simulated through the array of wires that fed into the gloves.

She glanced at Mark, to see him looking equally disappointed. His visual patches were still over his eyes, making him look kind of wasp-like.

She removed her patches and the room looked a little brighter. Eve had entered the room and stood in front of them.

"Apologies. Yuko has been in touch, and she's waiting for us in the parking lot. It's time to go."

Jacqueline sighed, popping the patches into the holsters attached to the horse-like body she was sitting on. Mark did the same, and they carefully dismounted onto the blue padded mats.

"It's another world here," Jacqueline commented, shaking her head. "Whoever would have thought about riding a horse just for fun?" She chuckled to herself.

Mark was also in good spirits despite the initial disappointment of having their experience interrupted. "I haven't ridden many horses in my time," he confessed, "but that felt pretty realistic!"

Eve smiled, satisfied that her invention had brought

them pleasure. "It's because the eye patches 'wire' into your ocular nerve using light pulses which trick your brain into all kinds of stimulated sensations. That's why it's so realistic—because your brain is telling you it *is* real."

"Without wires or electrodes!" Mark exclaimed excitedly.

Eve nodded. "All through light pulses. Neat, huh?"

Jacqueline still looked impressed. "That's pretty awesome," she admitted. "And I like the non-invasiveness."

Other riders were already heading into the room and mounting the pretend horses. "Yeah, I'd happily be hardwired into some tech for the experience, cyborg-style, but knowing there is a way where you don't have to…"

Eve nodded. "Much more convenient, especially when it's for entertainment purposes."

Eve led them back along the long wide corridors of the entertainment palace toward the parking lot at the rear of the building. They passed several of the experiences they'd had and games they'd played, discussing briefly which were their favorites or the trickiest as they passed.

Eventually, they reached the back doors and headed out into the parking lot. Eve guided them directly to the black box, which was parked in the same amount of space it would normally take to park a few hovercars. The three of them carefully crossed to the box and hopped in, finding Yuko fiddling at the computer screen.

She looked up as they came in. "Did you have fun?" she asked, smiling.

Jacqueline and Mark started telling her all the things they had done and played since she had left them several hours ago on the main street.

"Sounds like you've had quite the time!" she exclaimed brightly as the box swooped through the sky to a quieter location.

Jacqueline was brimming with enthusiasm. "I had no idea civilization could be so advanced. I mean, I know tech has its uses, but this is almost…excessive." She grinned like a kid in a candy store.

Eve sat quietly on the other side of the container at another computer. She turned. "They had *Wata kashi* too," she stated simply.

Yuko nodded sagely. "You have experienced good things today, then."

When the excitement had died down a little, Eve looked at Yuko pointedly. "And you? How were your 'errands?'"

Yuko flushed a little. "Good. All is well."

Eve glanced at her screen and back to Yuko. "Anything you want to tell me?"

Yuko slowly shook her head. "I don't think so. Why?"

Eve nodded at her screen. "Because I see the location the box went to. And the glow in your complexion," she added, trying hard to stifle an excited giggle.

Yuko blushed a deep red, lowering her eyes and then quickly covering her face with her hands.

Jacqueline suddenly cottoned on to what was being discussed. "Has she been to see a boy?" She gasped.

Mark frowned, looking at each of the females in turn. "How on Earth did you come to that conclusion?"

Jacqueline chuckled. "It was obvious from her reaction," she said simply. "So who is he?" she asked, turning to the faceless Yuko.

Eve answered for her. "He's a police inspector we met

on a job not long ago. He helped us, and it turned out his family has a long history of fascination with our operation. He's also super cute. 'Inspector Hottie' is what I call him. And he's into Yuko."

Yuko had calmed herself a little and lowered her hands. She was still flushed and her eyes were focused on her lap, but she seemed to be composing herself.

Eve continued. "The real question is, when are you seeing him again?"

Yuko's eyes came up to meet Eve's without any other part of her body moving. "Tonight," she whispered.

Jacqueline clapped her hands with excitement, and even Mark gasped and laughed at the same time. Eve brimmed with enthusiasm and approval. "That is the best news I've had for a long time."

Yuko blushed, but her eyes remained on Eve. "You ok to watch the kids again?"

Eve smiled. "Of course! They'll have a blast."

6

Kirk was standing on the roof of a six-story building near the outskirts of what was left of their side of Old Paris, just looking to the west and thinking. He had on his vest, with cartridges in the sewn-in loops and his sawed-off shotgun slung at his side.

The Were groups might have been destroyed, but nobody went out at night in Paris without protection, not even him.

He heard some boots shuffle along the roof, step over a small block wall he knew was there, and continue in his direction.

"Tim," he called, not bothering to look behind him.

"Kirk," Tim responded as he ambled up beside his boss.

"She's out there, isn't she?" Kirk asked his friend. "She isn't going to stay."

"I'm not sure if she is waiting or watching. Hell," Tim reached up to scratch his nose, "I think she is hoping something is coming in the night. Something she can release her pent-up, screwed-up sense of protection on."

Kirk glanced at the other lookouts on the buildings around him before he turned back to Tim. "She told you no."

"Several times," Tim admitted.

"Can't say you didn't try, and I got to say I'll never call you a quitter."

"You?" Tim asked.

"No," Kirk shook his head slowly. "I decided I would be better off with someone who wants to stay at home, not be out there," he nodded to the plains, "fighting the Darkness."

"Good man," Tim told him. "I've been relegated to a casual friend. I think something else has her heart."

"The vampire?" Kirk asked. "Akio?"

"Not some*one*, some*thing*," Tim said. "Those are people who fought with us, and you know it."

"Not Eve," Kirk pointed out.

"She's got enough humanity to be all right in my book."

"But it's a technicality. She isn't really a person."

"You know, Kirk," Tim clapped his friend on the back, "sometimes you can be a dick."

The two men turned when they felt something different, Tim to the left and Kirk to the right, looking for whatever set their danger senses off. Moments later, Kirk popped Tim on the arm and pointed up.

Both men watched as something black moved across the stars in the sky. Kirk put his hands up to his mouth and yelled, "Don't you point your guns unless you want to shit them out later!"

There were chuckles around them as they smiled, recognizing the ship.

James joined them on the rooftop as the Pod landed and the cockpit started to open.

Tim was the first one to speak. "Michael?" he whispered and walked forward, heedless of the ship.

"Oh...damn," James whispered under his breath. "She didn't make it." The two men watched as Tim reached into the plane and took the young boy from Akio, who handed him up.

"Mr. Timothy," the little boy was groggy from sleep, "I saw the stars so close I could touch them. But Mr. Akio said they were still too far away."

Tim held the boy in his arms, then adjusted him and allowed his head to fall to his shoulder. Seconds later, little Michael was asleep once more. Kirk and James walked up next to him.

Michael was the first to jump out, his coat flapping as he vaulted easily out of the seat and over the side to land next to the Pod. Akio followed him out.

"It seems," Michael nodded to the young boy, "that his mother met the Duke in the city. She sacrificed herself to allow little Michael to run back to their hotel. William didn't follow the boy. And I am sorry, but he had another bad scare right before we found him. He will need someone to take care of him."

"I got this." Tim was rubbing the little boy's back. "I told her not to go, that..." He choked up a moment. "That... It doesn't matter. I told her not to go."

James told them, "Tim was close to Michael and his

mother. They didn't see eye to eye on everything, and he has been worrying since they left."

Tim spoke into the silence. 'Thank you for bringing him home."

Akio?

Hai, *I will go to her and ask.*

I'll be here. Let me know when you are ready. I'll come to you.

Hai.

The three men watched as the shorter vampire nodded to them and then walked toward the stairs. They turned back to Michael, who said, "He is going to see if Sabine has made up her mind."

"Hell," Kirk shrugged. "I could have told you she is beyond ready to leave. I wouldn't have thought it, but she is a changed person."

Michael looked around, noting the different people on the tops of the buildings. "That kind of experience does change a person, when they were fearful for so long."

James walked over to the edge of the building and looked down. He could see Akio three blocks away, heading for the area where James knew Sabine liked to hide in the shadows and guard in the night. "He sure gets around quickly."

The other three joined him, watching Akio's last few steps before he slipped into darkness.

The three men never noticed when Michael disappeared from behind them.

I am coming, so don't shoot me.

Sabine's head whipped to her right. "Akio?" she whispered, trying to find the man who helped give her back her sanity. "Where are you?"

A hand touched her left shoulder. She slapped it off and pulled a pistol, but it was stopped halfway up by another hand on hers. "Why do you think," Akio told her, his face only a few inches from hers, "I just told you *not* to shoot me?"

"Sorry." She slipped the pistol back into her holster. "I wouldn't have shot you, but pulling it is normal." She smiled. "So, can I get a hug?" Not waiting, she reached for the stiff man, hugged him, and released him. "So, are you here like you promised to give me a choice? Here to—"

"Shhh." Akio stepped around her and started walking toward the plains. "I'm going to leave you here if you keep talking."

She followed him out of the deep shadows of a building into the starlight. "So I get taciturn Terry as my *sensei* now?"

Akio looked back at the woman. "I am not offering myself as your sensei," he corrected before she could get a good pout going. "I am offering to teach you. Perhaps at some point you will figure out your future." He pointed to the stars in the night. "I will tell you the same thing Michael told Jacqueline and Mark. We go into danger, and there is no promise you will not die tomorrow."

Sabine turned around to look at Paris. "I know it isn't a nice thing to say, but I'd rather have a fast death with you, Michael, and the others than a slow death in a city that died decades ago."

A new voice called into the night, "Then we can continue, young one." Fortunately, she stopped herself from reaching for her gun again.

"Michael!" She smiled, then a puzzled frown took over her face as she looked from Michael to Akio and back again. "How messed up am I, that I now have two vampires for friends and there is no one else I'd rather see right now?"

The black Pod slipped down out of the sky, the cockpit already opening as it settled nearby to float a few feet off the ground. "I would consider that the beginning of wisdom," Michael replied.

Akio spoke up. "Sabine, take the back seat," he told her as he walked toward the Pod. "I will take the front."

"Wait, what about..." She looked around. "Where's Michael?"

I am all around you, his voice said in her head, *and I am in the ship. We don't have the room, and I have a location for the Duke's chalet, so we must go.*

Nagoya, Japan, Hirano Residence

Yuko appeared in the same spot she had landed the box earlier that day. In the dark, it looked more like that first time she had dropped Hirano here after the operation all those weeks ago.

The Pod door slipped open, letting her jump gracefully onto the pavement. She headed straight for the door, far more confidently than she had the last time. Just as she approached the front door to the apartment building it opened, spilling yellow light onto the porch. Hirano stepped out, dressed smart-casual and even holding flowers. As she got closer, she saw they were daisies. Her favorite.

She immediately suspected Eve but decided to refrain from spoiling the moment by wanting to know the ins and outs.

"Good evening, Yuko," he called as she approached.

She bowed nervously. "Good Evening, Inspector," she replied, making light of the formality of their meeting.

He handed her the flowers. "For you."

Yuko blushed for the hundredth time that day. "Thank you," she said softly. "They're my favorite."

"I know," he admitted, giving her a telling smile.

Hirano nodded toward her Pod. "Are we taking your vehicle or mine?" he asked coyly.

"It's up to you. I don't know where we're going," she admitted, having already agreed to him picking the restaurant.

Hirano grinned. "Well, can yours take an address and get us there?"

She nodded.

"Well then, perhaps we could go in your… What do you even call it?" he asked.

They started walking in the direction of the Pod, whose door was already sliding open. "A Pod," she told him.

He bobbed his head as if she'd just told him the name of her pet poodle.

He helped her in and then hopped in himself. Yuko explained the harness, and they told the EI interface the address. Within moments the door had slid shut and the Pod lifted into the air.

It hovered twenty feet above the immediate township for a brief time to allow them to take in the view and then it shot higher, the town disappearing from view.

Seconds later it descended, appearing again over a different part of town.

"We should probably drop into an alley or something. No point in flaunting the technology," Yuko said modestly.

Hirano nodded, his eyes wide and mouth still hanging open. He had not said a word since giving her the address of the restaurant.

The Pod slipped into the alley next to their destination, stopping less than a foot from the ground. The door opened, allowing them to exit. Yuko got out first and Hirano followed, turning and practically stumbling backward, trying to take in the whole concept of the machine as he disembarked.

Yuko waited for his bewilderment to subside.

"So, the restaurant is this way?" she asked, pointing to the street.

Hirano seemed to remember himself. "Yes. Yes, it is," he confirmed as he watched the door close and the Pod disappear into the stratosphere again. "Is it... Is it safe on its own?"

Yuko chuckled, covering her mouth. "Why? Did you want to stay with it while I go to the restaurant?" she asked jokingly.

Hirano took her point and directed his attention back to her. He offered her his arm and she linked her arm around his, thrilled to be that comfortable with him so soon.

Once on the street, Hirano got his bearings and then led them to the restaurant he had booked.

Saint-Genis-Pouilly, France

The Duke looked around the large room in surprise and a little wonder. "They all work?" he asked aloud.

Evan nodded to his boss. "Yes. Damned surprising that so far nothing has been stolen and everything is in working order."

There were five people in the room with William and Evan. The others were checking the machines, comparing their findings to the notes that had been left by those who had shut the buildings and equipment down.

"We just knew, absolutely knew, that it had been completely destroyed!" Evan spoke to himself in wonder. "No one ever came to look."

William broke his personal thoughts and commented to Evan, "That isn't true. I noticed some bodies, skeletons really, to the north. At some point there were fights, so it probably became a myth and a warning to not come here. Eventually those protecting the place either died in the fights, died of old age, or finally drifted away."

"Still," Evan turned back to his boss, "I would have thought the effort to keep it complete would have failed."

"Sir?" One of the men William had tapped to join them on this expedition called from a desk some thirty feet away. Both William and Evan turned to look. The man pointed down. "We can't seem to get this machine to boot up appropriately."

William watched Evan walk between the desks and make his way to the computer in question. A moment later, William watched Evan's face show confusion as he bent over and started typing on the keyboard. It took the scientist a couple of minutes to finally exhale. "There," he told the guy as he stood up. Then Evan bent back down and typed some more. "Oh, hell." It was another minute before he stood back up and turned to William.

"Sir," Evan said, "we are going to need some more."

"More what?" William asked, his annoyance flaring.

"Minds," Evan answered as he played with something on the computer.

The Duke ground his teeth together. "If I didn't need you in a good place," he whispered to himself. "I would leave your blood-drained corpse for the crows to eat in the sun." William waited a moment, then spoke louder. "What kind of minds, Evan?"

The scientist looked up. "What? Oh, we need the best minds."

William nodded and turned around, then walked to the door and stepped out. His physical demeanor would have told anyone paying attention to stay away. Unfortunately, William was very familiar with this type of human called a 'scientist' now. They seemed to have way too much of the curiosity gene, and way too little of the self-preservation one.

The first attribute furthered his plans, but the second tried his patience. Moreover, he had learned that should you ask a scientist how to kill practically unkillable people, they would start rattling off ways as if they were making a list to go to the store.

He didn't want that effort focused on himself, and he needed them to have access to the tools which could kill Michael.

Or him.

So for now, he would hold onto his anger.

7

Nagoya, Japan

"I must admit, I still can't really believe you're here," Hirano confessed.

The restaurant had one of the most romantic settings Yuko could ever have imagined. They had been seated on a balcony overlooking the city. Fairy lights framed the handrail and trickled from above and down the sides of the framed structure in strategic places.

The city itself looked more beautiful from this vantage point.

"How do you mean?" she asked. "We arranged it."

Hirano smiled, appreciating Yuko's literal interpretation of what he was saying. "I know, but I'm still pinching myself. It's like, maybe I didn't really get up this morning. Maybe I'm still dreaming this incredible dream, and you didn't really show up on my doorstep."

Yuko smiled, fidgeting awkwardly with her napkin.

Hirano moved the conversation on. "Tell me about your

world. What do you do when you're not fighting bad guys?"

Yuko chuckled quietly to herself as the waiter arrived with the bottle of wine Hirano had selected. He and the waiter went through the tasting routine and the glasses were filled.

"I research. And explore. And build things with Eve," Yuko tried to explain succinctly. "It would be rather boring to anyone watching, I suspect."

The waiter placed the bottle down and left. Hirano leaned forward, holding his glass up in a toast. "I don't think you could be boring if you tried," he told her confidently.

Yuko raised her glass to his and they chinked. "I hope this is the case," she answered demurely.

Hirano smiled, holding her gaze. "I know this is the case."

Yuko blushed. Again.

Hirano changed the subject, taking the pressure off her. "I've never had a bad dish here," he said, picking up his menu. Yuko, glad of the task-oriented distraction, picked up her menu too.

"But the duck is especially good, whichever way they cook it," he added.

Yuko started reading the menu, basking in the romantic atmosphere. She briefly found herself wondering if this was what Bethany Anne experienced when she was on a date with Michael.

The butterflies, the ambiance. The anticipation.

Suddenly there was a crash.

Yuko thought she saw a couple of black shapes swing

over the balcony in front of her. There was a woman's scream, and then a shuffling of chairs and some movement. She heard something behind them, too.

In a heartbeat she was on her feet, slipping her Jean Dukes out of the thigh holsters she had worn under her dress. She pinpointed the targets immediately. They were dressed all in black with their heads almost completely covered by their masks and hoods. She recognized the way they moved.

This order she had fought before.

"Get under the table," she told Hirano calmly but clearly. Hirano looked shocked. He had drawn his weapon too. "You're kidding?"

She shook her head. "You don't want to mess with these guys." Seeing the sudden agitation in her eyes, he conceded and did as she had instructed.

And with that, she started firing. She took out the two ahead of her, beautifully avoiding any of the patrons. Then, as if she were merely dancing as the evening's entertainment, she shifted her weight onto the other foot and turned to face behind her. Two more fighters had made their way from the roof onto the balcony. She fired two shots, taking them out almost silently.

There were more shouts and cries from staff and guests alike, but Yuko kept her focus. She scanned for the next wave, and sure enough, fighters were entering through the doors and climbing over the balcony.

She took out three as they came through the main restaurant, despite one trying to use a passing waiter as a human shield. Again she turned, picking off the black suits as they appeared over the railings. One, two, three, four…. And then another four in close succession.

By the time she had finished, a number of her fellow diners had already moved off the balcony and into the main restaurant to take cover. Only a few remained, paralyzed by fear.

Yuko walked over to the balcony and searched above and below to make sure the threat had been neutralized. Satisfied as she could be without sweeping the entire place, she headed back to her table and sat back down before she remembered that her date was under the table.

She ducked her head under the cloth. "You can come out now," she told him casually.

A somewhat befuddled Hirano shuffled awkwardly back into his seat, holstering his weapon and looking at the destruction around them.

Yuko took a sip of her wine as if nothing had happened.

"So," she said, "what do *you* do in your free time?"

Hirano looked at her in utter amazement. She winked, and the pair burst out laughing.

After the shock had dispersed and the staff started venturing back into the public areas and talking to their guests again, Hirano found the presence of mind to ask her what had just happened.

Yuko looked fleetingly concerned. "I'm not sure," she confessed. "I recognized the fighting style and have no doubt they were here for me. Though why—and why now—I'm not sure. Our operation has only been back in town for a matter of days, so I guess they must have been waiting since our incident last time."

Hirano looked confused. "You think it was the same organization we messed with?"

Yuko shook her head, tidying the table as she contemplated her answer. "I don't think so. I think this is another group. Maybe something to do with the fact that Michael is back."

Hirano searched his mind, trying to get everything straight. "The ArchAngel, who has been in a different place?"

"Exactly," she confirmed.

Hirano whistled through his teeth, then looked at the chaos in the restaurant. "I think we're going to have to go somewhere else if we want to eat tonight," he commented, looking at the confusion.

Yuko agreed. "I know just the spot."

"Ok," he said, smiling despite the disarray that surrounded them. "Let me go settle up and then we'll go."

Yuko sat there for a moment more looking at the cityscape, mulling who on Earth might be trying to make their presence known to her. She tapped her communicator and filled Eve in.

"I'll monitor cameras and see if they give us anything," Eve told her. "Are you coming back to base?"

Yuko saw Hirano approaching. "Not yet. Don't wait up," she added mysteriously.

Eve started to protest about her safety and the like, but Yuko ignored her and concentrated on her date.

"Ready?" Hirano asked, holding out his hand to help her up. Yuko took it and allowed him to lead her out of the restaurant and the chaos.

Dukes Chalet, France

The Pod descended in the barely increasing light, the sun just cracking the eastern horizon as Akio adjusted a few controls.

As the craft approached the ground the canopy cracked open. Before it had risen enough for Akio to get out, Sabine had a gun out and was looking around the creepy chalet. Michael had already exited, and was fairly stomping toward the house.

Sabine nodded toward the rapidly receding Michael. "Is he nuts?" she whispered. "Who knows who is here?"

Akio touched the side of his head. "There is nobody here, Sabine," he replied as the Pod took off into the sky. "We would know already, have a feeling, if you will. I'm sure Michael is searching to see if there are any hints or suggestions as to where our target has gone.

Sabine looked around for a moment, taking in the dark recesses and shadowy areas. "This place gives me the creeps." She looked up at the three-story-tall roof. "A few weeks ago while I was running across the plains, I would never have thought I'd be helping chase down the scary monster who was in command of the evil *branleurs* pursuing me. The one who was behind the problem in the first place."

Akio kept his own vigilance, understanding Michael didn't want the human with him at the moment. "I'm afraid I don't know that term," he finally replied.

Sabine brought her gaze down from the chalet's roof and turned to Akio. "What term?" She thought about what she had just said. "Oh, *branleur*? It, uhh…" She thought about it a moment. "'Wanker,' the English would say 'wanker.'"

Their discussion was interrupted when an explosion occurred out of sight.

"Shit!" She turned and was going to run toward it, but her arm was held fast. She turned to Akio, who was looking toward the chalet but didn't seem concerned. She tried to pry his fingers off. "Michael—"

His fingers didn't budge. "Is ok. You can keep trying, but you won't be able to pull them off, and trust me, the Archangel is fine. The reason he went ahead is so you don't run into that," he nodded toward the chalet where the explosion had occurred, "and have your body parts become part of the wallpaper."

Her head turned from Akio to the chalet and back. Akio released her arm and she surreptitiously rubbed where his hand had grasped it. "You're kinda strong for a short guy."

Akio grunted and tried another smile. "Big things come in small packages."

Sabine looked at Akio for a moment, then her eyes narrowed. "Was that a comment about, uh…" Her eyes glanced down and then back up to Akio's face, which was a study of calm and repose. "No, never mind. I'm sure my mind is just making things up."

They both turned when they heard boots crunching on gravel to see Michael coming down a path between the chalet and the tall brick wall some fifteen feet away.

Sabine stepped away from Akio and looked at Michael's coat. "How did you…" she started as she walked around him. Michael stood still, his head turning around first one way and then the other, tracking her. She put out a hand to rub his arm. "How did you not get anything on you?" Looking at him, she asked, "You can switch into your misty stuff that fast?"

"I can and did," he answered. "However, if you were there I would have had to grab the two of you as well. Doing that is a bit of a pain, and I would have been less than pleased with myself if I had missed. Better to skip the mistake than court disaster."

"How many?" Akio asked Michael when he turned toward him.

"The one fire trap I accidentally tripped. Three more of those, once I figured out how I missed it. Five normal traps and some poison." Michael turned to look back at the chalet. "I think I found most everything. Sabine, you might want to stay out here."

Sabine nodded. "I'm good, but I'm not indestructible. I'll keep the perimeter clear."

Michael turned and walked back to the chalet. Akio patted her shoulder as he stepped past her. "Keep your guns handy. We don't know if anyone has been notified."

Sabine's head swiveled to the gate. Moments later she was heading in that direction. "God," she called over her shoulder, "I hope so!"

Akio heard her open a door as he entered the house behind Michael.

William received a buzz on his small phone. He lifted it and listened for a moment before he replied in a gruff tone to the person on the other end of the line. "Take ten and go find out who is messing with my home, the home I wish to come back to someday." He paused as the other party asked him a question. "No, I doubt it is him. Not if we have explosions happening. Hmmm? Yes, if you find anyone in the house, you may do with them as you please. Just don't kill them in the chalet if you can help it. I don't want a complete mess to clean up. Also, don't let them go. Either kill them or enslave them. Yes, you can do that as well. Ok, goodbye."

He snapped his phone case closed and went back to reviewing the extensive architectural drawings of the Hadron Collider. He marked the exits and other places he might be able to make exit holes out of the large ring and sub-ring for his new permanent lair.

Sabine looked around and considered the difference between when she had first been saved by these two men and now.

Her reunion with her cousin James and spending time with his friends Kirk and Timothy had been enjoyable, but she had still wanted to see Akio again. She smiled, trying to figure out if the Japanese man had been joking or not. Had he actually made a sex joke? She didn't get the vibe that he liked her.

Dammit, it was all too confusing. Sabine wasn't sure if she was attracted to him because he saved her, because he gave her a way to fight back, or because he had a hot body that oozed sex appeal.

Maybe all three.

She sat herself down in a corner where two walls came together. She was in the dark. *Not that it would have mattered*, she thought to herself. The sounds of people coming toward the chalet were loud enough to wake the dead.

Well, shit. She thought about Michael and Akio. *That includes the mostly dead.*

"It's feeling too damned weird," Adlar whispered to his boss. Adlar was dark-skinned, but Derick was so dark Adlar thought he could make a moonless night seem like daylight at times.

"Yes," Derick agreed and turned to the others in the squad. "It feels wrong, people. Shut your mouths and try to be silent." He pointed to the three in the back who had been talking. "You three swing around to the north and come in from the garden side."

"Why do we have to swing around?" Hoary hissed.

"Because you three are going to give the rest of us away with your constant joking around," Meinard, another in the squad, hissed back.

"You need to get a life," Hoary commented.

"You need to get laid and grow the fuck up," Meinard retorted.

Hoary's friend Darnell chuckled, "Well, he's likely to grow up before he gets laid."

"Probably," Derick's voice broke into the conversation, "that won't happen because of your childish behavior. Now, go north and enter through the garden." His eyes fairly gleamed at them in the dark. "And if this is a vampire, I hope he chokes on your bones."

Hoary slapped his two friends. "Derick said 'boner!'"

"Bones, you ass!" Derick shook his head in frustration. "If you fuck up the Duke's chalet, he will probably end you and my life will be better for it."

The three started toward the north, still whispering amongst themselves.

Adlar watched them go. "What do you call those three?"

"I call them bait," Derick admitted when they were out of earshot. He turned to his number two man. "If we don't hear any screaming in a few minutes, we will go in the front."

Adlar and the others who had stayed behind chuckled.

"I doubt it," a female voice told them. "I think your people are dead, and if you don't slowly step back and return to where you came from, you will be too."

"Where the hell?" Derick's eyes were trying to figure out where the voice had come from. The Duke's chalet had high stone walls, and the voice hadn't come from up top.

"On the left," Adler whispered. "I think she is hiding in the shadows by the wall."

"Hiding?" The female chuckled. "Boys, I don't need to hide from you. I just need to stay outside of the blood."

"What blood is that?" Derick asked. Behind his back, he was giving instructions to his team with hand gestures.

"You know, the blood from your wounds when a sword cuts you open?"

Derick smiled, his teeth gleaming in the moonlit night. "I doubt that anyone is going to sneak up and cut anyone, little girl. I see you in the shadows in the corner. Me and my men," he waved behind him, "will be enjoying your cries of pleasure this evening."

"I'm sorry," she said. "You and who?"

"Me and…" Derick turned to point to his team and stopped. He saw five of people dead on the ground and a short man with brightly glowing red eyes and a gleaming sword staring back at him.

"Finish them," Akio commanded, and two shots rang out in the night. Both men's heads snapped around from the power of the bullets, and both bodies slumped to the ground. Sabine walked out of the shadows and holstered her pistol. "The other three?"

"I killed them before I came over here," Akio told her.

"I thought as much," Sabine admitted. "Michael?"

"Felt them from quite a distance, and had me come out to hunt."

"Oh." She looked at the men. "Did you, uh, need to…"

Akio smiled. "I don't drink blood from humans, Sabine."

"Right." She looked around. "Do we have much more to do inside?"

"Come on in." Akio walked around the bodies and went toward the house. "I know the front is clean of traps."

Sabine looked him over as they went into the chalet. "How did you not get any blood on you?"

"Practice, little one. Lots and lots of practice."

8

Nagoya, Japan

The black box was almost invisible against the night sky. Yuko figured that if it weren't for her vamp senses, she might have had difficulty locating it in the middle of the park where they had landed. She sniffed the air—no trace of Were scent.

Strange, she thought, not too concerned.

She trudged up to the container and opened the door, stepping into the semi-lit cabin.

"And what time do you call this?" Eve demanded playfully from the other side of a bank of consoles.

Yuko glanced around. "Where are—?"

Eve smiled. "Still out. I checked them in, to the arcade's hotel for when they've worn themselves out playing games. We can collect them in the morning. Besides, I didn't want them to see your example," she said, winking.

Yuko giggled. "Right," she said, contemplating a protest and then deciding she was too tired to be witty right now.

"So," Eve pressed, "what happened after we spoke?"

Yuko pulled out a seat and slumped down. "Not much. We left the restaurant and finished our date elsewhere."

Eve's voice was serious. She peered at Yuko from between two computers. "No more attacks?"

Yuko shook her head.

"So," Eve continued impatiently, "tell me about the date!"

Yuko's complexion flushed slightly. "It was…wonderful. We ate fish and chips sitting at the port. And we talked and talked. He told me all about his parents and his grandparents and about the stories they used to tell about us."

Eve raised one eyebrow. "I thought we wiped their memories."

Yuko bowed her head for a moment as she spoke and sat up in her chair a little. "Yes, but they would record it on paper and then extrapolate in between. Hirano swore that his grandfather's recountings were exaggerated each time he retold the story, and with no real memory to go off, he was just inferring from his incomplete notes."

She paused.

"Though he did get something right."

Eve held her gaze intensely. "What was that?"

Yuko grinned. "That you were the most intelligent and overwhelming non-human entity he could ever have imagined."

Eve frowned. "He wrote that?"

"He did," Yuko confirmed. "Even made Hirano question whether you might have been fiercer than the fiercest vampire or Were!"

Eve stood up and walked around the computers so she

could see her friend better as they talked. "Wow. And yet he didn't seem scared when we met."

Yuko pursed her lips. "I think he figured that since you were with me, it was one of his grandfather's confounded suppositions."

Eve chuckled. "It sounds like they've been quite fascinated with our comings and goings."

Yuko sighed, looking across the room as she sat back in her chair. "Yes, this is true." She paused, remembering their conversations. "You know, he seems pretty fascinated with this whole concept of space and Bethany Anne having put ships up there. He kept asking all kinds of questions."

Eve paused, processing. "You don't suspect he's a spy, do you?"

Yuko shook her head. "Oh, no, not at all. Just, he's curious. Fascinated. It's a good trait if we're going to spend time together again," she hinted noncommittally.

Eve grinned. "You mean you're going to see him again?"

Yuko smiled. "Yes. Well, he asked me, and I said yes. So…"

Eve looked concerned for a moment.

"What is it?" Yuko asked, sensing something was wrong.

Eve shook her head. "It may not be a good time. What with Michael being back and the danger factor rising… I mean, you were attacked tonight for no good reason."

Yuko started nodding slowly. "You have a point. Those guys weren't run-of-the-mill criminals. They were trained professionals, and they were after me, for sure."

Yuko thought for a minute more, her glow and excitement gone.

Eve cocked her head. "What are you thinking?"

Yuko's eyes seemed to turn down at the edges. "I think I need to tell Inspector Hottie I can't see him anymore."

Eve was quiet. "Are you sure you want to do that?" she asked finally. "You've waited so long to have a relationship with someone who gets your world."

Yuko's eyes had dropped to the floor of the cabin. "I know," she said distantly. "But if he had gotten hurt tonight, I wouldn't have been able to forgive myself." She sighed. Eve could sense her pain. "And besides, just knowing he's alive in the world brings me happiness. I need to make sure it stays that way."

Yuko shook her head, hauling herself out of her chair. She busied herself with tasks—anything to distract her from the hollowness growing in her chest where before she had felt so full she had thought she would burst from happiness.

Eve stood quietly for a moment before broaching her next question. "Do you have any more idea who they were? I haven't got any footage from the restaurant at all."

Yuko glanced up, her mood much soberer. "None at all?"

Eve shook her head. "They just don't have it."

Yuko frowned. "That's…odd."

She mused for a moment, looking around the Pod before continuing her thoughts. "Well, as to what we do know… We've made a lot of enemies over the years, but I have no idea why anything would have changed now. Unless…"

Eve blinked. "Unless?"

Yuko pursed her lips and pulled herself closer to the computers, booting one up. "Unless news of the ArchAngel has spread and these forces want to try and take us out before the ArchAngel crushes them."

Eve frowned, voicing Yuko's counter-thought. "You'd think it would make them want to keep a low profile."

Yuko shrugged, watching the computer screen. "Unless they feel desperate." She tapped a few keys and brought up a map of the country. "Either way, we need to be away from here to regroup."

Eve stepped over to her screen to look at what Yuko was doing. Seeing the map, she placed her hand on the back of Yuko's chair. "Where are we going?"

Yuko pointed at a lake in the middle of the country. "Otsu," she said quietly. "It's remote, and it will give the others some downtime to normalize from the battles they've been in recently."

Eve nodded. "I'm sure they'll appreciate that. However..." She hesitated a moment. Yuko looked up, and Eve put her hand on her shoulder. "You don't have to run away from Hirano."

Yuko lowered her eyes. "I'm not, I swear. I'm trying to keep him safe."

Eve didn't push the issue. She nodded and returned to her computer to make some preparations for their trip the next morning.

Yuko added softly. "I'll go see him in the morning. Let him know."

Eve nodded again and went back to work.

Peckham, England

"In that building there," Officer Oscar Williams pointed

to the dark brick building. His partner looked to where Oscar was pointing.

"Put your damned finger down!" Leo hissed. "You're going to get us tagged!"

Oscar yanked his hand back. The two officers were in the shade of a tall edifice three blocks from the large black building, soot having stained the bricks of the outer walls centuries back.

"What'd'ya mean?" Oscar asked his salt-and-pepper-haired partner. "We got the tip that the man we're looking for is in that building."

"And he is going to stay there," Leo told him. He slapped his partner on the arm and nodded down the street away from the black building. "Let me buy you a pint, and I'll explain something I was hoping to keep you out of for at least another six months."

Leo swept his fingers through his hair and started walking away, tucking his hands into his uniform jacket. Oscar took one more look at the building, then jogged to keep up with his partner.

Leo shook his head to quiet his partner when Oscar tried to start a conversation. As they walked, the two officers nodded to the ladies on the street and shook a couple hands. "Here," Leo called over his shoulder and dipped into the Green Antlers Pub.

Oscar was surprised when Leo waved to the barman and kept walking toward the back. The two stepped out of the smoke- and beer-fume-filled bar into a hallway, and Leo reached up above a door and grabbed a key. Ten feet farther he reached up on the wooden wall, twisted a small piece of wood aside and inserted the key, then turned it and pushed open the portion of the wall that was a hidden door.

He waved Oscar inside the room after making sure no one had followed them.

Closing the door behind them, Leo pulled off his hat and tossed it onto a chair. The room was fairly large and included a couple desks up against one wall, a table large enough for ten, and a bar at one end. "They keep the bar stocked for us." He waved Oscar to the bar. "Take a drink—you're going to need it."

"Well," Oscar walked over to the bar and grabbed the bottle of whiskey he recognized, "not going to argue with a free drink." Oscar stopped before he poured and turned to Leo. "It *is* free, right?"

"It is," Leo answered. "I'll wait till you finish it. Wouldn't want to waste your drink."

Oscar chuckled. After pouring the drink into the glass, he stoppered the bottle and placed it with a *thunk* back onto the bar. Leo had found a bottle of lager from somewhere. "Drink up," Leo told him and tipped his bottle back. It took Oscar a second to down his drink.

Oscar's slight coughing spell amused Leo. "Going to have to practice by yerself a bit harder with the good stuff before you do that again."

"I'm good," Oscar replied, setting the glass back on the bar. "Didn't realize my throat was so dry."

"Uh huh." Leo pulled out a chair at the table. "Might as well sit down. I've got a story to tell you."

Oscar dropped his hat on the table. "Ok, I'm warmed up well enough. What's up with those in that building?"

"You ever heard of blood-baggers?" Leo asked. Oscar shook his head. "Ok, how about vampires and Weres?"

"Well, of course, them," Oscar answered, and leaned forward. "Wait, those street rumors are true?" He reached out and started playing with his hat. "That would explain a couple of the killings in the park."

"We keep as much of the truth from the citizens as we can. Usually, the paranormals stay out of the city with their problems because of the blood-baggers."

Oscar shrugged. "Not following."

"It's like this." Leo tapped his fingers on the table. "The blood-baggers drain vampires and sell their blood. It gives humans some damned good benefits, and the blood-bagger is only killing the undead anyway. The Weres aren't as big a draw, 'cause taking their blood is a good way to die if you happen to mix them. But the blood-baggers are willing to grab an occasional Were or two who isn't associated with any of the local packs for a little R&D. So, in general, they don't come into town, and especially not this area."

"So the guy who was pointed out?"

"Is a blood-bagger, and based on your description it's probably Noah. He's the Number Two over there and a real asswipe. The other three are George, Thomas and Harry. Harry is the leader, and you can figure which one he is 'cause of his white hair and youthful face. He has a baby-like appearance."

"But don't mention it?"

Leo shrugged. "I've never heard of him reacting to a comment on his age. However, I wouldn't push any of the four. Noah is a jagoff who seems like he is on angry drugs all the time. George is tall and about as wide as a stick, and

Thomas is kinda short and a little frumpy. None of them are in bad shape, and for God's sake don't get into a fight with them."

"Fisticuffs?"

Leo shook his head. "Any of it. They are wicked fast and strong 'cause of the vampire blood they suck down, and they have some of the best weapons cause it's like their asses print money—selling that blood and all." Leo eyed his partner to see how much of this warning was sinking in as he sipped his beer.

Oscar was quiet, but a few moments later he leaned back in his chair. "You were going to wait the six months why?"

"Most pubes like you quit in the first six months. Was trying to save you from the darker side of our work."

"There's more?" Oscar asked. "I mean the freaky-deaky stuff, not the normal human stuff."

Leo used the bottle to scratch an itch before taking another swallow. "Some stuff even *we* find hard to believe, like those people who seem to be losing themselves when they sleep and finding some sort o' gray mist place. But most of them have checked out ok, just having a common dream. The psycho-doctors all give them a thumbs-up, so we write it up as bad digestion."

"So the people in that place are off-limits?" Oscar finally asked.

"Only the four I told you about," Leo admitted. "They have an agreement with the higher-ups. They keep down the paranormals, we look the other way. If we have an issue with some of their people, we take it to the captain. If the captain and whoever talks for the blood-baggers decide their guy was in the wrong, then we are ok to grab him whenever he isn't on their property."

"The black building."

"The very one," Leo agreed. "About now is when most need a second drink."

Oscar pushed his chair back and turned around to step over to the bar. "Yeah, I think that would be a good idea."

Leo played with his beer, turning it around and around while he waited for Oscar to pour and toss back his drink and finally cap the bottle once again.

"What's special about this room?" Oscar asked, taking in all the paper and notes scribbled on the walls."

"Well, that's the reason you are going to need a third drink," Leo told him. He looked around the room before returning his gaze to his partner. "Not all of us are happy about the agreement. We think one of these days we will have to go into the black building, and we wish to be ready."

Oscar thought about one of the dead bodies he now associated with the stories Leo was telling him. He turned back and grabbed the bottle, pouring himself a double. Capping the bottle, he took a sip and went back to his seat and sat down. "I'm in."

"Boy," Leo laughed, "you wouldn't have been in the room if I didn't already know there was no way to keep you out of that building." He pointed to different parts of the room. "I showed this to you, so you know we got plans. So you won't go get yourself killed before you can be part of those plans and do it right."

Oscar picked up the glass, noting how the dark amber whisky reflected the light and took a sip. "How many have tried to help before me?" he asked as he looked at the older cop.

"You are the seventh. Two are dead because they wouldn't take my word for it. I'm sure that bastard Noah killed one and I think it was Thomas who killed the other. Four are on the force and waiting for our time, and the other was killed in a freak accident over off Carnaby."

"Did I know any of those killed?" Oscar whispered.

"Sorry, son," Leo told him. "One of them was your brother Jack."

Oscar thought about the closed casket funeral he had attended. His mother crying as her oldest was laid into the ground. The number of police officers who had attended the funeral had surprised the teenaged Oscar. Seeing them all there in their uniforms had solidified his desire to be a cop—over the objections of his mother.

He lifted the glass to his lips and tossed back the rest of the whisky. When he had set the glass back down gently on the table, he looked at his partner, his eyes obsidian. "Just tell me what I've got to do, sir."

Leo nodded. "Don't think I won't, young man." He pointed his beer at Oscar. "We will both," he pointed the end of the bottle between the two of them, "make damn sure that asshole is dead and buried."

9

Peckham, England

Harry sniffed and reached up with his handkerchief to wipe his nose. "Damned dust," he commented. He and his top three men were inside the core meeting room of their fortress.

Noah was to his left, George was in front of him and Thomas was to his right. They were sitting around their personal planning table. Two bottles of clear alcohol rested in the middle along with three bottles of stout.

George pulled up his shirtsleeves. The fabric did nothing for his lean physique. The vampire blood he consumed gave him excellent strength for what should have been a man you could break over your leg. The lids of his eyes were drooping. "So it's true?"

George was never one to waste time.

Noah poured some of the liquor into his glass and put the bottle back down on the table. "Yes, it's true." He tossed the drink back and smacked his lips. "It took two of my men and three of theirs, but we got the right proof." He reached into his pocket and tossed some pictures onto the table. "Watch the blood."

Thomas *oof*ed as he shoved his chair back to give him room to lean forward and pick up one of the pictures. "That's the Dark Messiah?"

"The very one," Noah agreed. "The team that had this information wanted too much money for it."

"Who's the other guy?" George asked. "Captain of the ship?"

"Yeah." Noah reached for one of the stouts. "From what I can tell," he held the bottle a couple inches from his lips and winked at George, "he's English, and the vampire told him to shout out that he was coming for another vampire in Europe."

"The Duke," Harry said, his deep voice cutting through the talk. "We have dueling deadly vampires."

"Either the score of the century," Thomas commented, "or a good way to die."

Noah leaned forward and put a downward-pointing finger on the tabletop. "I choose to think of it as a good way to rid mankind of a couple monsters and make ourselves the most powerful humans in existence as we sell their blood." He looked at Thomas and George as he spoke. "We can get a shitload of money for mere *drops*." Noah leaned back and smiled. "Drops, guys. Not ounces, *drops*. We lock these freaks down and feed them, right? We are damned near immortal, I bet you."

George looked at Harry, his blue eyes contemplative under his bushy white eyebrows. It was quiet for a few moments. "It'll probably be our final score." Harry agreed and looked at all three men in order: Noah, George, then Thomas. "We need to either leave these two vampires to—no pun intended—duke it out, and we go after the winner if there is one. Or we go after the new guy who probably doesn't know his way around too well, and once we have his blood, we go after the Duke himself."

Thomas rubbed a finger under his nose while George pursed his lips. Noah just sat in his chair grinning. *His mind*, Thomas thought, *was probably already made up.*

"We got enough blood?" George asked, looking across the table. Harry nodded.

All three men looked at Thomas, who shrugged. "What the hell, we been together since we all beat the shit out of Charley William in fourth grade. We can beat another bully, right?"

Harry smiled and leaned forward, grabbing a beer. "To our last Charley William!"

All men grabbed a drink, the sound of clinking bottles and glasses hitting each other breaking up the quiet as the men toasted.

"I've got home fort," Harry told the three. "Each of you take a team and a copy of the pictures and find this Dark Messiah. Let's crucify him on the cross of pain and agony."

Noah grinned as he pushed his chair out far enough to stand up. "That's down on dungeon level three, right?"

Nagoya, Japan, Hirano Residence

Hirano was surprised but excited when Yuko rang his bell at eight o'clock the next morning.

She made her way to the second floor to find his door

ajar and the smell of coffee wafting into the hallway. She went in, closing the door quietly behind her.

"You drink coffee?" he called from the kitchen.

"No, thank you," she responded. "I can't stay long, but I thought I needed to say this in person."

The clattering of cups in the kitchen stopped and Hirano emerged into the living area drying his hands with a dish towel. He slung it over his shoulder, now looking concerned. "Why?" he asked. "What's wrong?"

Yuko stood motionless, her eyes fixed on the floor, trying to find the words.

Hirano approached her. Before he got within two steps of her, she looked up and spoke, stopping his advance. He dropped his arms to his sides. He'd been reaching out to her.

"I've been thinking about the incident last night," she started.

Hirano nodded. "The army of ninjas you took out single-handedly. Hard to forget."

She dropped her eyes again, clearly distressed. "I… I can't see you anymore," she blurted quietly. "I'm sorry."

He stepped forward again, but she shrank from his outstretched arms. "Why?"

"It's too dangerous. You were in danger last night because of me. And if they find out that you mean something to me, then we might not be so lucky next time."

"Is this because Michael is back?"

Yuko nodded solemnly. "It may be. We just don't know anything yet."

Hirano looked pained. "But I don't want you to just disappear."

Yuko looked back up at him. "I don't want to either, but I have to. I have to get my team away from here, and we need to let you be safe."

"When will I see you again?" Hirano asked, now moving closer and holding her shoulders between his hands.

Yuko shook her head, looking down again. "I don't know. Maybe never," she confessed.

Hirano frowned, holding her more tightly. "What do you mean?"

Yuko sighed and stepped back a little, forcing him to let go. "Well, if our mission goes according to plan we'll be leaving Earth soon," she explained.

He looked bewildered and torn up inside. "So that's it? You just leave?" he pressed, unbelieving.

"Yes," she confirmed. "I'm so sorry. I shouldn't have gotten in touch. It was unfair. I wasn't thinking of the repercussions. I was selfish, I wanted to see you."

Hirano moved closer again and put a finger on her lips. "No, you weren't," he told her firmly. "And whatever happens, I will always be glad that you came to see me, even if our time was brief." He dropped his finger from her lips and leaned in and kissed her, just as a tear ran down the side of her face.

Yuko headed out the front door of the apartment building and back to her Pod. Hirano's last words rang in her ears. "Always know you can come back to me. I will wait for you. Come back to me when you feel ready. We have something that is worth holding onto."

She swiped at another stray tear as she hopped into the Pod. She thumped down into the seat and contemplated not even doing up her harness. Right now she didn't have the energy for trivial things in light of what she had just had to do.

Her heart ached with a pain she had never known before.

Happiness, she thought to herself. *Is it really worth all this hurt?*

The Pod lifted off, and Hirano looked out of his living room window in time to catch sight of it out of the corner of his eye before it was gone from his world for good.

Otsu, Japan, Lake Biwa

The large black box rested on the lush greenery on the banks of Lake Biwa. Given the relocation into the middle of nowhere, Jacqueline had encouraged the team to take a day off to rest and recoup from the excitement of the city.

Eve suspected it had more to do with Jacqueline wanting to spend some time with Mark, but there were many things Eve could do given a little downtime from the incessant battling they'd been doing since the return of Michael.

Yuko, on the other hand, was busying herself in distraction from her brief encounter with actual happiness.

Eve cocked her head, processing something abnormal.

Yuko noticed. "What is it?"

Eve held up one finger, and then a moment later resumed normal functioning. "I was communicating with Akio. We have new orders."

Just then, Jacqueline stepped back into the black transport box, cum office. Her hair and skin were wet, and it looked like she had just slipped a dry set of clothes over the top, that was consequently now damp in patches. Around her neck, she had slung a towel from the gear that Eve had issued them when they entered the box.

Yuko glanced up from her computer terminal. "Where's Mark?" she asked casually.

Jacqueline's eyes narrowed. "Why?" she asked suspiciously.

Yuko shook her head. "Jacqueline, it's ok. I'm not after him. I was just inquiring."

Jacqueline's face relaxed a little as she caught herself acting like the needlessly jealous girlfriend.

Eve turned to join the conversation, adding a semblance of logic. "She's not interested because she's got the hots for Inspector Hirano, remember?"

Yuko lowered her eyes, her cheeks flushing a bright shade of pink. "We have a job to do," she said, changing the subject.

Eve agreed. "We have new orders from Akio," she explained. "He'd like us to investigate the whereabouts of the pieces of the Kurtherian ship."

"The Kur-what-ian-what-now?" Jacqueline asked, her mouth skewed to one side, perplexed by the strange words.

Yuko smiled at Jacqueline's reaction. "The Kurtherians. The name of the alien race. Didn't Michael explain this to you?"

Jacqueline shrugged. "He may have mentioned something, but as you know, he's not the most wordy or explain-y of people." She pulled the towel from around her neck and ruffled her hair vigorously, drying the dripping ends.

Just then Mark came stumbling up the steps into the black box, grabbing Jacqueline's butt surreptitiously. Jacqueline's face lit up at the attention of her boyfriend, which Yuko and Eve could only imagine she had spent the morning trying to exhaust.

"What did I miss?" he asked, pulling a t-shirt on over his enhanced vampire six-pack.

Jacqueline turned to look at him, his arms now around her waist. "We have another mission. To find some pieces of a boat."

Eve shook her head. "Not boat. Spaceship."

Mark's eyes widened. "No shit?"

Eve nodded. "Yes shit." She realized what she had just said and clamped both hands over her mouth, giggling at herself.

Yuko stretched her legs out a little as she began to explain. "Ok, it looks like there are a few things you still need to know. You might have heard how Michael's love, Bethany Anne—our Empress—is off amongst the stars?"

Jacqueline and Mark nodded. Jacqueline spoke for both of them. "Yeah. I mean, it's pretty intense, but we've gotten that much of the story."

Yuko bowed her head slightly before continuing. "Well, the Kurtherians took over the Yollins, and sent them to Earth with the hope of subjugating the human race the same way.

"Bethany Anne and her team of scientists were able to get into space and took out the scout vessel before it could bring through the rest of the army. And when I say 'through,' I'm talking about through a gate which joins two distant points in space."

Mark's eyes flashed in amazement. Yuko continued her story. "Bethany Anne and her team effectively chased the Yollins off, following them back through the gate that had brought them here from a far region of space. But then it exploded, leaving them stranded."

Jacqueline had stopped drying her hair and was listening intently, her eyes betraying uncharacteristic signs of distress at the lovers' plight. "So how will they get back to Earth?"

Yuko jumped in. "They're rebuilding now, but it's taking time. I understand the distance is considerably farther than anything which Bethany Anne's Kurtherian technology could handle."

Jacqueline became more agitated, emotion welling in her chest. "But she knows that Michael is alive? She's coming for him?"

Eve continued to explain calmly. "Yes. We're able to get short messages to her, but our communications with her are limited to a few words."

She turned to her computer screen and pulled up a new interface. Mark and Jacqueline shuffled over to see. Eve indicated with a nod of her head. "Here," she told them. "This is what we showed her."

The words within the message envelope, separate from some code that looked like a foreign language to even Mark, were clear as day to them.

"ArchAngel lives," Jacqueline mouthed breathlessly.

A tear welled in her eye. There was silence in the gray

office while the pair of newcomers absorbed the information.

Eventually, Jacqueline spoke, her voice cracking with emotion and determination. "We've *got* to help them!"

Yuko nodded, her own eyes a little damp. This conversation only accentuated the feelings she was already experiencing from her morning's trip. "We need to find the pieces of the ship, put it back together, and get Michael into space."

Mark took a deep breath, clearing his head. He frowned. "Hang on. Let's say we manage to get the pieces of the ship put together and we launch it. How on Earth are we going to find Bethany Anne in all of space? And if the gate is destroyed and she's trapped on the other side, then at best we'll just be hanging around waiting for them to finish repairing it…in space?"

He shook his head, feeling foolish for even entertaining the possibility that he, a random out-of-place geek-turned-vampire, was now seriously talking about going into space.

Yuko moved to the computer that Eve and the others were gathered around so that she was in their line of sight. "We have maps. Kurtherian maps. We can find the gate. And as you said, Michael isn't a detail kind of vamp. Getting through the gate is something we'll figure out once we get to that…er…bridge."

Jacqueline was nodding her head as she listened. "Well," she said, pulling herself out of her brief emotional interlude, "I guess first things first. We need to find the pieces of the ship and get them put together."

Yuko nodded. "*Hai.*"

Jacqueline flicked into tech-seeker mode. "Ok, so what

can you tell us about the ship?" she asked. Mark noticed the change in her demeanor and looked at her.

Jacqueline noticed his gaze. "What?" she asked, a little distracted by the task at hand.

Mark shook his head. "Nothing. It's just, you're on the case all of a sudden. I've only seen you like this when you were ready to tear someone up."

Jacqueline smiled. "You didn't know me before I met Michael. This was what I spent my life doing—scouting for lost technology." Her smile widened. "This is what you might call 'my gig.'"

Mark's eyes widened. Yuko was sure she saw something else behind the new admiration he had for her.

Yuko sighed quietly to herself. "We know more, yes," she continued. "The ship belonged to the third Kurtherian group, known as the Sacred Clan. We have some of the pieces safe in our warehouse already. However, the ship was broken up into sixteen boxes by the Queen of the Leopards before Bethany Anne executed her for her part in killing Michael."

Jacqueline closed her eyes. "I think my head's about to explode," she said, a little bewildered at this point.

Yuko nodded. "It's a lot to take in," she agreed sympathetically.

Mark's face was lit by a grin, hardly believing his ears. He barely wanted to seek clarification in case someone burst his fantasy that this kind of tech might be real.

Eve started programming coordinates into her computer. "I guess it's time to pay your friend in Yokohama a visit," she called to Yuko.

Yuko nodded. "Yes, I believe so. Jacqueline, Mark, we should leave soon."

Jacqueline glanced out the door at the green vegetation and the glimmering lake. She remembered that they had been trying to have some quality downtime, but nodded her agreement, trying to hide her disappointment.

Mark, on the other hand, tried to hide his excitement at the prospect of new, advanced, and alien tech. "Suppose I better go grab the rest of our gear then," he said, keeping his voice as level as possible.

Jacqueline mumbled something about drying her hair and followed him out.

Eve smiled. "Looks like personal lives will have to wait just a little longer."

Yuko paused, registering Eve's reference to personal lives. "What do you mean by that comment?" she asked, somewhat suspicious.

Eve shook her head. "Oh, nothing. Just, Mark and Jacqueline will have to wait for more vacation time until this is squared away. And then they can resume. That's all."

Eve turned back to her computer, sensing Yuko's eyes still on her and hoping that her point had been received.

10

Peckham, England

Noah, George, and Thomas all stood on the small stage in the warehouse, with seventeen men and four women at the tables in front of them. George moved to the center and raised his hand as the afternoon sun shone through the antique glass on the second level, bathing the old brick warehouse in natural light.

George waved to his two partners to the center with him. "We all appreciate you coming on such quick notice." He hitched his thumbs in his belt. "I know most of you have your ears to the ground to find the next vampire and get one of our bounties."

There was general murmuring in the group, which George allowed to die down for a moment.

"Well," he continued, "we have good information about two."

"You're going after the Dark Messiah?" Alfie Cimmons called. Tina, who was next to Alfie, slugged him in the arm.

George frowned at the outburst. "Alfie, keep your mouth shut or we will have to sew it shut for you. Wait until my message is over and then ask." He returned his attention to the whole group. "All of you know about Europe's Duke, and now most of you know about the one called the Dark Messiah. This one's an addition to the list. None of us have heard of him before so we are thinking he must be relatively new, but he is very powerful. If you believe," he looked around at the tables of bounty hunters, "even half the rumors, he can call down lightning out of the sky and walk on water."

The chuckles around the room were mirrored by the three on the stage. "I know," George continued, "enough lead will make anyone drop to the bottom of the lake."

"Nothing out there I've ever fought," a guy named Henry commented to no one in particular, "was able to ignore a judicious application of lead poisoning."

"Or a shit-ton of fire," the woman next to Henry added.

George put up his hands. "Noted, and I think we all agree. However, none of us are here because we are stupid. We have two powerful vampires that need to be captured."

Noah spoke up from behind George. "Preferably painfully."

"Very," Thomas agreed. "No telling how many innocent humans have been eaten by them in the dark of the night."

George turned to look at his two partners. "Well, it's definitely the darkest before the dawn."

"And dawn kills," three of the bounty hunters called out.

"For those who are willing to join us, we will have three teams. One with Noah, one with Thomas, and one with me. Everyone will be outfitted with blood for the fights."

Thomas spoke up. "Which we will sign out to you, and if you don't need it, we will charge you for it."

Several laughed. Trying to keep an extra vial of vamp blood was a damned game for the bounty hunters. The blood-baggers would charge them eventually, but every once in a while, if you got clean away, the extra vials could save your ass.

"How many vials we going to be issued?" Henry asked.

George turned to answer him. "Each person will have five."

Henry whistled. Five was unheard of. "The good shit?"

"Yeah," Tina called back. "I don't want the cheap pansy blood you sell to the little jerkwads trying to play 'big man on their block.'"

"Listen," Thomas answered from behind George, "each of us will be leading a squad, so we don't want you sucking wind in the middle of the fight."

"We will all," George finished, "be packing the good stuff."

Yokohama, Japan

The black box landed in the corner of a lush green park. Mark was the first to exit, a renewed spring in his step. He looked back at the container, waiting for the others to disembark almost like a terrier waiting for his owners to take him for a walk.

Yuko was the next one out, her sword strapped across her back for the first time in several weeks. It felt strange, having hardly worn it for so many decades and then to have been battle-ready constantly during the days with Michael.

She shook her head, noticing how different she was feeling since embracing the less than diplomatic side of her. It was no longer an intellectual conversation with her friends, but rather it integrated into a new way of seeing herself and her role in the world.

She wandered across the grass, taking in the skyline of the city of Yokohama juxtaposed against the immediate surroundings of the manicured gardens.

She inhaled the clean air and the fragrance of grass mixed with blossoms, remembering how much she had loved her time here, training in the mornings and evenings with Kashikoi and working on her projects with Eve in the afternoons.

While Akio had always given the impression that he had just been waiting, she really felt she had managed to live some semblance of a life despite the loneliness. And no matter what dangers they might face now that things were heating up with Michael's return, she had no regrets.

Jacqueline tumbled out of the black container as she scrambled to strap her holsters and weapons to her body, clearly not thrilled to have her dirty weekend plans interrupted. And yet, secretly she now had a sense of purpose. Not just born of honor, but a real desire to get back in the saddle with the next mission and achieve something.

Not that she was going to admit it to Mark.

Eve jumped down after her, closing the door remotely by whatever synaptic connection she had with the box. "Remember where we're going?" she called to Yuko.

Yuko nodded. "It's been a while, but yes, I remember,"

she confirmed, striding across the green carpet of grass toward a main path. The others followed her, feeling a little surreal at being in the middle of a gunfight one minute, lakeside the next, and now in a beautiful Utopian park.

Jacqueline hurried to catch up with Mark. "You're excited about all this, aren't you?"

Mark looked suddenly defensive. "Well, it's extraordinary. But it doesn't mean I'm any less excited about us," he clarified, slinging one arm around her shoulder as they walked.

Yuko led them through the park and onto a main street with cars running along and above it. She found the nearest crossing, then led them deeper into the maze of buildings and skyscrapers. After a while, they found themselves in an area of town that wasn't quite as pristine as the park where they had landed.

Yuko slowed and called, "Just down here on the left." The group closed the spaces between them, suddenly more alert.

Jacqueline felt Yuko's attention sharpen. Her head started moving more often, presumably looking for signs of trouble. "Thought we were going to see a friend of hers," she whispered to Mark.

Mark raised his eyebrows. "Suppose it depends on your definition of *friend*," he retorted, using his first two fingers on each hand to air quote the word "friend".

Jacqueline drew a deep breath. "I guess so…" she said, suddenly not feeling at all comfortable about what they might be walking into.

Yuko stopped outside an inconspicuous door between a

disused computer hardware shop on one side and a shuttered shop front on the other. She flicked her attention up and then down the street.

There wasn't a soul around.

There hadn't been for about three blocks now.

Jacqueline unsnapped her holsters, thinking that a gun would be less messy than claws in the close-quarter environment they were heading into.

Mark clenched and unclenched his fists, getting ready to move if he had to.

Yuko took a breath and then marched up the two stone steps to the white door with its peeling paint. She rapped decisively on it and waited.

Nothing.

She tried the handle.

It opened.

Yuko started to glance back as if to look to the others for reassurance, but then breathed in her own courage and pushed through the door into the darkened hallway.

The others followed.

Once inside she took a few paces forward, then paused for her eyes to adjust to the dimness.

There was a smell of damp in the air, and a hint of old food. She stood still, waiting. Listening.

There was a cough from upstairs. Her head tilted upward, still waiting.

Mark could hear her elevated heart rate.

"Hello?"

There was another cough and a shuffling. And then a muffled voice responded, "Come."

Yuko seemed to relax a little once she took off her

boots. As she headed to the stairs and started climbing, holstering her Jean Dukes. Three steps up, she turned to her friends. "Probably best you wait down here for a few."

Eve nodded and stepped back off the first step, then turned to look at Mark and Jacqueline as the Diplomat walked up the staircase. After arriving at the top she headed left, farther into the building, and disappeared from view.

"Konnichiwa," she said, bowing at the door and then entering the clean, spartan training room.

"Konnichiwa, Yuko," the old man replied. His quiet voice traveled through the space as if powered by some unearthly force. Or chi. There was a moment of silence as Yuko paused, acclimatizing.

His voice traveled to her again. "To what do I owe this honor?"

Yuko approached the *kamiza* side of the dojo where he was seated. "The honor is mine," Yuko responded, bowing in respect to her old comrade.

The old man struggled to his feet stiffly. He returned the bow, then used his wooden walking stick to support his weight as he sat back down on his cushion.

He motioned for her to join him.

Yuko picked up a cushion from a pile in the corner and dragged it over to place herself directly in front of the old man. She sat down and breathed, becoming present with her old friend. "How are you, Kashikoi?"

"Better in health than temper, my dear," he said, smiling

sagely. "It's been quite a while since I saw you last. How go your projects?"

Yuko relaxed as they talked, catching him up with some of what she had been doing. They chatted for several minutes before Kashikoi brought them around to the obvious question. "What brings you back after all these years?"

Yuko shifted her crossed legs, considering where to start. She found her place and took a deep breath. "As the keeper of knowledge of the Sacred Clan, I have supported your quest to grow your following of the worthy and to maintain your secret."

Kashikoi closed his eyes and bowed his head. "For which I am very grateful."

Yuko bowed slightly in acknowledgment before continuing. "You're welcome," she told him. "But I come to you with new information which may change our agreement."

Kashikoi's face remained unchanged. "Our agreement for you not to ask and for me not to lie to you?"

Yuko nodded. "*Hai.*"

Kashikoi's old face cracked into a smile as he paused to consider the prospect. "What is the new information?"

Yuko lowered her eyes. "The Patriarch has returned. And now he needs to reassemble the ship."

Kashikoi's face became grave. "You know I keep that knowledge from falling into the wrong hands," he responded, his tone taking on the weight of thunder.

Yuko was undeterred. "Yes, I know. And I have always supported that. But Michael's are not the wrong hands."

"But there are forces still active in these regions," he protested. "Forces who would take this knowledge and this technology and exploit it for their own ends." His manner remained sage and mostly gentle, but Yuko recognized the passion that burned in his eyes. This had been his project longer than most people had lived.

Yuko softened her tone. "This is true. But with Michael returned, these threats are no longer a risk to the knowledge or the technology."

The old man sighed, contemplating this unprecedented and unanticipated change in the status quo.

Yuko remained silent.

Eventually, he asked hesitantly, "What assurances do I have? That this will not end up in the wrong hands," he qualified.

Yuko thought for a moment, keeping her face expressionless in the negotiation. There was a slight glint in her eye for a moment before she spoke again. "Your followers...you trust them?"

Kashikoi nodded. "Of course. When I leave this mortal coil, they will maintain the *'vallitseva tila.'*"

Yuko nodded her understanding. "Yes, dedication to the *vallitseva tila* must be continued. So, do I assume that your willingness to leave them as the sole protectors means that you might send them as your proxies to assist my team and me in securing the relics?"

She paused, letting the old man contemplate the idea. "You always said you relished the idea that one day they might be brought together again, all other things being equal," she added, this time allowing a warm smile to grace her lips.

The old man put up a final defense against her logic. "I did," he agreed, "but things are not equal. The Chinese government still has some knowledge of the components, and as long as individuals in their ranks lust for power and profit, there will always be a risk."

Yuko returned her expression to neutral. "And if your followers are able to mitigate that risk, along with my own assurances, under the protection of the Patriarch?"

The old man looked across the dojo, his eyes unfocused as if imagining the possibilities. Eventually, he returned his gaze to Yuko. "Then it would be a wonderful thing to see," he confessed. He sighed a little, leaning forward in confidence with his old friend. "My concern is not that you are true to your word, but that the forces you will face are too great."

Yuko considered his words for a moment, then stood, turned, and walked out.

He heard her voice call down the stairs, and then she returned to the room, bowing again on entry. She waited near the door as three other individuals appeared. She instructed two of them to bow on entry out of respect for the training space, and then led them over to where they had been talking.

"These," she said, presenting the three, "are my friends. My allies in this pursuit. Eve, you know."

Eve bowed her head to the old man, who returned it with a nod.

Yuko indicated Jacqueline, who waved. "This is Jacqueline and her partner Mark." Mark bowed quickly and awkwardly, improvising.

Kashikoi acknowledged each of them and turned his attention back to Yuko.

Yuko was wearing a slight smile, her conventional

poker face unconventionally neglected. "Perhaps you would like some of your disciples to come up here and see if this is a team they would find adequate for the challenges we might face."

Kashikoi looked the four of them up and down, moving his eyes from one to another. He stamped his stick on the floor three times and continued to regard the three newcomers.

A few seconds later a horde of agile young fighters in traditional gear jogged into the training space.

Yuko's smile didn't falter. She counted at least twenty of them and glanced at the others. All of a sudden this was becoming exciting for them, after too many moments standing around waiting.

Kashikoi regarded Yuko again. "Are you sure you want your friends to be a part of this?"

Yuko looked at her team, who were already preparing, discretely limbering up where they stood. She nodded and joined the old man where he sat.

Kashikoi nodded his head, hiding his surprise that she didn't feel compelled to help her allies in the test.

"Very well." He lifted his voice so the others could hear clearly. "Open hand combat only. No drawing blood. Whoever is left standing is the winner."

Jacqueline frowned. "What does he mean by 'open hand combat only?'" she whispered loudly.

Eve translated for her. "It means no weapons."

Mark sighed. "Oh, well. And the 'no blood' means no teeth either?"

Eve nodded. "That's right. Think you can restrain yourself?" She smirked at him.

Mark chuckled. "It's not me you need to worry about. It's her," he said, winking and tilting his head in Jacqueline's direction.

Jacqueline scoffed. "Don't you worry about me, Geek-boy! I'm the picture of reserve."

Kashikoi leaned closer to Yuko to speak with her. She crouched to put her ear at his level. "Do they always talk this much?"

She laughed. "Yes. They're from a different discipline," she explained, standing up again.

"Discipline?" Kashikoi muttered. "Interesting choice of words."

He knocked his stick on the ground once and his squad of fighters sprang into action. Some charged. Others performed jump-kicks and shouted intimidatingly.

Yuko's team countered their attacks either by stepping aside or allowing individual fighter-boys to land inelegantly on their fists.

The exercise lasted about forty seconds, during which time Jacqueline actually tossed one of the larger humans to Mark, saying "Here you go, honey. Try not to break him too much when you put him down."

When all movement had subsided, the three stood on the same side of the room where they had started, with a carpet of bodies strewn around them.

Kashikoi, maintaining a neutral expression as much as he could, leaned on his stick and hauled himself to his feet. "Did they leave any of them alive?" he asked, confounded by the display and now looking to Yuko for an explanation of how this was possible.

Mark cocked his head and listened for a moment before answering. "They're all alive," he confirmed casually.

Kashikoi nodded and wandered onto the training floor as if inspecting the damage up close was going to make his decision easier.

He turned and looked at Yuko. "Very well. You can take some of the disciples of the *vallitseva tila* and start gathering the knowledge."

Yuko bowed respectfully, accepting her victory.

Before Jacqueline or Mark could speak and potentially undo her diplomatic efforts, she quickly requested they wait downstairs, telling them she would follow shortly.

11

Saint-Genis-Pouilly, France

William pursed his lips and enjoyed his new quarters. He was under so much rock that even the famed ArchAngel wasn't going to be able to get down the long shafts and through the air-sealed chambers.

He reviewed the schematics and knew that he probably was going to have to wait to get a couple more of his hidden exits dug out. However, he had enough right now for him to feel fairly comfortable.

The team had brought down a table that would seat ten comfortably. The Duke tapped his fingers on it, thinking. Moments later, there was a knock.

"Come in," he said. Gerard stepped into the room and shut the door behind him.

"We have news," Gerard told him. William nodded.

"There have been sightings of the ArchAngel, and rumors of him being the Dark Messiah. A ship landed in Frankfurt bearing his name. Our contacts in England have said that the blood-baggers have pulled together a team to try and capture him."

Gerard stopped speaking when the Duke started laughing. "They are going to try and capture Michael?"

"Yes, their thought is to capture Michael, use his blood to ramp up, and then either capture or kill you."

"Peasants," William spat. "Ignorant peasants. If I hadn't needed those blood-baggers to keep down the vampire population, I would have killed them long ago." He smiled. "But since this provides me an idea on how to lure Michael, I think I will hold off helping them and suffer with the knowledge that their deaths will support me in my endeavor to rule the world." He sniffed. "I would have had to kill them sometime anyway."

"Yes, Your Grace," Gerard replied.

"We need a team of four mercenaries," William told him.

"Where would you like to meet them, sir?"

"Here."

"Here?" Gerard's eyes opened in surprise.

"Well," William waved a hand toward the ceiling, "up top. I want them to know where we are."

"May I ask why, sir?"

"Yes, you may." William smiled. "Because when they go to kill Michael, he will read the fact that these four have seen my face and where I was when I gave them the commands." He stood up from the table. "Come, let me find my scientists and plan for the next phase of the project."

William opened the door and stepped through. Gerard had started closing the door when he asked his next question. "Did you find out how to turn on the power, sir?"

"Yes," William's voice floated back down the large, manmade cutout tunnel, "but it isn't something we have a lot of fuel to run."

Yokohama, Japan, Kashikoi's Dojo

Kashikoi returned to his seat, his back to the blacked-out windows on the street. Daylight streamed in from the skylights, softly lighting the space and the dust carried in the air.

"Before you embark on this mission there are things you should know," he told Yuko.

Kashikoi's tone was more serious than Yuko had ever heard it. She quietly sat back down on the cushion opposite him, and they waited for the last of the unconscious bodies to be cleared out of the dojo.

The moment the door at the end of the training area closed, Kashikoi spoke again.

"We know that there are a number of locations in China. When *she* had the pieces boxed up, she dispersed them across her realm so that they could never be used by someone who didn't know their locations."

Yuko nodded, unsurprised, indicating to Kashikoi that this information was familiar to her—at least in principle, if not the details.

Kashikoi continued, "Since then, what was left of the Chinese government has been trying to track these pieces down. They even tried to interrogate me at one point, thinking I had some knowledge of their whereabouts."

Yuko frowned, concerned. "But you didn't?"

Kashikoi carefully placed the stick he had been holding on the ground in front of him. "Not at the time."

"And now?"

Kashikoi put his hands on his crossed legs. "Now I know that a map was made and the locations recorded. The Chinese government acquired this in the years following the WWDE."

Yuko's breath became shallow as she listened intently to the Mysteries she had never been privy to.

Kashikoi lowered his eyes to the floor in front of his crossed legs and cane. "We have since learned the rough areas of three of the pieces, but we haven't the means to find the precise location or the resources to dig them up and protect them." His thoughts drifted as he spoke. "Which is why we've merely maintained the knowledge."

Yuko raised her chin slightly, indicating her growing understanding.

"The other challenge we face," Kashikoi continued, "as I have always understood it, is that even with the pieces, being able to assemble and activate them would require knowledge of the Kurtherian language."

Yuko's eyes glimmered with her secret, but she quickly lowered her eyes so as not to divulge what she knew. It wasn't that she didn't trust the old man. It was more that telling him would put him in danger. And the fewer the people who knew about the missing piece of the puzzle, the better chance they had at seeing this mission through to completion.

She looked back up at him and saw he was studying her carefully. "It seems you have been holding knowledge of the Sacred Clan too," he commented, hoping she would offer the information.

"My friend," she told him, her voice as even and respectful as ever, "there are things that we must keep from each other still if this mission is to be a success. *Vallitseva tila*," she added, invoking the concept of maintaining the status quo for the good of all involved.

Kashikoi nodded understandingly, although the boyish glee that had briefly inhabited his eyes was replaced with a mild disappointment. "*Vallitseva tila.*"

Yuko felt the reversal of the tables in the information game and found herself wanting to share with her old sparring partner. However, circumstances made it impossible. "I suggest," she offered instead, "that I return tomorrow for your chosen representatives to escort us on our mission. If you are in accord?"

The old man agreed and bid her farewell until tomorrow. Yuko rose, bowed, and exited the training room, leaving the old man alone with his thoughts once more.

France, the Duke's Chalet

Akio and Sabine found Michael in a large room, its ceilings twenty feet high. There was a long wooden table that had eighteen chairs around it. The one on the far end had a much larger back.

Michael had pushed it back and was sitting on it with his feet on the table. There was a pile of papers on the table in front of him and he had a pair of round glasses perched on the tip of his nose.

Akio snorted and Michael looked at him over the top of the glasses. "They are not prescription, merely decoration."

Sabine walked down the righthand side of the table opposite Akio, who had chosen the left. Michael turned his head and smiled. "I trust your target practice was adequate?"

"Just barely," she replied and pulled out the first chair to Michael's left. She sat down, then considered her options and lifted the chair up to move it back. Finished with the chair, she placed one foot, then the other on the tabletop. "I take it we aren't worried about messing up the furniture?"

"Fuck it." Michael turned back to his papers. "Since I don't think this chalet will be here in a few hours, I'm sure I don't mind a little breakage if you are feeling particularly vandalistic?"

"This asshole," she commented, looking at the numerous nice paintings on the walls, "has hurt a bunch of people. I'm thinking that destroying one of his hidey-holes will piss him off."

"Yesss," Michael replied slowly, picking up one of the documents he had been reading. "I think it will annoy him to lose this residence, even though he is safely in another location. Anything to piss him off and push his buttons."

Sabine stood up and started walking back down the table, then stopped and turned around. "Are there any more traps?"

Michael looked up and glanced over the glasses, a smile on his face. "There aren't any more traps that I know of. But then, if you get blown up, the best I can give you is 'oops.'"

Sabine's lips twisted, then she shrugged. "It isn't like I'm not living on borrowed time right now anyway." She turned and headed out of the large dining area. Moments later, they heard a loud crash from the front of the house.

"I believe," Akio commented, "that the bust of Wolfgang Amadeus Mozart—"

"An original," Michael interrupted as he licked his thumb and removed a page, lifting it off his lap to set it upside-down on the table."

"The *priceless* bust of Wolfgang Amadeus Mozart," Akio amended, "is now in pieces."

"Irreparably destroyed, I do believe," Michael agreed when they heard what sounded like a chunk of rock go crashing through fragile china.

Akio smiled. "I fear we are turning her to the dark side."

Michael glanced over his glasses again, the small smirk on his lips telling Akio he was having fun playing with the spectacles. "Is she your first?"

Akio's eyebrows narrowed in confusion for a moment before relaxing. "Oh, you mean student."

"Yes," Michael replied. "Why, what did you think I meant?"

Akio waved him off. "Doesn't matter DM," Michael grunted and returned his attention to the paperwork in his lap. There was another crash, then what sounded like a rip.

Michael spoke as his eyes scrolled down the page. "I think she just found the exquisite twelve-foot painting of Napolean. The last time I saw that painting it was on the wall in Versailles."

Another rip, then a crash.

"There goes the gold-filigree frame," Akio commented

as a loud *bang* and more breakable plates and glasses crashed to the floor some distance away.

Michael looked up, taking off the glasses and opening his coat to slide them into a pocket. "Tell me," He scratched his leg, "you have the basic information to build Pods, but nothing that is going to help us go into space. Do I understand that correctly?"

Akio pursed his lips. "*Hai*. We have the Pod technology to a large degree, but we don't have anything I would trust to go to the moon and back too often. Although, remember I told you that Bethany Anne is supposed to be coming back."

"I understand that, Akio," Michael replied, putting another piece of paper on the table as he reviewed the next document. "However, I am not going to wait around only to find out she ran into a problem." His eyes glanced up, "Or she was late getting ready," He looked back down. "Or she needed me, and I was still here on Earth, twiddling my thumbs waiting for a ride." He moved another document to the table, putting the period on that discussion. "Back to my question about the technology. I sense a serenity inside you, so out with it. You have an idea," Michael commanded.

"The Sacred Clan has a ship."

"Spaceship?" Michael asked.

"Yes," Akio clarified. "A spaceship."

"But?" Michael asked, his eyebrows raised.

"How did you know there was a 'but?'"

"There is always a 'but' involved; nothing can ever be easy. I've lived a long damned time, and anytime I thought

I'd gotten out of a predicament without a 'but,' I just hadn't looked *hard* enough."

Akio nodded toward Michael. "You are correct. The ship is in pieces."

Michael pursed his lips. "That doesn't sound too bad."

"We don't know where they are, exactly."

Michael raised an eyebrow. "How un-exactly do you know?"

"They are within the area what we used to know as the country of China."

This time, Michael paused a moment before he finally asked. "The country? To be clear, you don't know where the pieces are in the whole *country*?"

"The pieces that matter are in at least five caches secreted by the Sacred Clan right before their future was destroyed."

Michael put up a hand. "Wait a minute," he told him. "Are you telling me that they hid the parts of the spaceship that I now need almost two hundred years ago—"

"Less than one-seventy," Akio interjected.

Michael ignored the clarification. "Right before the story you told me about Bethany Anne killing their Queen—"

"Empress."

"Whatever."

Akio nodded. "She was a tad upset about your death."

Michael paused. "Did I receive a nice eulogy?" he asked, his eyes sparkling.

"It caused people all over the world to shed tears," Akio admitted. "Bethany Anne was very moving."

"Where was I buried?" Michael asked, amused to be talking about his own death and burial.

"The sun," Akio replied.

Michael blinked a couple times. "The *sun*." Akio nodded. Michael opened and shut his mouth a couple times. "The *goddamn* sun?"

"She consigned your empty coffin, plus those of the others who perished, into the sun," Akio repeated.

Michael looked at the ceiling as if he could find answers there. "Remind me never to sleep in a coffin as a joke. I'd hate to be accidentally sent into the sun."

"It would hurt," Akio agreed, and Michael chuckled.

"Ok." Michael moved the papers off his lap to the table and pulled his feet down to set them on the floor. They both could track Sabine by the continued sounds of destruction throughout the chalet.

"I believe she is working out some anger." Michael paused and thought for about ten seconds before he asked Akio, "Do you think she will lose her edge?"

"For shooting?" Akio asked, and Michael nodded again. "No. I believe this is the worst we have to deal with. Sabine is not going back, no matter how much anger she gets off her chest."

The guys could hear female grunting as she struggled with something heavy. Both heads turned to look toward the other end of the room when they heard a grating of something heavy rubbing against the stair railing from the third floor. A moment later something slid off the rail. There was a humongous crash when a three-quarter-sized statue crashed to the marble floor outside the room. Some white dust blew in and Akio turned to look at Michael. "Donatello?"

"I think so," Michael concurred. "She is setting a new world record for 'Most Priceless Objects Destroyed in a Single Afternoon.'"

"I'm so proud," Akio admitted and pantomimed wiping a tear from under his eye.

Michael started chuckling. "You are getting the hang of humor."

Akio winked. "It is liberating."

"It can get you in trouble," Michael told him. "And speaking of trouble, we have five pieces of an alien ship to find, then put together."

"Archangelsk." Akio turned back to Michael. "Boris can help."

"Boris?" Michael flicked his eyes to the end of the room when he heard Sabine yell in frustration, then returned them to Akio. "He has the knowledge to put the ship together?"

"No, Lilith does," Akio answered.

"I'm fuzzy here."

"Lilith is a Kurtherian brain inside a computer."

"Another one?" Michael searched his mind. "I seem to remember…"

Akio shook his head. "No, that was ADAM using a Kurtherian brain. So, not a Kurtherian brain inside a computer, but rather the opposite."

"True."

Michael held up a finger. "So if we find the major ship components, we know someone who can help put them together and probably help figure out how to fly it."

"Assuming the parts exist and they work." Akio agreed.

"Well, yes." Michael shrugged. "If they don't, we will create a company to R&D the technology." He looked at Akio, his eyes granite-hard. "I will get back to Bethany Anne. I made a promise on my honor."

Akio bowed his head in understanding. "*Hai.*"

"That leaves us needing people, resources, and know-how to build the spaceship. Do we go to Japan for them?"

"They are the most advanced for the job, but I have issues with them."

"Such as?" Michael leaned forward and started moving the papers into an organized pile.

"They are the most advanced and skilled people for the job. The issue is security."

Michael's eyes went flint-black.

Akio held up a hand. "The problem is that Japan is the most advanced, which was Bethany Anne's point. She wanted a country that was mostly intact."

"So, the problem?"

"They are the most advanced in stealing secrets as well," Akio admitted, looking sheepish.

"They are human, what do you expect?" Michael asked, knowing full well that Akio was asking the whole country to step up to his romantically remembered version of his people. "Never mind, I see it in your eyes." Akio just shrugged. "You have been through the end of the world, Akio," Michael pointed out, "so you have endured the worst that humanity has ever dealt with, excluding perhaps the last Ice Age."

"My people didn't change for centuries."

"Yes, but for as long as I have known them, a sense of

self-importance was always a temptation just below the surface." Michael chuckled. "The Japanese have always been the elves in my version of European myths."

Akio's eyes narrowed.

"No, really." Michael leaned forward. "Think about it. You have the body build, the long hair, and if we bleached your skin…"

Akio made a face, but Michael spoke right over it. "If you had blond hair and pointed ears, with your personalities, you would fit right in with elves."

"I have no idea if you are being serious or playing." Akio grumbled.

Michael leaned back. "I guess you will have to figure it out." He turned and grabbed the top few pages from the pile on the table. "So you are saying we need to use Japanese labor, but not be on Japanese land?"

Akio pursed his lips and nodded. *"Hai."*

"Ok." Michael looked in the direction Sabine had departed. "I don't hear much in the way of destruction."

Akio stood up. "I'll see if she has worked it out of her system."

Michael stood and pushed his chair in before grabbing the papers. "I'll find some energy." He started walking toward another door out of the room. "Chalet on fire in five."

"Meet you in front," Akio called over his shoulder.

Twenty minutes later the three figures watched as the roof of the chalet, engulfed in flames, crumbled down into the center of the outer stone walls. Sabine rubbed her nose. "I don't suppose I had to be so effective with that large picture of," she looked at Michael, "who was it?"

"A short man with a large ego," Michael replied. "His name was Napoleon."

"Where was it from again?"

Michael smiled. "The last time I saw it was hanging in Versailles."

A minute later a black Pod drifted down out of the sky. The three walked toward it.

"Where are we heading?" Sabine asked.

"Back to Frankfurt," Michael replied. "The Duke has a residence there we need to check out."

"Shotgun!" Sabine called and raced toward the Pod. She screamed in frustration when the Pod lifted out of her reach. She stomped a foot, turned around, and pointed at the retreating Pod. She stared daggers at Akio, whose eyes glinted in humor. "You dick!" she shouted. "That's not fair!"

"How does she even know what 'shotgun' means?" Michael asked.

"Some phrases," Akio answered, "resist change by time and circumstance."

"Yes," Michael agreed as the approached the red-faced woman, "but we are talking about a century and a half and the end of the world as we knew it."

Akio just shrugged. Some things even he still couldn't figure out, and he had lived them.

1 2

Yokohama, Japan, Kashikoi's Dojo

Yuko and Eve arrived at the door to the dojo and this time made their way straight upstairs.

Kashikoi was in his usual spot, but this time was instructing a small group of new disciples in their training. They continued, despite the presence of the strangers.

He called for someone, who came in through the far door, listened to an instruction the old man gave him, and then disappeared through the door again.

Yuko waited patiently and Eve stood almost motionless, but for her small efforts to maintain an appearance of being human.

As they waited, Yuko observed the techniques the young fit students were using. She noticed that their applications deviated a little from when she had trained here, and she judged that they were a little more effective.

She smiled, wondering if perhaps Kashikoi had perhaps bowed to her influence in effectiveness over style after all.

The young boy appeared again and bowed to Kashikoi, receiving a nod in return before he disappeared. Kashikoi pulled himself to his feet and issued his final instructions to the group training.

"*Yame*," he instructed.

The fighting stopped immediately. "*Rei.*" They bowed to their respective opponents. "*Kurasu shuryo,*" he finished. The group gathered the pieces of gear and training equipment they had left strewn along the side of the hall and jogged out of the training room.

Kashikoi beckoned Yuko and Eve over. They bowed and walked around the mats to meet him.

Just as they approached, four slightly older students arrived at the far door dressed in outdoor clothes. Yuko turned to acknowledge them with a bow.

"Konnichiwa," she said politely.

They lined up and bowed to their master and then to the visitors.

Kashikoi was on his feet already, aided by his stick. "Yuko, Eve, may I present my best students?" He waved his hand at them, taking a few steps onto the training floor. "Haruto, and Riku." The two Japanese males stepped forward and bowed before returning to their place in line.

Kashikoi continued, "And Akari and Ichika." A small, proud smile reaching his lips. "Ichika is, in fact, my granddaughter. And, even though she causes me much trouble, she is nevertheless one of the most courageous warriors I have ever met." He paused before continuing, "All four of these disciples I offer to you as the most dedicated to the cause of all of my students. They will assist you on your mission and represent our interests in maintaining the *vallitseva tila* no matter what."

His voice took on a warning tone. "While our interests are aligned, we are faithful allies. If the integrity of these relics were to become compromised, rest assured that these warriors you see before you would do whatever it took to ensure that the packages were kept from falling into evil hands."

Yuko bowed her head. "I understand entirely. Let's hope it doesn't come to that," she added optimistically. She turned back to the four new team members. "I am Yuko. This is Eve. We welcome your assistance and hope that we remain allies on this task."

She looked at Kashikoi. "Thank you, old friend."

Kashikoi smiled and said something in Japanese. The four bowed to him and jogged the length of the training room and out toward the front entrance that Yuko and Eve had used.

Eve watched them leave.

"Go ahead." Yuko nodded to Eve. "I'll catch up."

Eve narrowed her eyes, deliberately conveying her mistrust about automatically being excluded from the conversation that was about to happen. Regardless, she turned and headed out the door after their new teammates.

Yuko turned her attention back to Kashikoi.

He smiled, the essence of a young boy returning to his field. "You're ready for your next clue?" he asked her almost teasingly.

Yuko smiled. "*Hai.*"

Kashikoi lowered his eyes before he spoke. "We know the Chinese government has some of the salvaged boxes. I gleaned that much from their early interrogations of me. The person you want is someone deep within the remaining organization."

Yuko sighed. "Looks like we're heading to China then," she said, resigned to the prospect.

"*Ie*," Kashikoi insisted. "You must stay on the island. During the time you've been gone, anyone with any power or money has migrated to the place which can offer the most comfort and security. Consequently, most of the remaining governments and tech powers have relocated to Tokyo."

"China, as you know," he continued, "is mostly destroyed. Their citizens don't live as we do. They have villages interspersed over large areas of land. You will find the individuals who govern the country in Tokyo. The man you are looking for, if he is still alive, is Qin Shi."

Yuko frowned. "The emperor himself?"

"*Hai*," Kashikoi confirmed. "He wasn't always the emperor, though."

Yuko understood. "And where in Tokyo will I find him?"

Kashikoi's face took on a seriousness. "Shouldn't be hard. I'd start at the Chinese Embassy."

Yuko couldn't believe it might be that easy. "You mean we'll just be able to walk into the Chinese Embassy and make these demands?"

Kashikoi smiled, bemused. "No one said it was going to be easy, though the Diplomat gaining access to an embassy should be what your American friends call 'child's play,' no?"

Yuko smiled. "This is true. I will proceed. Qin Shi," she said, repeating the name of the man she needed to locate.

"Good. Very good," Kashikoi concluded. "You always were an excellent warrior, Yuko. And from what I've heard over the years, an excellent diplomat. I look forward to hearing of your success."

The old man bowed to Yuko.

Yuko returned the bow. "And I look forward to reporting our success to you, old friend." She smiled at him before heading out of the dojo to join the others on the street.

She pounded down the stairs in her boots and out the front door, finding their four escorts and Eve huddled in a group on the sidewalk. She pulled the front door closed behind her and headed over, interrupting their somewhat awkward "getting to know you" conversation.

Yuko smiled faintly as Eve turned to her. "You have the information?"

"I do. Tokyo is our next stop," Yuko divulged, setting off down the street. The warriors exchanged puzzled glances and followed her, Eve bringing up the rear.

Yokohama, Japan, *Yokohamakeon* (Park)

Yuko and Eve strode across the lawn of the park where they had left Jacqueline and Mark to make preparations.

Ichika jogged up to Yuko to speak with her. "Excuse me, Yuko-san? Shouldn't we be going to a train station if we're to go to Tokyo?"

Yuko instantly understood Kashikoi's warning when he had introduced his granddaughter. Hiding her smile behind her practiced blank expression, she glanced at the young woman as they walked. "*Ie*. We're going to Tokyo directly. The fast way. But first, let me introduce you to our friends. Our other allies on this mission."

Ichika glanced back at the others nervously. They had heard about the incident the day before when Yuko's friends had laid waste to nearly thirty attackers in a demonstration. The atmosphere around the trained warriors turned from mission orientation to one verging on dread.

Eve noticed they had slightly slowed their pace.

They approached the container and Eve led the way up the steps into it. Yuko and the others followed.

Eve was vaguely aware of scrambling and the shuffling of a chair being repositioned. As she entered the doorway she saw Jacqueline zipping up her jumpsuit and Mark tucking his shirt into his pants. Mark's hair was somewhat disheveled.

She ignored what they had walked in on and headed straight for her computer to get the box underway.

Yuko ushered the Japanese contingent into the office and lined them up to meet their new team. "Jacqueline and Mark, may I present to you Ichika, Kashikoi's granddaughter."

Ichika bowed, and Mark and Jacqueline awkwardly tried to mimic the strange bobbing custom.

Yuko continued, "This is Akari. And those are Riku and Haruto at the back," indicating each in turn.

"*Gakusei-no* Kashikoi," she said, addressing the group of their new allies, "this is Jacqueline and Mark. I must warn you that they are enhanced; you'll have heard the stories."

It was Haruto who spoke this time. "You mean like Weres?"

Jacqueline, still a little flushed and embarrassed, tried to cover up being caught off-guard by venturing into the conversation. "I'm a Were, but he's not." She jerked her thumb at Mark, who was now standing a complete arm's length from her.

"Vampire," Mark said, grinning and baring his teeth. He allowed his eyes to glow red.

Akari, Haruto, and Riku all shuffled back in response, their hearts frozen in their mouths. Only Ichika remained relaxed. "Ahhh, *that* explains how you could overcome our troop in combat!" she exclaimed excitedly. Then she frowned. "How come you left them alive?"

Jacqueline frowned too, stepping forward as her skin color normalized. "Why would we want to kill them?"

Ichika chuffed. "It's what your kind do, no? You can't help it, I thought?" She glanced at Yuko for clarification.

Yuko frowned. "You know that *I'm* a vampire?"

Ichika nodded. "Of course, but you are the Diplomat. You enforce the strictures in the absence of the Patriarch. But other vampires and Weres..." She looked puzzled.

Yuko laughed, waving her hand at Mark and Jacqueline. "No, these are also good Weres and vamps. They have both trained with the ArchAngel. You can trust them. They have honor as well." Her eyes took them all in. "There are additional good vampires and Weres around the world, not just myself and Akio. Not many, but certainly more than the two of us."

Ichika seemed to understand, and the others relaxed a little too.

With the introductions out of the way, Jacqueline and Mark pulled up separate seats in the far end of the container. The others found places to sit or perch and Eve gave her chair to Akari, explaining she wasn't human and didn't need to sit. Akari thanked her cautiously before sitting down.

Yuko felt herself stepping into a leadership role, something she had barely had cause to do in all the time she had been stationed here with Akio. "Kashikoi told me where we might find at least some of the other boxes," she began, bringing Jacqueline and Mark in on the information she had to share. "He suggested that we talk with someone in the Chinese government.

Mark glanced at Jacqueline. "China, here we come!" he exclaimed, the excitement of the unfolding adventure piquing his curiosity.

Yuko shook her head. "The government is here in Japan. Tokyo, to be exact."

Mark's brow furrowed and then quickly smoothed as his eyebrows jumped up. "Because Japan is the place to be? With all the tech and stuff?"

Yuko nodded.

The warriors had started looking around the container, their eyes taking in all the computers and equipment this strange team of renegades had at their disposal.

She continued, "The man we need to see is Qin Shi. We will most likely find him at the Chinese embassy."

Eve was already typing away on the computer. She looked up, pulling Yuko's attention.

"What is it?" Yuko asked.

Eve checked her screen again. "I think the reason we'll

find him at the embassy is because he is the emperor, not some run-of-the-mill official."

Yuko pursed her lips.

Eve held her eyes. "But then, you already knew that."

Yuko nodded and paused, waiting for a reaction from Eve. When none was forthcoming, she said, "I suggest we request an audience with His Highness. Could you put in an official request?"

Eve nodded. "Adding us to his schedule now," she reported.

Ichika had a look of amazement on her face. She gazed at Eve in awe. "You're *the* Eve. The legend that only a few have ever encountered."

Eve thought back to the written account the detective's family had been keeping, realizing that someone through the generations had indeed been paying attention despite her efforts to cover their tracks digitally. She sighed and confessed, "Yes, I am she."

Ichika glanced at Akari. "So cool," she mouthed, her face alight with excitement.

Eve continued her work. "Plotting a course for the *Chinese* Embassy. In *Tokyo*," she added, lacing her tone deliberately with a hint of irony.

Yuko noticed and smiled. "Those human algorithms are working out all right when you use them."

Eve shrugged. "I suppose now that we have more people around, I will make more of an effort." She glanced at the two young men, who had barely said a word. "And maybe in return, they might also feel comfortable in sharing some facial expression with us," she added cheekily.

Haruto and Riku exchanged puzzled glances, but Ichika sniggered, understanding Eve's comment precisely.

Yuko grinned. "To Tokyo, then," she concluded, moving to a computer herself to do some research before they arrived.

Tokyo, Japan, Chinese Embassy

The group of warriors stared at the embassy building. Like the rest of Tokyo it remained, not just intact, but had been enhanced over the last several decades as the economy here flourished. Though they had arrived in less than fifteen minutes—much to the amazement of the new crew—they waited patiently until their appointment time.

Now, with the sun low in the sky and many of the embassy personnel dispersing for the evening, they stood outside the main gates.

"Ok, here's the plan," Yuko told them, her eyes still fixed on the building. She rehearsed in her mind where all the exits were from the rapid research she had done on the way there.

"Eve and I will go in first. We will ask for their help. If and when that fails, we will try more extreme measures."

Mark chuckled. "You mean measures Michael would approve of?"

Yuko nodded, her expression once again blank and matter-of-fact.

He sniggered. "Why even bother asking them nicely? They're not going to give up this information easily."

Yuko turned to face him. "Because it's something I need to do before we break hell loose over them. It's good form," she said, suddenly aware of Akari and Ichika paying close attention to their exchange.

She changed the subject. "We'll move inside the gate now. When you hear the signal, you can come inside and lend assistance."

Jacqueline frowned. "What's the signal?"

Eve transformed her hand from a five digit implement to the enormous gun she had used in battle previously. "You'll hear it." She smiled.

Yuko couldn't keep her face straight. It was almost like there were two personalities still duking it out within her. This Yuko— warrior Yuko—smiled with satisfaction at Eve's Michael-approved response.

Yuko raised her voice a little so all the allies could hear her. "Jacqueline, you're in charge. Try not to kill anyone until we get the intel we need."

Ichika looked a little put out. "How come she is in charge?"

Yuko glanced at the young woman and allowed her eyes to flare red. "Because I said so," she told her quietly.

Ichika backed down immediately.

And with that, Yuko and Eve marched ahead of the others to announce themselves for their appointment.

The rest followed, slipping through the gate behind Yuko, who was readily granted access. Once inside they peeled off in opposite directions, finding their respective ways in the deepening shadows and staying out of range of the cameras despite Eve's assurance that she had them "taken care of." Ichika and the others went right, Jacqueline and Mark left.

Once Eve and Yuko were safely inside the front door,

Ichika turned to Haruto. "I thought she was a diplomat, not a dictator!" She *hmmpfed*, still pissed about not being left in charge.

Haruto shrugged. "People change, I guess."

Mark watched them from the other side of the lawn, debating whether to let them in on Yuko's decision to become more warrior and less diplomat since Michael's arrival. He caught Jacqueline's eye and she shook her head. "Let them find out," she winked mischievously.

Mark smirked playfully and kept his mouth shut. He looked back at where the other four had been on the other side of the lawn, but they were gone.

He grabbed Jacqueline's arm. "Hey, where'd they go?"

Jacqueline scanned the area quickly, then sniffed the air. She shook her head. "Ninjas," she said, rolling her eyes.

13

Frankfurt, Germany

The short frumpy Englishman was shadowed by a woman and another man. All wore coats in the middling-cold weather.

The sun was high in the sky.

Thomas, in the lead, walked around the corner, his eyes darting to all the possible hiding places along the dark brick street. There were slight shadows under doors and in alleyways where tall buildings stood close together, blocking out the sun.

There were plenty of people around to provide the feeling of safety, but Thomas had not lived as long as he had by assuming enough people meant enough eyes on their surroundings.

Some things that went bump in the night could go bump in the day. And furry or not, they were enhanced beyond a human.

"Third building on the north side," Thomas said as the

three of them made their way slowly down the street, walking at the same speed as others on the sidewalk.

"Look," Samantha said softly. Her job was to pay attention to the south side of the street ahead of them. Thomas and Jack both grunted.

"How could we be so lucky?" Jack asked. His eyes flitted back to his area of responsibility when he recognized the one from the picture.

"Dammit," Thomas hissed in annoyance, "he can walk in the sun. Fucker must be stronger than we thought."

"I don't know," Samantha replied as he walked across the street with a female beside him. "He doesn't walk like he is weak."

"And the female with him doesn't look subjugated," Thomas murmured. "Well, we have a challenge wrapped up in a riddle." He nodded to his left. "Let's hold there and discuss next steps."

"How are we getting in?" Sabine asked as the two of them crossed the street under a couple flying cars that floated above them. They walked up to the three-story stone building, which had definitely been built before the fall of civilization.

"I believe in knocking," Michael replied. Sabine's eyes looked at him in confusion.

Michael climbed the five steps to the landing and stepped to the door. It had a four-foot covered porch. "Knock," Michael said as his leg lashed out and slammed into the door near the door handle. The whole door erupted off the hinges and was flung inside of the residence.

Michael stepped in and moved far enough inside to allow Sabine to come in behind him. "Knock," he finished.

"Keep your guns handy," Michael told her. "We are probably going to encounter more goons." He looked around. "I see he likes to have multiple homes."

Sabine unsnapped her pistols' holsters and slightly lifted each pistol, making sure they would be easy to yank. "Is that why Akio is behind us?"

"Yes," Michael called from another room in the residence. "Oh, and cops."

Sabine rolled her eyes. "Great, now I have to fight the men in uniform, too."

"No." Michael's voice was right next to her, causing Sabine to jump.

"Dammit!"

"Situational awareness," Michael told her as he swung past and went up some stairs that were five feet on the other side of her. "I suggest finding a place to hunker down for a firefight."

"Ok." Sabine looked around the attractive first level of the residence. The floors were made of marble, and the furniture looked like it was centuries old. "What did he do, rob museums?"

"PROBABLY!" Michael yelled from somewhere on the second floor.

Sabine moved into the large living room area and looked around. "Well," she started pushing a large couch, working her way from one side to the other to get it to move, "it's not like this will need to stay pretty, I suspect."

"The woman?" Jack asked.

Thomas considered the question, then shook his head. "We have enough trouble. If we are all in agreement that she is there of her own free will, then she will be collateral damage."

"I think so," Jack answered. "My intuition says she is on the same side as our mark."

Both men looked at Samantha. "Hell, even with no hair that man is flat-out gorgeous. She could be along for the ride." She slapped Jack when he snickered. "Do you always have to go there?"

"Do you always have to say something that makes me go there?" Jack asked, eyebrow raised.

"He's right," Thomas added. "You always set up the easy ones."

"Whatever, you two. The girl goes whether she knows what he is or is just there to clean the pipes." She stared at Jack, who looked back at her, confused.

"What?" he asked.

"No comment?"

"No comment," Jack replied. "That was on purpose. You don't have to snicker at the obvious ones."

"Men!" Samantha huffed and looked toward the large home down the street.

Thomas glanced down at his watch. "Let's call everyone to get ready." He noticed that Jack had a question on his face. "First group to snag the new guy gets an extra share."

"Well, why the fuck are we yacking here about sexual innuendos then?" Samantha asked.

Thomas punched the last button to call in the rest of his group. "Sam, there is *always* time for sexual innuendos."

"It's how you know you're alive," Jack added.

Sam decided that shooting her two partners would be premature. At least, at this particular moment, it was.

Akio noticed the three talking in the front doorway of a building three doors down. His eyes continued to roam the street as he stayed in what little shadow he could find on the top of the building one down from the residence Michael and Sabine had gone inside.

"To run down there and read their minds, or stay here..." Akio's eyes found another group of two walking down the street from the opposite direction.

Michael? Akio sent.

Yes.

We seem to be attracting a large number of people with long coats.

Hiding weapons?

Give me another ten seconds, and two will be in my range.

I'll warn Sabine and check the back.

Hai.

Michael sped down the steps. Sabine caught his movement out of the corner of her eye.

"Look sharp," he told her. "We have an early warning from above."

"Goons?" Sabine asked from behind her little fort.

"Not sure. Only know they aren't expected to be cops," he answered as he went to the back of the house. "Be right back."

The door opened a little crack and he disappeared.

Thomas got a response from each of his four team members. Nodding, he punched in the code. "Ok, everyone is set. Let's drink our juice and bag and tag us a vampire." He reached inside his coat and pulled out a vial. Like the others, he uncorked it and tipped it back to allow the contents to spill into his mouth.

"*Gah!*" Thomas corked the vial and slid it back inside his jacket. "I hate that stuff."

Jack grunted an affirmative and Samantha didn't say anything as she finished her vial and slid it into a pouch around her waist.

"Love seeing the new colors," Samantha's eyes were moving from one tree to another. "It's a shame I can't live on this stuff."

"Well, technically..." Jack began but then went quiet, when Thomas gave the signal that the operation was starting.

Thomas had seven green "Go" symbols from his team. He stepped out of the doorway and started down toward the building.

Ok, definitely hostile. Akio's lips pressed together. *They are looking to bind you and kill Sabine.*

How many?

Seven, Akio provided.

I've got two here. Seems long coats are not very popular in the early fall in Frankfurt. Makes them stand out.

I've got these two. Akio turned and raced across the roof toward where the outside fire escape went down to the street. In seconds he was halfway down the fire escape, his eyes barely catching the shadows as three humans passed his alleyway.

SABINE! He yelled through his mind. *Shoot whoever enters!*

Moments later, as his feet hit the concrete from his two-story drop, he heard the beginning of a firefight coming from the building next to him.

SABINE! Sabine heard Akio's mind voice. *Shoot whoever enters!*

Sabine dropped into the zone, the place where she was more than normal, more than who she had been before.

She aimed her first pistol at the door and squeezed.

Jack raced ahead of Thomas. While he wasn't normally a

lead-from-the-front sort of person, if he was the one to do the most damage and allow them to grab the vampire, he would earn a second share. From what they had talked about, just one share was probably going to set them up for life.

All he knew was two of something that would set him for life was going to make his future sweet.

Thomas was excited; the vampire blood was a damned drug to all of them. Hard to come down when you felt such power in your veins, throbbing and allowing you to effortlessly accomplish feats no human could.

Over the years, he and others had put down a handful of mercenaries who had become blood junkies. They would do anything for the blood, including stealing it.

Occasionally they could save those types of people. It was the ones who bagged a vampire and were forcing it to change them that they killed with extreme prejudice. Their people didn't need new vampires who knew all the tricks and would be out to get rid of the competition when they built up their strength.

So far they'd had only one instance of all-out war in England. A mercenary by the name of Johann Williams had successfully faked his death, figured out a way to be turned, and started picking off blood-baggers in an effort to reduce the number of those hunting him.

Thomas remembered it was Jack who took Johann down. He had half-decapitated the man with a shotgun blast. Johann's head was lolling to the side and he wasn't as observant as he could have been.

No big surprise there, when you are trying to hold your head on and allow it to heal. Unfortunately for Johann, Jack was still powered up and swung around behind Johann, shooting his heart out through his back.

They burned his body. No one wanted that tough sonofabitch coming back.

They saw that the door had been kicked off its hinges as they raced up the stairs.

Jack would go through the door first and head left, while Thomas would go right and Tina would go forward if possible.

Thomas was almost to the door when Jack's body, blood spraying from a damned hole the size of Thomas' fist, was tossed violently into him, clipping him and throwing him back.

What the hell had gotten through Jack's body armor?

Tina jumped over the two of them. Once committed, you trusted the plan. Besides, her inertia was going to carry her in some even if she tried to slam on the brakes, so to speak.

As Thomas rebounded off the side of the front entryway, he heard Tina's guns fire and then stop.

"Tina?" he called. He had two more coming from above, and two from the back. He needed to support his team.

He flipped the semi-auto fire switch off and was pressing the trigger as he turned the corner. He was laying down enough pain to keep anyone with sense hiding behind some protection or give those without sense the option to stop his bullets with their heads.

He made it around the corner into a large room full of living room furniture and saw Tina—her head was gone. Something had hit her so hard her skull had exploded.

His speed was still jacked up and he sprayed the little fort of protection with the last of his ammo. With his off hand he grabbed a magazine and readied to switch them out.

When he was reloaded, he would walk up on the protective little fort and finish whoever was on the other side.

Sabine watched with little emotion as the first person she shot with her Jean Dukes special was blown back. His body armor took some of the kinetic energy and transferred it to throw him back out of the doorway, following his guts that were leading the way.

A moment later a female came around through the door, having jumped the body Sabine had shot. The mercenary turned in her direction and shot from her hip. Sabine barely registered that the wall close behind her was showering her with pieces of plaster.

The lady's head disappeared in gore when Sabine's bullet hit her.

That was when all hell broke loose. Sabine's eyes were large as she dropped behind her furniture protection when the *BRRRAAAAAPPP* of an automatic started showering her area with bullets.

Pumped up on adrenalin, Sabine believed she could count the bullets as they slammed into her fort. Twice she twisted as bullets found their way through the furniture, whizzing by her head and slamming into the wall behind her.

For the first time since her run from the werewolves, she was starting to feel fear.

Aim and shoot, Akio's voice told her. *Trust.*

Sabine allowed the calm to combat the fear and twisted her hand toward the door. She neither considered nor cared that there was furniture between her and her adversary.

She merely pulled the trigger.

Once, twice, three times she pulled the trigger.

Moments later, the only noise she heard was the clatter of a gun on the stone outside.

Then Michael's voice cut through the loud beating of her heart. "Well done, warrior. Well done indeed."

"I'm telling you," Stephen hissed as he pulled his weight up the fire escape one building over from their target, "I'm going whoring with the first part of the money, then I'm going to invest the rest."

Gerry shook his head, stepping over the rusted rung. "Careful," he hissed back.

"Got ya," was the reply.

"The only thing you invest your pay in," Gerry stopped talking and peeked over the top of the ledge to check out the roof before turning back to finish his comment, "is a higher class of whore!"

Stephen shrugged. "They have mouths to feed too. It's

not like they aren't in business. Tell me your wife doesn't treat you better in bed when you come home with the bacon!"

Stephen made sure he skipped the rung Gerry had warned him about. "That's right, got nothing to say…" Stephen grabbed the ladder and reached for Gerry, who was falling backward. "The hell?" he yelled in surprise.

That was when he saw that Gerry would not be speaking anymore. Stephen's hand jerked back as the headless body fell past him. The left boot slammed into his head, but his vampiric strength was enough to hold on as the body flipped past him to career downward, slamming into the concrete below.

Stephen looked up to see an Asian man staring down at him.

The man's eyes were glowing red.

Jerry nodded when Frank touched his back. Both men stepped around the trash-strewn area and slid through a break in the fence between the street they had come down and the back alley of the building they were going to enter.

Jerry preferred working with Frank. The man was a professional and damned good. There wasn't any bluster, he rarely talked, and he didn't get excited and chatter in the middle of an operation like Stephen and Gerry.

Those two, he figured, were probably talking like two girls who just went clothes shopping.

Or out for makeup. Ever since one of the companies in East London had found a cache of makeup ingredients in a warehouse that had gone unmolested for so damned long it bordered on fantastical, Jerry had been consigned to listening to the women in his circle speaking about Cherry Red or Sublime Rose or goddamned Passion Pink.

It was enough to make a man take jobs killing vampires as a way to create a win-win opportunity. He either bagged the vampire and won or the vampire killed him, and that wasn't a bad second-place finish if going back to listen to more makeup talk was his third choice.

Jerry felt cold wash through him and stopped in his tracks, looking to the front and his left. Frank had the back and the right. He put up a fist to stop Frank as he glanced around, trying to figure out what had tripped his senses.

He couldn't see anything.

He turned his head enough so that his mouth was angled a little more toward his back and whispered. "Not sure what tripped me. You see anything?"

The voice that answered chilled Jerry's blood.

It wasn't Frank's.

Michael swept out of the house as Myst and worked his way over to where the two mercenaries were making their way through an opening in the fence to take the house from the back.

All in all, it would have been a rather sound plan if you were going for a typical vampire.

However, he wasn't typical, and frankly, he could tell what their plans were and that they had the vampire blood running through their veins.

Michael floated down behind the two men and swept the one in the back into the Myst, his body disappearing.

Michael sped to a building behind the Duke's house and dropped the mercenary from the Myst. The man hadn't made any effort to speak when Michael slapped his rifle out of his hands, but as the gun clattered toward the street, the mercenary reached for a pistol.

"I think not," Michael told him and palmed his own pistol. Michael was almost immediately back into Myst form, speeding down from the top of the three-story building as the dead mercenary's body collapsed on the rooftop.

Michael solidified behind the first mercenary, who was holding up a hand to tell his now non-existent partner to stop.

Michael smiled.

He was waiting for the man to do something when the first merc turned his head slightly and hissed, "Not sure what tripped me. You see anything?"

Michael answered, "I saw your partner a moment ago when a round from my pistol exploded his head like an overripe melon."

Michael swept his hand out; an incredibly small line of Etheric was riding on the edge, providing him with a marvelously sharp cutting edge. The scream of pain from when Michael's hand took off Jerry's arm at the wrist was cut short when Michael palmed his left pistol and shot him between the eyes.

Michael heard gunfire erupt from the house and his body disappeared as he headed toward the building.

Michael solidified just as Sabine's shots slammed into the last attacker, grabbing what information he could before his mind was in too much pain for Michael to be able to read anything else.

He noticed that Sabine had felt where her adversary was and shot through the furniture, and he checked out the placement of the holes in the body. All of them were close together. He turned to where Sabine was still hiding. "Well done, warrior. Well done indeed," he told her. His footsteps crunched on some broken glass spread around the floor.

"You can come out now. We have places to go."

There was a scream and a thud as a body hit the ground somewhere near the back. Moments later, Akio came in through the back door and stepped up beside Michael, who was scratching his bald head.

"Next?" Akio asked.

Michael started walking toward the front door, the crunching continuing when a shot-up bookshelf finally crashed. "First," he said, "I need a hat."

"Then?" Sabine asked as Akio helped her get out of her little furniture fort.

"We go into the sewers," Michael answered from outside.

"*Sewers?*" Sabine replied, disgust coloring her voice. "Couldn't we just, I don't know, go anywhere else?"

Akio had followed her as she headed for the door but stopped when he noticed an old military weapon on the bandolier of the man Sabine had shot in the chest. He reached down, turned it sideways to read it. Sabine turned to watch him take a round tab and yank it. He chunked it into the furniture fort.

"What was that?" she asked as Akio grabbed her and moved quickly out of the house.

"We have to go," Akio told her as the two turned left and walked up the street following Michael. "That was an incendiary grenade."

"Ohhhh," Sabine responded, looking over her shoulder. "Which means?"

"It's going up in flames," Akio replied.

Sabine turned back and worked to keep up with the quickly walking men. "What is it with you boys and fire?"

14

Tokyo, Japan, Chinese Embassy

Using Eve's intel, Yuko and Eve navigated purposefully through the embassy corridors toward the emperor's office.

When they arrived, Yuko stopped suddenly. Eve looked at her.

Yuko mouthed, "There are three people in there."

She touched her chest to indicate she was listening for heartbeats.

Eve nodded her understanding. Having controlled all the other security checks and personnel either by sending them messages to take them elsewhere or home for the day, it seemed that there had indeed been unforeseen events that kept Qin Shi from being alone.

Yuko took a breath. Her sword was stowed respectfully but was reachable on her back. She pushed the office's double doors and they swung open against her weight.

There had been low voices talking, but on hearing the

door open, the voices subsided. Yuko stepped into the large, ornately furnished office, followed closely by Eve.

"Good evening, gentlemen." She addressed the three men sitting on sofas in the lounge area of the office.

All three turned in their seats to look at her. One stood up. "Good evening, young lady. I see my assistant wasn't at her station to invite you to wait." He looked from her to Eve and back again.

His face had changed from friendly to "not amused" in the fraction of a second it had taken for Yuko to disturb them.

"We have an appointment," she told him. "Forgive me, but the matter is urgent." She bowed to the three of them, lowering her eyes to allow their egos the opportunity to do the right thing.

The two men with the emperor looked to him for his lead on the situation. It seemed like one of the men was ready to rise and excuse himself. Yuko held the emperor's gaze.

A moment passed before Emperor Qin Shi made his decision. "I'm busy. It will have to wait."

Yuko bowed again. "I'm afraid it can't. The reason your assistant wasn't at her post to ask us to wait is that we've taken the precaution of removing all personnel from the building. The matter we have to discuss with you is of utmost importance, and your cooperation would be very much appreciated."

The emperor looked confused, and then his expression turned to anger. "How dare you! I will be speaking with the Japanese Prime Minister about this. Who are you? I shall have your career!"

Yuko smiled slightly. "Emperor Qin Shi, I answer to an authority much greater than any you might have access to."

She paused and glanced at the other two officials, who were now on their feet. "May I suggest," she continued, "that we get to the reason for our appointment?"

One of the overweight men stepped forward. "I think the emperor has made it clear that he doesn't want—"

Yuko sighed and glanced at Eve, who nodded. Yuko drew her sword, the motion eliciting gasps from the three men.

The two men moved to protect the emperor. "State your business," the other official pressed, his tone less commanding and more focused on getting to the business at hand so the intruders might take what they wanted and leave.

Yuko lowered her sword. "We're here for information. Information about the remaining boxes of the Sacred Clan ship."

The two men in front of the emperor looked at each other, confused.

Their expressions immediately made them unimportant to her mission. "Sit down," Yuko told them, waving her sword in their direction, "or lose your limbs."

Eve glanced at her. "Whatever happened to asking them nicely first?"

Yuko shrugged. "I already did the diplomacy thing," she explained, turning her head in Eve's direction. "I guess Michael must have rubbed off on me," she muttered under her breath, turning her attention to the emperor as the other two sat back down on their sofas. "I assume you're Qin Shi?"

The man looked less arrogant as the gravity of the situation dawned on him. "I am, but I haven't got the knowledge you're looking for!"

Yuko narrowed her eyes. "And why would I believe you?" she asked unemotionally.

The emperor put his hands up, now shaking in fear. This may have been a powerful and greedy man who was formidable politically thanks to the money he wielded from his country, but, faced with a weapon in the absence of his security detail, he was nothing but a weed.

"I swear to you that I don't know the details," he protested. Yuko stepped closer.

"You need Chang Feng, my technology officer. He knows about that project. It was deemed too important for me to know about it."

Yuko regarded him carefully, making up her mind.

Just then Eve lunged forward, having spotted the man on the right slipping his fingers underneath the ornate coffee table in front of him.

"Shit. He's just tripped the silent alarm," she called to Yuko.

Yuko's eyes glared red. She was about to swing her sword at the pompous official when she saw that Eve was already on it, having launched herself at him over the sofa and tackled him to the ground. She punched him in the head, knocking him out cold.

The doors they had just burst through were opened again, this time by a tide of armed guards flooding into the stately office.

Within seconds guards lined the office's walls, surrounding Yuko, Eve, and their captives.

Yuko growled in frustration. "I wanted to do this diplomatically, but evidently that isn't an option here. Eve, send the signal, please."

Eve blasted her weapon in the direction of a second influx of armed guards gathering around the other door, taking out half a dozen of them.

Meanwhile, Yuko swiped up and around with her sword, taking out two approaching her from behind.

The guards on the side of the room farthest from the first door started firing, only to be jumped by two black figures that seemed to appear out of nowhere. The firing guards disappeared onto the floor behind the desk on the far side of the room, just before their shots could be maneuvered onto Yuko's position.

A second later Jacqueline and Mark appeared, taking out five armed guards from behind. They had entered from the next office.

Other black figures slipped like shadows around the room, dropping the paramilitary security guards, breaking necks and trigger fingers without mercy.

Within moments there was no more gunfire; everything was once again still and peaceful.

Yuko stood, blood dripping from her sword, as the three men trembled in terror.

"So tell me, where might I find this Chang Feng?" she inquired politely, her diplomatic air returning to her.

Frankfurt, Germany - small shop

The ring-a-ling of a small bell notified Jan Zwerven he had customers. The older man put down his leather mallet and lifted his too tired body off of his chair. He smiled at the piece of leather he had been working on.

Jan leaned down and studied the last few imprints from his tool. He was creating a flower and the leaf tool embedded the impression as he turned the leather.

Turn, strike the tool with his mallet. Turn, strike the tool with his mallet.

From time to time, he would grab the old sponge and squeeze the water from it. Then, he would rub the remaining moisture on the leather and allow it to soak up the water. The leather would bloom, the outside becomes soft as the moisture was wicked into the tough skin.

His was a happy life. The smell of leather was something his late wife had never understood. He even enjoyed the effort of tanning hide, something even he recognized as weird. However, her not liking the smell of leather was something he never understood.

He made his way out of his back workshop and pushed aside the leather strips that provided some privacy from the front of his store, to his workshop and living quarters above.

Inside were three people, and Jan stopped. All of them wore weapons. Even the pretty woman acted as if they were part of who she was, not something she just belted on each morning.

His voice was confident if a bit diffident, "May I help you?" The shorter man, perhaps Japanese if he guessed correctly, turned and bowed his head just a fraction in his direction.

The woman had turned and graced him with a beautiful

smile. One that he would wager would cause a thousand ships to sail. If perhaps, he was the one commanding them.

Then again, his wife had always said he was a sucker for a pretty woman who smiled at him. It was why she would take over the task of negotiating for his services when he had a pretty woman for a customer.

Or hell, any woman that would smile at him.

The taller man was wearing a long coat, from a material he didn't recognize. He had no hair and was looking at different hats that Jan had done in the past. Some he did as potential sales and others for customers who never came back.

The man turned around. His eyes were sharp, his smile was genuine as he lifted a hat. "This style?"

"That is an old American style," Jan told him reaching out for the hat the man was holding. He handed it over. "I've copied a style made famous by a man called John Batterson Stetson." He turned the hat over, "Inside here," Jan pointed inside, "Is the bow that I make to look like the original skull and crossbones."

Sabine moved closer and looked inside, "Why would you do that?" she asked.

"It's a nod of respect from us in these times, to those who started our profession so many centuries before. Way before the end of our civilization that we had to crawl out of." Jan told her. "The old professionals would use mercury to make their felt hats." He held the hat in his right hand and used his left to point to his head. "The mercury would poison them, give them brain damage." He pulled his hand down, and moved it like it was spasming. "They would get violent and uncontrollable muscle twitching."

"That's..." Sabine paused a moment, "That's horrible!"

"That is life," Michael told her. "It is the reason we got the phrase mad-as-a-hatter."

Jan looked up at the man, "No one I've ever talked to knew that, mister."

Michael held out his hand to shake. "Michael," he told him. "This young lady is Sabine, and my other friend here is Akio."

"Oh, Japanese!" Jan smiled and bowed a bit, "I love meeting those from other countries." He turned to Sabine, "You are French?"

"*Oui*," she replied.

He turned to Michael, "And you, sir?"

"Most recently, America," Michael replied. "But I've been known to travel other countries."

"If only Gertrude were still here," Jan whispered, "She would have kept you here, drinking beer to get your stories."

"Too many stories, young man, too many stories," Michael told him.

"Ah!" Jan waved a hand, "You would do better to get this one to smile at me to cut my prices, flattering me by calling me young won't do it."

Akio smiled, a bit of humor in his eyes.

"I need a special hat," Michael told him.

"Fabric?" Jan asked.

"Leather, something appropriate to match my coat," Michael told him as he held out his coat for Jan to feel.

"Going to need something...Different." Jan reached up and scratched his face. "Design?"

"Roses!" Sabine answered before Michael could say anything. He looked down at her in surprise.

"Roses?" He asked.

"Yes!" Sabine started looking around, "Do you have something I can use to draw?"

Jan turned and made his way to the back, "One second, oh patient lady." He called out and disappeared behind his leather strips.

Akio whispered. "He obviously does not know this young lady." He said and laughed when Sabine tried to pop his arm.

He wasn't there to receive the hit.

"Dammit, you move fast!" She grinned and turned around when she heard Jan coming back. She walked up to his counter and accepted the pen, and paper. "What I'm thinking…"

Michael and Akio glanced at each other with Akio asking, *When did she take over designing your hat?*

When have you ever known a woman to need permission?

Hai.

The two men turned back to Jan and Sabine.

"… Right here is a skull, dead center. Behind the skull are Angel wings, with roses laying this side and the other side. There should be flames in the eye sockets…No, no. Scratch that." She marked on the paper, "Now, here we need two pistols crossed, above the skull and between the wings."

"What do these pistols look like?" Jan asked. Sabine turned around to look at Michael with a raised eyebrow.

Michael walked forward and pulled his coat out of the

way. He drew his pistol, confirming the safety was on and the power turned off. He laid it on the counter.

Jan whistled. He looked up to Michael and back to the pistol. "That's unique, isn't it?"

"It's before the time of the world falling," Michael told the man. "Made for me."

Jan looked back up, staring at Michael, "You don't look that old."

Michael smiled, "From where I stand, your age is that of a *baby*."

Jan's mouth opened in shock. "Oh … oh oh oh!" He turned excitedly to walk to the back, but then turned around, "Don't go anywhere!" he told Michael and then turned back around and went through the strips again.

Michael read his surface thoughts and shook his head. "Who knew."

Akio just nodded.

"I really hate it," Sabine eyed them both, "when you two go all silent and mind-talky between yourselves."

She was interrupted when Jan came walking back out, holding a large book reverently. "This was Gertrude's." He laid it out on the counter after Michael picked up his pistol. Jan waved at the gun, "I've got that up here, no problem with my memory." He opened the book. "This is her secret research." He told them. "It's what got us started, we both loved history, finding out the secrets of the past." He turned the pages, scanning them and occasionally pulling down clippings that were affixed inside.

On the third turn, he found was he was looking for. "These are the stories of the one, the Patriarch," Jan read, his finger scrolling across the page. "The man who brought honor or swift death to those who would change in the dark of the night. They would follow the strictures, or they would die. He left his children here in Europe, to travel to the colonies, never to come back to Europe again. When he left," Jan looked up at Michael, his voice solid, but soft, reverent, "He was already ten centuries old."

Michael pressed his lips together, "That might have been off a few decades."

A tear was forming on Jan's face, drifting down his cheek. He never felt Sabine pick up a piece of cloth to wipe it for him. "She was right," he whispered. "She knew that the Patriarch wouldn't let us down." This time, he pulled his glasses and dabbed at his eyes. "You're here to take out the Duke, aren't you?" He asked Michael.

"Among other things, yes," Michael admitted.

"Then may I ask a favor?" Jan closed the book and set it to the side.

"Let me hear it," he replied.

"I would like to add Vampire teeth to the skull, and tiny red pinpricks of red to the eye sockets." He said, but Michael stopped him before he continued.

"I need something quick," Michael answered him, "I'm not sure we have the time…"

Jan shook his head. "If you will just promise to wear it when you yank that sonofabitch's heart out of his chest, then our daughter will be avenged," he told Michael. "You come back tomorrow morning, I will have your hat, Arch-Angel, you have my *word*."

Michael held out his hand, and Jan took it, "I will take some of his blood and consecrate your vengeance so that the hat knows."

A few moments later the bell rang again, but Jan heard nothing. He was already grabbing the leather he needed to work.

Tokyo, Japan, Chinese Embassy

Chang Feng, forsaken by his emperor, found himself being dragged from his office through the now-deserted corridors of the embassy and into the state office.

Riku held him unceremoniously by the scruff of the neck, his grip so tight that Feng dared not resist for fear of tripping and being strangled with his own collar.

Haruto followed them in, closing the bullet-riddled doors behind them. Plaster from the ceiling had been strewn all over the previously pristine carpets, and a film of dust covered everyone who had been in the room. Consequently, on arrival, Chang Feng looked a little out of place. His uniform was still clean and untouched by the white dust.

Riku released his grip and pushed him roughly over the mess of debris and dead bodies to a chair in front of Eve and Yuko.

Ichika stood menacingly behind the two men who had been in the meeting with Qin Shi, proud that Yuko had indicated for her to keep them quiet and out of the way of the ensuing interrogation.

"We're here for information," Yuko said quietly to a petrified Feng. "You tell us what we need to know, you get to live."

Chang's eyes darted to his emperor, who nodded his assent to answer the questions.

He glanced back at Yuko. "How do I know that if I tell you what you want you'll let me go?" he queried uncharacteristically bravely.

Yuko moved toward him, her eyes glowing red again. "Because some of us operate by a code—a code of ethics. If I give you my word, you are lucky indeed," she told him, her voice still low but definitive, making it even scarier than if she had shouted at him.

He nodded, glancing down to where a wet patch was forming on his pants.

Yuko stepped back a little, averting her eyes. Akari glanced at Ichika and nodded at Feng's pants. Ichika smiled in delight at the fear her new leader had instilled.

Yuko turned her back for a moment, glaring at Ichika for her childish, uncompassionate reaction. She walked away a few paces before turning back to Feng. "We're here about the Sacred Clan boxes," she explained. "They don't belong to you, and now we have a use for them," she declared, strategically assuming rightful ownership. "I want to know where they are."

She paused, holding his fearful stare steady, ready to flash him the red eyes again. As it turned out, there wasn't any need.

He raised his hands, flinching without her needing to move a muscle. "Ok, ok. I tell you."

"They buried all over China," he explained in his imperfect English. "We have no way of finding them though. The intel was stored on a physical server, but during the earthquake of 2045 it was lost."

Eve's eyes darted from side to side as she accessed information to confirm or reject his story. She nodded, affirming to Yuko there had indeed been an earthquake in this area at that time.

Yuko had taken a necktie from one of the security personnel who lay dead on the floor and was carefully cleaning off her sword. She sighed and told Feng flippantly, "I've just started getting this clean. Don't make me mess it up again."

He raised his hands in panic again. "No, no…please. Let me explain," he panted. "The earthquake destroyed our secret base. It was under the Kurobe Dam. When the quake hit, it not only destroyed the dam but the bunker we had built underneath it. As far as we could tell, it was completely flooded and the servers with all the information on them were lost."

He added, "It wasn't just the location of the boxes that was lost, either. Japan suffered a great deal, for reasons that were never released to the people." His eyes darted over to his emperor, looking somewhat sheepish for having divulged potentially embarrassing information about their tentative allies.

He tried to cover his tracks by returning to the technicalities of the matter of the servers. "Ever since then we have worked to find better ways of protecting our data, blockchain protocols being one of them."

Mark stepped forward, his eyes lighting up in interest. "You mean spreading sensitive information over multiple client terminals?"

Feng looked momentarily surprised that someone might understand his discourse. "Yes."

Yuko glanced sideways at Mark, pulling the conversation back on track. "You built a bunker underneath a dam?

Surely that was a high-risk location?"

Feng nodded. "Yes," he agreed, his attention peeled from Mark and his potential geek-out, "but—forgive me—you're thinking about this the wrong way."

Yuko frowned, thinking that if Michael were here, Feng would not dare to be so casual with him.

Feng continued, "Why do you think they built the dam in the first place?"

Eve had stepped a little closer, being unable to smell the urine Feng had excreted into his pants. "For hydropower, of course."

Feng shook his head, looking down. "No. So they could construct secret bunkers."

Yuko glanced at Eve. "This means they had this in place long before we came here. Long before the WWDE and the need to protect Japan."

She turned her attention to the sofa where Qin Shi was being guarded. "Why were we never told of this? We had an open relationship with Japan."

Qin Shi shrugged. "Perhaps not as open as with the back channels of the Chinese at the time, though I cannot comment with any certainty. This was obviously something arranged by one of my many predecessors."

Yuko relaxed a little and sighed. "Yes. I suppose there is little to be done about it now." She turned back to Chang. "We need the location of the bunker, then."

He nodded. "It's located in the central mountainous national park in the eastern part of Toyama prefecture. If you had a map…"

Eve pulled up a map on a screen that opened out of her arm and Feng showed her the location. "The bunker, I believe, stretched over this kind of area," he explained, indicating a larger area under the water.

Yuko frowned and glanced at Eve. "Do you think we'll be able to do a seismic scan with the equipment we have?"

Eve processed the question for a few moments before her activity returned to normal. "I think it is possible. Yes."

His need to be right seemed to outweigh his desire to stay alive. "The servers were destroyed, though."

Yuko glanced at him. "Well, we'll just have to confirm that."

They tied the officials up and quickly left the building just as sirens approached the area.

Jogging into the night, Jacqueline found herself alongside Ichika as they left the rear of the building to avoid the crowd forming out front.

Jacqueline glanced at her. "Those were pretty nifty moves back there."

Ichika smiled back at her, carefully avoiding some street furniture as they bounded into a nearby alleyway. "You didn't do too badly yourself," she said, bowing her head in respect. "I wish I had that kind of power in my upper body," she added a little shyly.

The rest of the group arrived and the black container appeared, looming above them.

Mark inserted himself into their conversation. "Ah, that's nothing," he told Ichika. "Wait till you see her slip into Pricolici mode," he said, a hint of pride in his tone.

"Pricolici?" Ichika asked.

Haruto came up behind them. "As in the legendary beast?"

Mark chuckled. "You might want to refrain from using the word 'beast' around her, but yeah. Sounds about right."

The black box reached the ground and the group piled in before it disappeared into the fading twilight.

15

Frankfurt, Germany

The three walked down the street, Michael amazed that anyone in this time, so many years since he had last been on Earth, had tracked any of his whereabouts.

These people needed someone to believe in, and apparently, a man from the dark ages was what Jan and his late wife had chosen. Perhaps he had more to give than just ensuring he got back to Bethany Anne.

They made their way across two streets and walked through a park. Sabine was shocked by all the technology she could see, including flying cars in the skies. "It's like this isn't even a part of the same world," she commented aloud.

"It is a factor of where people are and where technology survived, including the knowledge of how to make it," Akio told her. "Germany had the skills and the technology was given to them by a group Bethany Anne saved in Antarctica."

"Is it like her technology?" Sabine asked, turning all the way around as she watched a flying car first circle and then land in the park.

"No," Akio answered. "It doesn't work the same, and is not nearly as efficient. Her technology would make this," he waved at the flying cars, "seem medieval by comparison."

"How?" Sabine turned and spoke directly to Akio. "We have flying cars. Your plane is impressive, but not that much more sophisticated."

"When we meet up with her," Akio looked around, "you will understand the difference."

"Speaking of meeting up with her," Michael said, "do you know any good Japanese technology workers we can trust?"

"We will have to mind-read them all," Akio admitted. "My comment from before is true. They are the best people to manufacture the equipment, but also the best to steal it."

Michael considered Akio's warning. "We will have to move our manufacturing location off the islands."

"I will speak with Yuko and Eve about locating the pieces we need."

The trio had started walking away from the park when Michael stopped and turned into a small store. "I'll be but a moment."

Akio looked at the store. It sold chemistry components.

A few minutes later, Michael stepped back out holding a small brown package. "Thank you," he told the two, and they continued their discussions as they walked down the street.

The little bell rang and Jan pushed himself out of his chair. Although his back hurt, he was ready to deliver the finest hat he had ever made. The skull was so realistic it could almost talk.

It had taken him until five thirty in the morning. He'd had an hour nap and had been drinking caffeinated beverages since then to keep his old body ticking. He might be pushing it, but there was no way he would miss this opportunity to complete his side of the bargain.

His beloved Gertrude and their daughter Holda would be able to rest easier now, knowing that he had set into motion an agreement that pitted the Patriarch against their daughter's killer.

He tried his best not to think about her death—how they found her, and all the research the two of them had done to figure out who had killed their daughter.

Although they finally solved the murder, they knew they had no options against one so powerful. Jan had turned his sorrow inside, but Gertrude had sent her sorrow into more research. She was the one who had found the truth.

And the truth had walked into his little small shop yesterday. It had been designated by the god of Justice, he knew.

He grabbed the box that held the hat and walked to the front. Michael was waiting for him, his hands behind his back. His two friends were with him. Jan had read Gertrude's notes and now knew who Akio was. He was probably the one Gertrude had expected to reach out to and ask.

But she had died unexpectedly.

Jan set the box down on the counter and lifted off the lid. He reached in and pulled out a black leather hat. It was a Stetson design, with the carvings of a vampire skull, roses, the pistols, and angel's wings on it. He handed the black hat to Michael, who took it and turned it, reading the words that Jan had chiseled into the leather of the band.

"Honor or Death" had been inscribed into the little band, and "ArchAngel" on the back.

Michael felt the leather, the indentations that made the skull look like it had been carved of ebony marble. He reached up and placed the hat on his head, then tipped it a little forward. Jan watched him smile. "You are a master of your craft," Michael told him.

"I'm a man, no more, no less. One who wishes justice be served," he told Michael, who nodded.

"Justice will be served," Michael replied, leaving the hat on his head. He reached into his coat.

"No!" Jan waved him off. "I will not take money for the hat. A deal is a deal."

"The deal was struck," Michael agreed, "but I will not allow you to give of yourself so deeply without something from me. Your heart is one of the purest I've met since I came back." He pulled out a vial. "When we leave, close and lock the door and drink this, then lie down." He handed the vial to Jan.

Michael tipped the hat in Jan' direction, who recognized the salute. "Make sure you destroy the vial and get rid of any evidence that it was around."

"What do I do when I wake up?" Jan asked, wondering if what he guessed was in the vial was correct.

Michael considered the man a moment. "Know that your vengeance is complete and your responsibility for your daughter to your wife is done. Allow your sorrow to go down the drain and decide when you look in the mirror in the morning, what the next stage of your life will be."

With that, the bell rang as the woman left, and then Akio and finally Michael, wearing his hat, stepped out.

The door shut behind them, the tinkling of the bell slowly dissipating as Jan stared at the vial in his hand.

After standing there for a couple minutes, he stepped around the counter and locked his front door, pulling the shade and making sure the sign said his business was closed.

He went back to his workshop, set the vial in a safe place, and looked around. He busied himself for twenty minutes cleaning up. He set the tools in the right places, making sure that no scraps were lying around. He wasn't sure what would happen, but if he died, he didn't want someone to see a mess in his workshop.

Finally, he took the vial and went to his apartment above. There, he first made his bed and then unstoppered the vial. He drank it quickly and re-capped it, setting it aside.

He laid down wondering how long it would take, and never realized he was asleep before a second thought went through his mind.

Late morning the next day, Jan's eyes opened. It took him a moment to get his bearings. He was alive! He thought it had been a dream, but no, the vial was still on his nightstand.

He rolled out of the bed easily and walked to his bathroom. The Patriarch had mentioned that he needed to…

Needed to…

Jan stared at himself in the mirror. He reached up and rubbed his cheeks. He looked at his hands, turning them so he could examine both sides. "I'm…" he whispered.

He looked in the mirror again in confusion before uttering the words he didn't quite believe.

"I'm *young*," he said aloud.

Tokyo, Japan, Chinese Embassy

The ornate old building stood against the dying light as sirens approached from a distance. The staff who had managed to escape stood outside the gates, huddled behind the few guards who remained, their weapons protecting those they could.

Alert and watchful though they were, no one noticed the slight shimmer in the darkness as numerous dark figures scaled the walls of the embassy.

Breaching the windows at several levels, they made their way through the corridors like an infection entering a bloodstream.

"What is the meaning of this?" Feng tried to rise from the seat he was tied to as the second wave of intruders swarmed through the two doors of the office and the window.

"We told you everything already. You talk to us of

honor, but now you're going back on your word?" he blurted in protest.

The masked ninja lowered his face to the restrained technology officer. "I'm sorry, you must have mistaken us for someone else."

Chang Feng craned his head back to allow him to look into the man's eyes. "Who are you?" he demanded, intent on drawing attention from the emperor if he at all could. Redemption was always something he could strive for.

The intruder stood upright and moved catlike around the room, taking in the details of the situation as he spoke.

"My name is Orochi, and we," he indicated the team of half a dozen ninjas who now controlled the room, "are the protectors of the Sacred Clan's secrets. We will do whatever it takes to preserve the technology and keep it from falling into the hands of outsiders and heathens."

One of the emperor's officials found his courage and his voice. "What do you want from us?" he demanded from the footstool where the three of them had been tied up together, separate from the recently interrogated Chang Feng.

Orochi turned on him like a snake and approached the lounge area of the office. "We want to know what you just told your captors." He paused and glanced at one of his minions. "Your *other* captors," he corrected, a hint of snide humor in his tone.

"We told them nothing," the other official protested. "Honestly."

"Honestly?" Orochi repeated. "You're lying! *He* already said you told them everything," he said, pointing in Chang's direction without taking his eyes from the terrified, overdressed official. "Plus," he added, "they wouldn't have left you alive had you not cooperated. We know of their leader. He is ruthless." He pulled a sword from its sheath on his back and placed it deftly at the man's throat.

"Tell us or die."

Armed police stormed up the stairs of the embassy, clearing sections of the building as they went.

"Get me eyes on this place," an annoyed voice commanded through the radio as various statements of, "Clear" echoed over the shortwave communicators.

A second voice reported back to him. "Sir, the central computer was compromised. We have someone trying to restore access to the cameras, but it may take some time."

Commander Ugaki looked dismayed as he nodded his understanding to Koga, his second-in-command, who acknowledged the information.

Ugaki scratched the back of his head as he turned toward the SWAT truck parked at the gates. "Looks like they got away already," he said, resigned to the inevitable cleanup that was going to have to happen.

"Sir," another voice said over the communicator, "we have found the emperor and some of his colleagues."

"And?" Ugaki responded. The agitation in his voice evident.

"Dead, sir," the voice on the radio reported. "They're all dead."

Commander Ugaki paled.

He walked away from the assembling camp of trucks

and flashing red and blue lights to gather his thoughts. Pulling up his secret communicator, he tapped a message.

You said you would leave them alive!

SEND.

Moments later he received a message back. "We did. Standby. Footage shows a second group."

The commander wiped his hands over his face as his second-in-command joined him. "Everything ok, sir?"

The commander shook his head. "No. We're in deep shit. Looks like our people weren't the only ones to pay the emperor a visit tonight. We're going to have to play this carefully if we're to keep our secret."

Koga nodded his understanding and walked back to the yellow and black tape that was being used to seal the entrance to the building.

16

Kurobe Dam, Toyama prefecture, Northwest of Tokyo

Ichika, Jacqueline, Mark, Akari, Haruto, and Riku stood overlooking the dam, taking in the view.

The morning light spilled over the lake, christening it in gold and silver hues. Though the team had had plenty of time for shuteye, because Eve had waited until morning to conduct her scans of the area, the living conditions in the container had proven a little cramped for the number of people who were now on the mission.

"I've never seen anything quite so majestic," Akari exclaimed, her eyes wide in wonderment.

Riku glanced at her. "Yeah. We're a long way from Yokohama."

Mark shoved his hands in his pockets. "Well, I agree it's impressive, but what about breakfast?"

Yuko must have heard, because a second later she appeared at the door behind them. "Eve says her scans are going to take another couple hours," she told them. "We have time to go into town for some food if you'd like."

Mark's eyes lit up as he rubbed his hands together quickly. "Would I!" he exclaimed excitedly. Jacqueline eyed him carefully.

Mark raised his hands in defense. "You're kidding! You're not jealous of food?"

Jacqueline noticed her knee-jerk reaction and her face softened. "No. No, I'm not jealous of food," she said, looping her arm into his and turning to face Yuko.

"I suppose using those super-speedy Pods to get to the village would be out of the question?" she asked.

Yuko nodded. "Afraid so. Eve is using all three of them to scan the area faster. The seismic devices we have are a little old and take more time to gather the data points."

Jacqueline shrugged. "No matter," she said, looking up at the sky. "It's a lovely day for it." She glanced at Mark, who nodded.

Yuko disappeared back into the box for a moment and then came out, closing the door behind her. "Ok, I've told Eve. She'll let us know if she gets finished sooner."

There were excited mumbles as the group headed out, following Yuko off the tree-covered mound toward a trail. Yuko glanced around, getting her bearings before leading them more decisively in the direction of breakfast.

Three hours later the team stood on the same spot they had been admiring the view from. This time they had three

Pods lined up, and were wearing waterproof suits that smelled like they'd been in storage next to a beer keg for the last two hundred years.

Jacqueline pulled at the suit's material. "Tell me again why you have watertight suits but no helmets?"

Yuko sighed. "I believe that they were prototypes developed by Team BMW for some side project they were working on, in case they needed to check water storage tanks. The helmets were probably re-engineered for space, though."

Mark wrinkled his vampire nose. "And they smell of stale beer because?"

Eve closed one of the Pod's storage units. "That'd be because Bobcat had a beer fetish," she joked, her face deadpan.

Akari glanced at her, unsure how much of this to believe. Their new teammates had just been talking about space and beer fetishes. She had known there would be surprises on the way and *Sensei* Kashikoi was never one to share all the details, but assuming she had misheard was just a simpler option at this stage.

"Ok," Yuko called to the six wet-suit garbed warriors. "Here's the plan… Eve and I will remain up here to make sure you find the point of ingress. From Eve's data, there is a cavern you can breach. This means you'll need to take the Pods into the lake and go deep enough to find the bunker. The entrance is completely flooded, but there is an air pocket just beyond it, and our guess is that beyond there the bunker is water-free.

"The difficulty is going to be getting access to it,

though. You'll take these charges," she said, holding up two small devices. "You need to plant them, then use the Pod to get away fast enough. Once they have exploded, you can head back in."

Mark raised his hand, a look of concern in his eyes. "But what's to say that the explosion won't break the seal on the rest of the bunker and cause the water to flood in?"

Yuko looked at Eve for the answer. "In my modeled simulation, there was a .011 probability that something like that might happen," she said dismissively. "But for the most part, it is held in stasis mechanically, meaning the arrangement of the air and blocks of concrete are arranged such that you should be ok. It was likely designed to prevent a single breach from overcoming it."

Jacqueline frowned. "Well, if that was the case, why didn't the Japanese already make this trip to salvage their servers?"

Eve looked at Yuko for the solution. Yuko frowned. "Perhaps they didn't know. This was built a long time before the earthquake hit, and I suspect they just accepted what previous generations had held to be true. It seems quite common in most civilizations."

Mark looked thoughtful for a moment. "Unless someone decided that the intel on those servers was better left buried."

Ichika nodded enthusiastically. "That would make sense. It's pretty much what *Sensei* Kashikoi has been advocating since I was old enough to understand the stories he told us about the legend."

Yuko registered the insight from Ichika but then turned

to Mark. "You think you'll be able to pull the information we need?"

Mark looked over his shoulder at one of the Pods, gesturing toward a rusted metal box wrapped in a clear plastic bag on the seat. "Yeah. If Eve's reading on that battery is correct, it should give me enough juice to tap into the mainframe and make the transfer. If your patch works, it shouldn't take too long to locate what we need no matter *where* it was stored. Then we should just be able to download it through a single server port onto this." He held up a dongle which looked high-tech but foreign, clearly from another time and place than the tech he had been exposed to.

Everyone else's eyes had glazed over. Mark turned back to Eve, slipping the dongle back into his suit pocket. "How on Earth did you get hold of a compatible cable, though?"

Yuko glanced at Eve. Eve responded. "We have friends in Tokyo who are collectors and, for the right price, they can find almost anything tech-related from since before…you know."

Mark seemed satisfied. "Well, as long as your friends' research is correct. Just a few years from now we might find that our cable or interface is incompatible, and then there won't be anything I can do down there."

Jacqueline noticed a tinge to his voice which she hadn't heard since he became a vampire—anxiety. Over tech, which was his bag. She looked at him, wishing there was some way she could reassure him, but the details were just a little beyond her area of expertise.

"Ok," Yuko said, looking at each of the six team members. "You know what you need to do. We're ready to go as soon as you get down there. We'll control the Pods remotely, but if you need to take control just use the voice command to flick it into manual."

There were nods and murmurs of acknowledgment as they headed for their Pods two by two.

"Feels a little ark-like," Riku mentioned to Akari as they jumped into their shared Pod.

Akari didn't understand the reference, but she chose to ignore the comment and swung herself in next to him with her game face on.

Moments later the Pod doors were closing. After they sealed shut, the Pods lifted and dropped elegantly off the side of the cliff toward the lake.

Yuko moved forward to peer over the edge and watched the three barely visible Pods move into formation and level out before they hit the surface. They skipped in the direction of the dam before hopping effortlessly over it to the lake's natural side and plunging to the depth at which Eve had defined their point of entry to be.

Yuko looked at Eve.

Eve recognized the concern on Yuko's face. It was the same look that she had observed on Akio's visage on more than one occasion before he sent them on a mission. "They will be ok," she reassured Yuko.

"It's not just them I'm worried about," Yuko confessed. "We need to find out who hit the embassy after we left, and see if there is a way to keep our commander out of harm's way."

Eve nodded and followed Yuko into the container, where they would control the mission together. "We have to assume they know what we know," she added as she followed Yuko up the steps.

Frankfurt, Germany

Sabine's third try amused Michael. "If we go into the sewers, you will get your beautiful new hat dirty."

The three of them were walking past a grocery store, following directions Michael had lifted from a man in a three-piece suit.

"If we *don't* go into the sewers we might miss William and this other group looking for him and myself," he replied.

She does not know yet that the Sewers is just a euphemism for the technology underground, Michael sent Akio.

That would make two of us. There was a pause. *I can't say I was looking forward to going through filth either.*

This is William, Michael responded. *He wants to be protected, not inconvenienced.*

There was another pause from Akio before he replied, *I am ashamed I missed the obvious.*

Michael stopped, and waited for Sabine to realize she was about to bump into him. "What?" she asked, looking up into his face. "Am I whining too much?" She saw the corner of his lip curl. "I am, aren't I?" She looked to her left. "Dammit."

"It is ok, Sabine," Michael told her. "The Sewers is not a place of pipes and disgusting water, it is a name for a place you can live here in Frankfurt."

Her eyes tracked back to Michael. "What kind of place?"

"It is something they built after the fall. It is underground, and it is large. There are places for the rich and places for the roaches to hide, and in the middle is a zone where they agree to do business. William has a residence at the bottom. You can get to it from the rich side or the roach side."

"Which side will the mercs be coming in from?" she asked, keeping up with Michael as he and Akio took off walking across the street toward some steps that led underground.

"They only know about the rich side," Michael replied.

"Why—" she started before Akio answered.

"There is always," he said as the three swung around the wall and started down into the subway area that held the entrance to the Sewers, "a back way out."

"Or in," Michael finished as they took a left into a less-than-clean-smelling hallway.

The fluorescent lights buzzed and hummed as the three walked through the passageways. Sabine was trying her best not to become overwhelmed thinking about how deep underground they must be as they descended their seventh flight of stairs.

On the eighth level, her body reacted while her mind was still contemplating being stuck down here for the rest of her life.

One moment Michael was in front and Akio behind her. The next Michael had downed two attackers in front, Akio had taken out one behind them, and she had another's head pressed into the wall, her pistol shoved against his skull. "MOTHERFUCKER!" she screamed at him. "I WAS BUSY WORRYING HERE!"

The guy—no, just a kid—was watching her pistol as best he could. Her finger was on the trigger and his eyes kept trying to see how hard she was squeezing. The noise in the landing came back to her in a rush. She could hear some moaning. "Kill him or what?"

"No!" The boy tried to get his nerves under control. "We weren't sent to kill you."

Michael walked up next to the young man and bent down. "Name?"

The teenager swallowed. "Erich."

You can put your pistol away, Sabine.

She brought her pistol down and holstered it.

"Well, Erich." Michael allowed his eyes to flash red a moment, mesmerizing the boy when he realized what kind of being he was looking at, "I need directions to a certain area down here in the sewers. Are you available?"

Erich's head jerked up and down.

"Good." Michael straightened up. "I expect you to provide the necessary signals so that we are allowed safe passage, or you will be my first kill of the evening."

Michael turned and headed toward the door. Erich called, "Herr...uh..." Michael turned and raised an eyebrow. Erich pointed. "There are more on the other side."

"You will do," Michael told him and waved him to the door. "There are none at the moment. We need to go to the Dark Corners area."

Erich stepped over the prone body of Frederic and grabbed the door handle. Yanking it open, he called, "It's me, Erich. Safe passage, and if anyone can hear me, we have three down."

No one responded. He stuck his head through the door and looked both ways. Stepping in, he was confused.

The man in the coat and hat walked in behind him. "Don't worry, they were scared and ran. They will be back later. Your friends live, and we don't have much time. The way, Erich?"

Erich turned to Michael's left and started walking down the passage. The walls were lined with white ceramic tile and the floors were concrete. There were LED lights every ten feet that lit the hallway enough that even Sabine could see very well.

"The Dark Corners," Erich started chattering, "have a bad reputation for people disappearing." He chuckled. "I think it's just someone trying to keep others away."

"Oh, it's probably true," Michael responded.

"Which part?" Erich asked as he turned and pushed on a door. It opened into another set of stairwells. "This will drop us another three levels to the main concourse. I'll get us through the toll there and then we have one hallway and another five levels to go down."

"Both parts," Michael read the instructions and directions from Erich's mind. "People probably *did* disappear, and it *was* so others wouldn't go there."

"But why?" Erich asked as they descended to the third level. He grabbed the door and opened it. Stepping out, he turned to his right and jerked a thumb over his shoulder. "Aren, Burk, these three are with me."

Aren was a big guy with blond hair and hazel eyes. He looked past Erich. "Are you playing with me?"

"What?" Erich turned around, but there was no one behind him. He stepped back over to the door to the stairway and pushed it open, then stuck his head inside and called out.

Aren's smile dropped when he saw the look on Erich's face. Reaching for a pistol and placing it in his waistband, Aren asked him, "What's going on?"

Erich saw him grab the pistol and shook his head. "You don't want to make them angry."

"'Them' who?" Aren asked as he waved to Burk to get his own weapon ready.

"I swear I'm not making this up." Erich looked down the way he had told the man to go. "His eyes glowed red, and he wanted to know how to get to the Dark Corners." Erich pointed back the way they came. "He and his two people took out the team I was on to require toll."

"Dark Corners?" Aren turned to the hallway that went in that direction. "Well, let's go lock the doors. If they got ahead of you somehow, that will stop them from coming back. They will have to bang on the doors to get us to open them."

"I don't think doors are their problem," Erich whispered.

Michael looked at the three doors in front of him. "Well, shit."

"He didn't show any doors in his mind, did he?" Akio asked. Michael had turned to Myst, grabbed the two of them, and gone down the hallway and into the correct stairwell.

Unfortunately, after five levels it stopped. There were

three doors and each one was going in a different direction.

"Nope," Michael agreed.

"It's easy," Sabine told them. She walked over and grabbed the left door and pulled it open. "After you two gentlemen…"

Michael raised an eyebrow. "What?" She pointed to the floor. "No foot traffic like the other two doors. This one isn't used much anymore. Trust men to not see dirt."

Michael resisted the urge to pet her head as he walked into the hallway beyond. She was right; this hallway still had light, but it wasn't used.

Akio was behind him. "Left or right?"

"Left," Sabine answered as the door clicked shut behind her. "and no, not because of dirt. It just feels creepy." She looked at both men, who looked back at her. "You guys don't feel it?"

Akio chuckled. "Sabine, *we* are the ones who make people feel creepy."

"Oh, right." She shrugged. "I guess I've acclimated to your version of creepy." She stepped around him and started walking down the hallway, muttering to herself, "What's that say about me?"

The security guard was standard-sized. *Which was to say huge,* Noah thought, looking up at him. The scar on the guard's face just missed his left eye and ended up somewhere under his brown hair. "We are here to meet our boss," Noah responded to the guard's question. "His name is William, but he goes by Duke."

"Not here," the man responded. He was looking at Noah's two compatriots with their eyes flicking everywhere.

"Of course he is." Noah slipped the man some gold and a note. "Let's make sure I have the right address, ok?"

The man's eyes narrowed and he reached out to grab Noah's wrist. In a second Noah twisted his hand, grabbing the guard's wrist and pulling him forward, then slamming his left fist into the guard's stomach.

His eyes bulged in pain, then rolled up a second later when Beatrice whipped out with a nightstick and popped him in the back of the head.

The guard dropped to the floor.

Noah looked at Keith. "What?" Keith asked. "Did I miss something here?"

Noah shook his head. "Pick him up and place him back in his booth," he said as he stepped over the huge man's back. "You have the extra strength, so use it."

Keith looked to Beatrice. "What did I do?" he asked as he reached down to grab the guard under his arms.

"You could have helped a little," she replied and stepped around him as well. Seconds later, four more team members swept into view and helped Keith move the guard out of the way.

"You take rearguard now." Keith's friend Tommy slapped him on the back as they left the little shack in the hallway. This was the least-used entrance into the rich area of the Sewers. The wealthy called it something else, but as far as everyone else was concerned, it was just the nicer part of the same place.

Kind of how you might expect hell to be. Nowhere in hell would be nice, but perhaps certain areas might be less hot.

At least, one could hope.

17

The Sewers, Frankfurt, Germany

The seven humans used their enhanced speed to rush down the tunnels. Noah had purchased plans to allow them to use some tunnels that were for infrastructure and stay out of the main hallways. Less chance of problems, they hoped.

It took the team three minutes to traverse to the Duke's residence in Frankfurt. One could hope that either the Duke or the new vampire would be here.

Noah was hoping to bag them both. His team had been notified of Thomas and his team's demise the day before.

He held up his hand. The team slowed down and stopped by a door, pipes all around them. Noah pointed through the door. "On the other side is a hallway. It goes both right and left. Right is back the way we came in, and to the left is the entrance to the living quarters the Duke has here."

"We know where his exit is?" Keith asked.

"Nope," Noah answered. "According to the plans, he would have to dig through fifty feet of rock to make a way to get out. I'm not saying it's impossible, and he might have started on it, but he seems to be the arrogant type and will probably believe he can just kill us."

"Don't they all?" Beatrice asked, and the guys chuckled.

"Oh no, humans!" Keith sing-songed in a high voice. "Whatever shall I do with myself?" He changed his voice to a lower pitch. "I shall kill you all!" The chuckles continued for a moment.

Noah paused, then continued. "Ok, we open this door, team one comes with me, we set the charge. We blow the door and go in. Second team sets up our defense. All shares are equal."

Noah might be a bastard—hell, he himself would admit he *was* a bastard—but he was also a team player, and those who protected your back door were just as important as those who rushed the door.

"*Go!*" he yelled. Beatrice yanked the door open and Noah slipped through.

"My, my, my." Michael heard a vase crash to the floor. "Hope that wasn't priceless," he murmured as he looked around a bedroom. Akio chuckled in the other room.

The three had found the back entrance to William's place nicely decorated with skeletons and other stuff that was just smelly and gross. He had made sure that anyone looking around would become another decoration that said, "Stay away."

Michael took them through as Myst and followed the rough tunnel into William's apartment, bypassing, Michael was sure, plenty of traps that would stop interested parties from figuring out where the tunnel led.

He doubted any who had helped build the tunnel were still alive. Well, he supposed they *could* be alive, just changed into vampires.

The bedroom was particularly opulent, with rich tapestries hanging from the walls and a bed so massive that Michael wasn't sure how they had brought it this far underground.

"Sabine?" he called. A moment later he heard her boots clop-clop-clopping down the hallway.

She stuck her head into the room. "You called?"

Michael nodded. "Would you be so kind as to leave some of the furniture? We aren't going to burn this one to the ground, and those who come later might enjoy what are," he pointed to the tapestries, "undoubtedly priceless historical artifacts."

"Sorry about that." She blushed. "I didn't actually mean to break that vase. I was scared by my own damn reflection and jumped."

Michael stared at her a moment. "You're kidding, right?"

She shook her head.

"Michael!" Akio called. "I believe we are going to have company."

Michael stepped around Sabine, who moved aside to let him pass. He walked down the small hallway into a much larger room. Akio was pointing down the hall with his right hand; his left was pointing to his head.

Michael released his senses too, and he focused in the same area Akio was pointing to. Soon Michael was shaking his head. "Well…hell."

Michael started walking down the hallway. "I'll be right back."

Sabine looked at Akio. "Is he taking them on all by himself?"

Akio shrugged. "He *is* the ArchAngel," he told her. "There was a reason that whole groups of the Unknown-World would move to other cities if he was coming to town."

"You're kidding, right?" she asked, and Akio turned and shook his head.

"You were blessed to meet Michael after he spent time with Bethany Anne." He turned back to the hallway that dogged right before going to the front entrance. "The old Michael would not have thought twice about killing first and not bothering to ask questions later. The new Michael will at least ask questions."

"What questions?" Sabine made sure her pistols were loose in their holsters. "I didn't hear him ask any questions."

"Up here." Akio touched his head. "He reads their minds and figures out what they are planning and what type of people they are."

"And what type are they?" Sabine asked. "You read them too, right?

Akio's answer was short and to the point.

"Dead."

Noah loved this part of a takedown. His senses were heightened, his speed enhanced, and his ability to dish out pain could damn near cause him to orgasm.

I AM THE ONE...

Noah, his feet driving forward, the door at the end of the ten-foot-wide hallway clearly in his sights, twisted to look behind him to see who was yelling at them.

I AM THE DARK MESSIAH...

Noah noted that his team had made it into the hall. Two right behind him, and the rest looking both ways.

MY NAME IS MICHAEL...

Noah put up his hand, fist clenched. "FORM UP!" he yelled and stopped running.

AND I AM DEATH, the voice finished.

"Welcome to hell." A male's voice caused Noah to turn around.

In front of the door was a man in a long coat with a black leather hat on his head. His eyes glowed red and the coat was pulled back to show two pistols in holsters on his hips.

Noah was lifting his rifle when the man drew his pistol and shot Keith, who was next to him. Noah's round blew a small hole in the door.

But the vampire was gone.

"What the hell?" Noah spun, noticing the look of shock in Keith's blind, staring eyes, half his skull blown out the back.

Remember those you killed? The voice was back in their brains. *Remember the ones you put on tables so you could bleed them dry?*

"They were monsters, just like you!" Noah called. "Everyone pull together, back to back. He can't…"

Beatrice's scream turned to gurgles. Noah caught just a hint of a hand appearing out of thin air, nails four-inches long. They sliced across her neck, her arterial blood spraying out as she collapsed to the ground.

That's two down.

"Come out here and fight like a man!" Bensen screamed.

But you say I'm a monster. Since when do monsters fight like men?

"You say you…*Argffhf*." Bensen, all two hundred and fifty pounds of him, had been lifted into the air, and the vampire was using his clawed hand to strangle him. Three guns fired simultaneously, but all they hit was Bensen.

The vampire was gone.

Three.

Noah considered whether he needed to cut his losses.

"Four, Five, Six," a voice called. With each word, another of his team was cut down by pistol shots coming from behind him.

Noah whipped back to the door and fired. He wasn't sure if the vampire was solid or stopping them from seeing him in their minds or what.

He just felt like he needed to fire his weapon.

Sabine bit a fingernail. "Seems like a lot of gunshots." She looked at Akio, who was reading a magazine. She bent down to see what he was reading; the front of the magazine had a car on the cover.

"Yes," Akio agreed with her comment on the bullets. "It says here the new Tellyson SP-600 aerodynamic antigrav car has room for six and a sixty-five kilometer range this year."

Several shots blasted the wall in the hallway, having come through the front door. Sabine looked at the damage, then at Akio still reading the magazine, then back to the damage. "They are blowing a hole in the door."

"Mmmm hmmm," Akio replied and turned the magazine in her direction, pointing to a picture of the inside of the aircar. "I do rather like this dark burgundy color for the leather. What do you think?"

"Oohhh," Sabine stepped closer and leaned in. "That *is* pretty." She looked at him. "You really aren't worried about Michael?"

Akio blinked twice before asking, "Are you?"

Sabine glanced at the wall and the holes that had been produced by the bullets a moment before. She shrugged. "If you aren't, why should I be?"

"That is correct." He took the magazine back and flipped the page. "Besides, he is having too much fun."

"Should we be doing something?" She gazed around the suite.

"For Michael?" Akio asked.

She turned back to him. "No, to see if we can find something to figure out where the Duke went."

Akio put down the magazine. "Yes, I suppose so. Michael isn't going to leave any for me to play with," He paused for a moment, then added, "I believe Jacqueline would add, 'the greedy bastard.'"

Sabine smiled, shaking her head, and walked away from the front door, ignoring the sounds of fighting.

Are you good and finished? The voice dripped malicious humor into Noah's mind. His gun was not responding, the action having locked open on the empty magazine as he squeezed the trigger.

Noah dropped the weapon and yanked a ten-inch silver-laced blade out of his holster, then moved backward until he was against the wall directly opposite Keith's body. "Bring it! I'm not scared."

"Who wants you to be scared, Noah?" the man asked him, his voice carefully neutral when he appeared close to the door that Noah and his team had used to get into the hallway.

"Certainly not me." The man walked toward Noah. "How about we go tit-for-tat, hmm?" He stepped over Benson's body. "You strike once, I strike once, and see what happens?"

"What the fuck are you talking about?" Noah licked his lips. "How about I kill you a final time?"

Noah, his reaction time increased with vampire blood, barely registered the movement as his arm twitched and thrust the knife blade out.

When time caught up, the man was smiling. Noah's blade was stuck through his shirt into his stomach. "The thing about living over a thousand years, Noah," he whispered, pinning Noah's knife hand to him, not allowing him to pull it out or move at all, "is that you learn how to handle pain. Real pain, not the stubbing-your-toe kind." Noah looked at the man's face. His teeth were growing sharp, eyes blazing red. "Can you handle pain, Noah?"

Noah felt his whole chest explode in agony and looked down. The vampire had punched into his chest, cracking his ribs and sternum in the center, right to his heart. "Now, you might have been able to heal using vampire blood." Michael looked down at the mess of Noah's chest. "Well, probably not. However," Michael pulled Noah's hand and knife out of himself, turned the blade, and, using Noah's own hand, shoved it into Noah's stomach. "I think I'll use your energy to heal myself."

Noah's voice squeaked; he could feel the life being sucked out of him. Energy…the energy he needed to try and fix his own body.

Soon Michael stepped back and allowed the emaciated corpse to fall to the ground. He turned and started walking toward the door of the suite. "May your sins stay on you until you stand in judgment," Michael pronounced and pushed the suite's door open, then closed it gently.

Seven dead bodies littered the hall behind him.

"Did you find anything?" Michael asked as he strode into the room Sabine was searching. "I only ask because I'm sure the security guards are on their way. I doubt they will want a friendly conversation."

"Are they a problem?" Sabine asked, looking up from the drawer she was rifling through.

"No, but I'd rather not kill innocents."

Sabine shrugged and shut the desk drawer. "This place looks like a plant. It only shows the stuff he was doing as a businessman. It has nothing like the plans we saw in his chalet."

Akio walked into the room. *"Hai."* He nodded. "I have found the same; nothing but business papers."

Michael looked around. "We need to visit England. Perhaps the group that is attacking William has ideas. We will ask them." He looked at Akio. "I think you will have some fun."

Five minutes later a group of security guards kicked in the door to the suite and quickly searched it, guns drawn, expecting to find more dead bodies.

All they found was a secret passageway leading somewhere. The captain in charge detailed two guards to *carefully* follow it and report back.

Many minutes later, one of the guards came rushing back into the hallway, excited. He pointed over his shoulder back toward the suite. "You guys are not going to believe what is on the other end of that trap-filled passageway…"

18

Below the Kurobe Dam, Toyama Prefecture, Japan

Three Pods hovered deep underwater just above a concrete protrusion.

"You must be right above it. Let me take you to the side," Eve's voice told them over the comm.

Mark had already released his harness and pressed his nose against the glass. "It's a bit murky down here, but I think I can see the break point."

Jacqueline sat firmly in her seat monitoring her breathing. "How do we know we're safe down here?" she asked. "I mean, if we leave the Pod, aren't we going to be crushed by the weight of the water?"

Mark tried to look upward out the front of the Pod. "Nah," he said, despite not being able to actually see how far down they were. "I think we'd need to be much deeper for that to be an issue."

Jacqueline wasn't entirely convinced, but she knew why she was here and she wasn't going to start being a chicken now. She'd made her decision when she sat next to her father's makeshift grave after he'd saved her. She was going to make her life mean something. And that meant being courageous.

"Ok," Eve confirmed. "The trackers in the Pods put you right at the location we talked about. You're good to go, Mark."

Mark glanced back at Jacqueline, a slight hint of childish glee in his eyes at the prospect of what he was about to do.

"Be careful," she warned him. "And make sure you don't go activating the charges until you're back in here," she added, undoing her own harness and wrapping him in her arms before releasing him to his task.

Mark shrugged her warning off. "It's ok. I'll be right back." He stopped. "Although… With the Pod filled with water, I wonder if that will impede its movement away from the explosion."

Jacqueline looked at him intensely. "I thought you had already done these calculations," she said, exasperated at his lack of rigor.

Mark pursed his lips. "I had. Approximately. But I'd rounded things up, and hadn't quite factored in the range of the remote for the charges." He thought for a moment. "Best we have a head start before we hit the button."

Jacqueline rolled her eyes.

"Also," he added, "let's tilt the Pod forward to conserve as much air as possible."

Jacqueline relayed the suggestion to Eve via the communicator, and the Pod tipped forward, forcing them to balance themselves on the outer frame of the see-through door.

"You ready?" He checked.

Jacqueline nodded, suddenly anxious again, and held onto the sides of the bench seat.

Mark hit the button to open the door and water started gushing in. Jacqueline instinctively scrambled to not get wet, but then remembered that most of the Pod was going to be submerged before they were done.

In fact, she was going to be going out there as soon as this first phase was complete. She dropped her feet back down and gasped as the coldness of the water met the outside of her suit before the suit corrected for the temperature differential. A moment later the water was up to her chest, and she was feeling quite comfortable.

Mark had moved out of the Pod and was swimming in the direction of the concrete slabs that were strangely juxtaposed on top of each other. Jacqueline waited, holding her breath and trying to see through the water she was now completely immersed in.

Mark placed the first charge, and then the second, then made a visual check that the other two Pods were a sensible distance back. He swam back to the Pod he had just left, hitting the button as he clambered back through the door. Immediately it started to slide shut, and a second after it had closed the water level started to go down. Within three seconds they had a small air pocket forming at the top. Both Mark and Jacqueline immediately moved to the top to breathe.

"Piece of cake," he told her, winking.

Jacqueline shook her head. "Let's just get out of here,"

she told him, sending the signal to move as a click over the intercom Eve had given her.

A moment later the Pod had whipped them out of the way, so Mark detonated the charge. The explosion blew all the Pods back, jolting them.

Despite the disturbance, the Pod had managed to replace around two-thirds of the water with air, leaving Jacqueline just wet and pissed. She slapped Mark hard on his arm. "Your calculations were off!"

Mark rubbed his arm while still standing and holding onto the grab rail. "Well, I thought it wasn't bad. There was a risk we'd be out of range for detonating the explosion," he protested.

Jacqueline was in no mood to concede, and Mark was smart enough to let it go. "As long as you're ok," he said. He ceased rubbing his arm and clutched her arm as romantically as he could under the circumstances.

They looked in the direction of the ingress they had created, but it was several more minutes before enough debris had settled enough for them to see what was going on. Even after that, there was a suspension of concrete and building materials which wasn't going anywhere.

Mark looked out at the mess. "Well, I think this is about as good as it's going to get for a while," he remarked, moving toward the door button.

Jacqueline pushed her bottom lip out, readying herself. "Doing this without an air supply sucks ass."

Mark nodded. "Couldn't agree more," he said, looking at her. "Thank goodness for superpowers," he added with a wink.

Jacqueline bobbed her head anxiously. "Yeah, but we

don't know what we're going to encounter down there. And it's a long way back to the surface."

Mark grinned at her. "Nervous, Little Wolf?" he asked playfully.

Her eyes flashed fiercely for a moment before softening to her true emotions. "Yeah," she admitted. "It's not like we can just tear through a bunch of Weres or low-lives and be ok. There'll be no fighting a lack of oxygen."

Mark sighed. "That's true. We'll be ok. You ready? I think we just need to head in there and keep going in the direction of that pipe you see running along the outside."

Jacqueline looked at the red pipe that ran the length of the concrete wall. "Ok, let's do it," she agreed, her expression more determined now.

The other two Pods had approached and were hovering next to them. Ichika had already managed to get hers open, and she and Haruto had exited and were making their way toward the blasted opening.

"Ok, come on," Jacqueline said, spying her competition. "Can't be seen as pussies," she added, hitting the button to open the Pod door again. The door slid up, flooding the airspace they had regained with water again. Jacqueline and Mark took deep breaths and ducked into the water to swim behind Ichika, who led the way.

Jacqueline turned to see Riku and Akari leaving their Pod and following.

In waterlogged silence, all six of them managed to get through the entry created by the blast. After they had swum deep inside, the man made cavern turned out to have an air pocket inside it. They surfaced, switching on the waterproof flashlights that Eve had distributed among them.

"Over there!" Riku shouted, pointing in the direction of a stairway. "That looks like it leads to a higher chamber."

Mark nodded. "Think so. From the schematics Eve managed to plot from her scans, it should be intact and dry."

Ichika shined the flashlight in the direction he was pointing, and the team headed over, guided by the light.

They hauled themselves up the steps and soon found themselves in a chamber that was more or less dry except for the water they tracked in.

Haruto glanced down at the sleeve of his suit. "Wow," he remarked, touching it with his hand. "Yuko wasn't kidding when she said these suits were quick-drying."

Jacqueline huffed. "Yeah, well, would have been good to have something that was oxygen-providing too," she grumbled, wringing the water out of her hair.

Akari was doing the same, but Ichika with her short dark bob simply flipped her hair back behind her ears and then squeezed the water out by running the flats of her hands over her head.

"Ok, this way," Mark told them, leading them deeper into the chamber and lugging the plastic-encased battery required for the job with him.

Peckham, England

George walked into Harry's office. He turned and shut the door quietly.

Harry looked up and frowned. "What's happened now?"

George ignored the tissues that were in the trashcan by Harry's desk. "Noah has gone dark."

"And another one of us falls." Harry sighed. "It seems that Charley William is trying to get back up off the ground."

Harry thought back to the bully. "I hated that little pecker. Let's lock down the building and start calling in favors. We can't let two of our own plus all of our mercs, assuming they are all dead, go without a response."

"Oh, we won't," Harry agreed and stood from behind his desk. "Call for a lockdown, and make sure the crop in the dungeons are tied down. We don't need any of those fuckers getting loose while we deal with someone coming in from the outside."

"You think they will be coming here?" George asked, pulling the door back open as Harry walked toward him.

Harry left his office, and George closed the door behind them. "Two of our kill-or-capture squads went after them. I doubt they are feeling very forgiving."

"Why not just go to ground, hide?" George asked. "We've seen it in the past."

"When you are a king, on the top of a sand pile," Harry answered, "you make sure to toss off anyone trying to get to you." The two men turned toward the operations room in their headquarters. "They won't run away from the sand pile or dig themselves a hole in it. They know we are after them now. Their egos won't accept us running, I don't think."

Harry opened the door to their operations room. His eyes swept to Thomas' and Noah's work areas, knowing neither one would ever be there to speak with again. "Call in everyone we can. Everyone we know who were friends with the people on those teams that were murdered." A second later, he called back to his friend, "Power up the trap, too!"

George nodded and turned to go make some calls.

Saint-Genis-Pouilly, France

The man was sitting behind a wooden desk in an office dozens of meters underground. His eyes glanced between two screens he had connected to his tablet computer.

"I could never hate another as much as I hate Michael," William whispered. He watched the video from one of his contacts, showing what was left of his chalet in France. In another window he had an open report about the attack outside his suite in Frankfurt. He didn't doubt that there was other damage to his suite, more than the expensive vase that was listed destroyed in the report.

More, his personal sanctuary had been destroyed by people rifling through his personal effects.

"Gerard!" William called. A moment later, his number-one man stepped in.

"Yes, sir?" Gerard motioned to the door with his head.

"Leave it open," William answered. "I need you to call the mercenaries and tell them their new location will be in Peckham, England. They will wait for Michael to show up. If he walks out of the building, kill him. Let them know if they can confirm his death, I'll pay double the agreed."

"As you wish, sir." Gerard nodded and left, closing the door behind him.

Peckham, England, Green Antlers Pub

There were seven police officers in uniform and three other men in street clothes inside the room deep in the back of the Green Antlers Pub.

Oscar sat down at the table. As the newest member, he had decided that keeping his mouth shut was his best course of action.

Leo, Oscar's partner, stood up so everyone sitting around the table could see him easily. "I asked you here to discuss the new information we've received." He picked up a bottle. "But first, we toast to those of our people who have fallen."

"Toast!" Eight men and two women raised their drinks in salute and then took a sip before putting them back down.

"We have good intelligence that Noah, may demons eat his corpse in hell, was killed during a kill-or-capture operation in Germany, and Thomas was killed the day before, also in Germany."

"Two down, two to go," Josiah Williamson grumbled.

Leo nodded his understanding and continued speaking. "That means we only have two of the leadership left, and we need to consider our next steps."

"Are we going to get a better time to take them out?" Mickie Clark asked. Her voice a bit gravelly as she chewed on a toothpick.

"Our latest intel shows them locking the place down," Leo told her.

"Probably think they are about to be attacked by whoever took them out in Germany," she mused. "Hell, I would."

Josiah rapped his knuckles on the table. "Watch and be ready to take the opportunity to rush them if a fight happens?"

Leo looked around the table, gauging the response to Josiah's suggestion. "How many could we get across all three shifts?"

"Hell," Mickie replied, "I'll take my shift and sleep in our lookout rooms during the other two. I'll grab a suitcase of clothes to be ready."

There were nods of agreement around the table. "Ok, let's work out the details. Who's closest to Judge Keeth to get the legal documents we need?"

The discussions went on for another two hours before the ten broke up and went their separate ways to inform their members.

The Green Antlers were going to war.

One of the reasons humans have survived the millennia is an ability to sense trouble at an unconscious level. Oftentimes science has been unable to ascertain just what caused the humans to react when there didn't seem to be any obvious trouble about to occur.

However, there would be many stories written about the fateful day in Peckham, England when the Dark Messiah and his followers took out the blood-baggers and rained fire down from the heavens to destroy their building.

Many would argue that he didn't bring any fire, but rather it was done by those in the police who had been secretly trying to dismantle the blood-baggers and help the victims they had grabbed over the years to escape.

Here is what no one argued...

It started at noon, the streets emptying as the blood-baggers' headquarters was boarded up. Gun-wielding men and women, hard as sheets of metal and carrying weapons and ammunition, went into the building in the light.

Then an advanced ship the likes no one had seen descended out of the sky, as if it had come down from the sun itself. It was black and made no noise that anyone who had been willing to stay near the black building could discern. When it hovered over the street three blocks from the blood-baggers, the canopy opened, and two people got out.

One was a woman who had two pistols strapped down and her hair tied back.

The other was a shorter man, Asian. He also had pistols, but reached inside the flying vehicle and pulled out a katana.

Suddenly there was another man with them. He had on a long coat and was carrying a black leather hat. Many swore they couldn't see any hair on his head as he looked around, taking in the street.

The Pod took off, rising into the sky and disappearing, leaving the three on the ground. The man in the duster put on his hat and took the middle as the Asian man went to his left side and the woman took the right.

All had checked their pistols, sliding them back into their holsters and preparing themselves.

Michael looked up at a window and nodded before returning his attention to his surroundings.

"You don't have to go with us." Michael looked at Sabine, who was busy ignoring him for the fifteenth time since they left Germany. Finally, she turned, Michael thought her eyes would have been fire-red if she were a vampire.

"If you tell me one more time you don't want me to go with you, Bethany Anne is going to be waiting awhile for you to heal from me sticking the Jean Dukes special up your ass and pulling the trigger!"

Michael's eyebrows raised as he turned to Akio. "What'd I say?"

Akio kept his face passive, but he was laughing on the inside. "I believe your effort to keep her safe is being taken as you telling her you don't believe she can do the job."

Michael turned back to Sabine, his mouth open. She was pointing to him. "Just one more Gott Verdammt word, Mr. ArchAngel." She pointed toward the black building. "You can use my skills right now, and if I die in there, then I'll fucking die taking down yet another level of dickheads that need taking out. You need to realize that you can't do everything. You need a team." She moved her hand to her pistol. "Even if any of your team die, we're fucking doing it because we wouldn't be any-fucking-where else than right by your side."

Michael reached up and pulled the brim of his cowboy hat down just a bit. "Sabine, I'm proud to have you fight with me." He turned and started walking down the street. Akio to his left, Sabine on his right.

"Damn right you're proud," she told him.

Then she added a moment later, "Now let's work on not dying, ok?"

The first shot was fired from inside the building. Well, at least that is what is universally assumed. The sheer amount of firepower unleashed by the three people on the street immediately after one or more shots came from the building, so overwhelmed those inside that no one could determine anything after that first shot.

"Wait until you see the red in their eyes," Harry directed the men and women peeking through the shutters over the windows. "I'll give the signal."

"How the hell are we going to see any red in their eyes?" George asked. "It's fucking noon outside, full sun, and these guys and girl are vampires. We sure about them being vamps?"

"Hey, didn't you see what's-his-face with the hat just appear?" someone called from the hallway near the south wall.

"Could be dust in my eye," came a reply.

"We've got forty guns, they have three."

"Six," George corrected.

"Whatever," Harry told him. "Just wait until I say 'go.'"

"Go?" someone asked.

Harry jerked around. "No!"

Too late; the man had fired a shot down the street. SHIT! Harry turned back, but it was in motion already. The wall erupted in explosions as if those people were using machine guns that were chambered with .50-caliber rounds.

Mercs hit the floor, and no less than three bodies exploded near Harry in a torrent of blood and guts as rounds found them.

It was all anyone could do to roll backward away from the windows and walls and make their way toward the stairs to go down into the center of the building where the weapons wouldn't be able to penetrate.

"WHAT THE HELL WAS THAT?" Terry yelled, an arm over her head as she raced down the stairs after Harry.

"Goddamned better guns than we got!" he fumed.

Leo was watching between the blinds in his little apartment. He had seen people leaving the street and not coming back for the last hour. At first, he thought it was his group that had caused the concern.

However, news came down that a lot of mercenaries were moving into the blood-baggers' building, and they had closed their protective window covers. They were getting ready for a fight; everyone could sense it.

"Hooooly shit," he muttered when the spacecraft came floating down into the middle of the street right in front of him. "Oscar!" In a few seconds his partner hurried into the room, tucking his shirt in.

"What?" he asked, coming up to the window and looking down through the slats. "Who the hell?"

"I think we know just who killed Thomas and Noah."

"Fuuuuuuck meee," Oscar whispered when a third person, a man in a long coat and a hat, just…appeared next to the other two. "You ever hear of someone who can be invisible?"

Leo was shaking his head, but his mouth said, "Yes…"

Oscar looked at him. "Who?"

"Oh my God," Leo whispered. The man seemed to look right at him and tip his hat. "Tell everyone to stay the hell away from those three."

"Why?" Oscar asked, and Leo looked at him. "Hey, I'm not saying I won't, but a guy's got to learn sometime, right?"

"Because," Leo pointed down to the three on the street as the vehicle lifted off again, "if I'm right, that is the baddest motherfucker on our planet." Leo looked back outside just as they stopped talking and started down the street. "All we need to do is cleanup and stay out of their way." He added a moment later, "Not necessarily in that order."

"He got a name?"

Leo's head nodded. "Dark Messiah. Before that, Arch-Angel. Before that, the Patriarch. But his first one was Michael."

Oscar watched them walk down the street. "That's a lot of names."

19

Under Kurobe Dam

Once they had made it into the second chamber, their journey became much faster, unimpeded by water now.

Ichika looked around with the curiosity and wonder of a child who had never experienced such a world. "Looks like Eve's calculations were correct," she remarked as the group traipsed through the deserted corridors.

Jacqueline grunted in acknowledgment, distracted.

"What is it?" Mark asked her, noticing her quietness.

Jacqueline glanced through the open doors at the deserted labs and offices. "Don't you think it's strange that we haven't seen any dead bodies in here?" she wondered out loud.

Mark slowed his pace suddenly, and Riku slammed into the back of him, jolting him forward. "Ugh," Mark grunted involuntarily as the wind was knocked from his lungs.

"My apologies." Riku bowed, blushing at his lack of situational awareness.

Akari swatted him on the arm. "Some silent warrior you are," she chuffed, rolling her eyes dramatically.

Jacqueline and Ichika sniggered quietly to themselves.

Mark was distracted, though. "You have a point, Jacqueline. Perhaps we should let Yuko know while we're searching this place? It does seem a bit odd."

Jacqueline nodded. "Ok, I'll do that," she agreed, pulling the strange communication device she had been given out of her pocket as they continued walking.

Just then something caught her eye up ahead. "Hey," she said, getting Mark's attention again. "This looks promising," she said, nodding toward a set of double doors.

Ichika frowned. "How can you tell?" she asked, curious as to what other strange superpowers these people really had.

Jacqueline smiled. "I spent a long time scavenging for technology back in my country. One develops a sixth sense for these things."

Ichika raised her eyebrows. "Oh," she said quietly, noticing that Akari was watching her strangely. "What's up with you?" she asked as they followed Jacqueline and Mark into the server room.

Akari shook her head. "Nothing," she said simply, following Ichika into the computer room and pretending to be immersed in the new environment of computer stacks.

Mark was already walking around the array, searching for the most strategic place to plug in.

Jacqueline looked around, a little out of her depth. "Honey?" she called. "I think I'm going to take a walk. See if there are any other clues about what really happened down here."

"Uh huh," Mark grunted, already on his hands and knees in front of a particular stack. He clipped something into place and a fan powered up. "Ok. Be careful. Take someone with you," he added. "And let Yuko know what's going on, would you?"

Jacqueline was already through the door before the two girls realized what was going on and decided to follow her.

Halfway down the corridor, they had just come from, they managed catch up to her. Ichika looked at Jacqueline as they strode. "Mark is your husband?" she asked naively.

Jacqueline shook her head. "Boyfriend," she corrected, before suddenly becoming suspicious. "Why?"

Ichika shook her head. "Making polite conversation," she protested, suddenly remembering that Eve had warned her about Jacqueline's jealous streak.

Jacqueline relaxed a little, but remained on edge, as she fiddled with the communicator. "Right," she mumbled, trying to get it to connect.

Akari was silent as she followed them.

Jacqueline finally connected with Eve. "Eve, hi. We're in."

Peckham, England

The first shot whiffed right by Michael's ear, his head jerking to the left while his right hand grasped the pistol butt and yanked. He had already sent four antigrav pulse-generated slivers of hot metal streaming back toward the building he believed the shot came from.

His eyes could see the implosion of the wall as his, Akio's, and then Sabine's shots destroyed that location.

Six guns, all turned up to the highest level each person could handle, started streaming shots down the street. They walked the shots to the left and right, each person taking an area based on their own location. Akio to the left, Michael in the middle, and Sabine on the right.

They walked down the street, continuing to fire.

The big building's brick facing was crashing to the street in front. Large gaps were being torn in bricks that had been there for hundreds of years by the fusillade of firepower destroying the outside. Anything inside was being pulverized as rounds ripped through walls to destroy what they could.

"Out," Akio commented. He calmly pulled out new magazines and put them in his pistols while Michael used his left gun to pummel the building in Akio's area. A second later Akio was back online and Michael took a moment to replace his own magazines. When he was done, Sabine took a turn and reloaded.

"These fucking hurt," Michael bitched as they reached the front of the building. He slid his right pistol into its holster and flung his hand back and forth. "Hellacious kick."

"Pussies." Sabine laughed.

"Try turning *yours* up to eleven," Michael told her. She looked at him, then looked at the setting on her pistol.

Six.

Eleven? "Oh, hell no! I take that back."

"Thought so," Michael told her. "You can stop. Everyone is farther inside the building now.

Sabine shot twice more and ceased fire, then watched as a chunk of the wall three stories up slowly slid off and dropped to the ground, crashing into the other chunks of brick. "Wow, now I know why guys like destruction so much."

"It is addictive," Michael agreed.

You going to watch out for her? He sent to Akio.

Hai.

Good, I don't need another verbal attack for caring.

Akio chuckled. *You need to stop saving people who then become willing to die with you.*

I don't think I'm responsible for this one. You are the one who taught her how to shoot.

Hai.

That's it?

What else would you have me say? You are right, I taught her how to shoot.

Just...just watch her, Michael finished, then stepped into the building.

Michael could feel the pain, the emotions of those beneath him in rooms under the ground. He read the thoughts, the agonies, the desires to die as machines sucked their blood out.

Some of whom he felt deserved it, many of whom did not.

His eyes flared red and he turned back around. "Akio!"

"*Hai!*" Akio turned from speaking with Sabine, his eyebrows raised in question.

Michael reached down and unbuckled his holsters' belt. "Take these. I'm not going to need them."

Akio noticed the granite in Michael's eyes and nodded. "We will be outside."

"What?" Sabine hissed, but stopped when Akio's hand sliced in front of her. Michael had turned around and was walking into the building.

Akio looked at her. "You have met a man who has been softened."

Sabine snorted. "Softened?"

"Somewhat," Akio clarified. "The Patriarch is here, so we need to step back."

Sabine looked around. "Like, literally?"

An explosion shook the inside of the building, and a portion of the roof seemed to crumble, pieces raining down across the street and bouncing off walls.

"Never mind," Sabine answered her own question, and the two took off running across the street, aiming for an alley.

Down the street, Leo and Oscar whistled as they watched the roof explode. "That man is pissed."

Leo had a smile on his lips, but it didn't touch his eyes. "I think he just found out about the captives underground."

"Why?" Oscar asked. "He doesn't like other vampires hurt?"

"Boy," Leo shook his head, "that guy is honor personified. He would do that if *you* were strapped there."

First, there were explosions…

Then there was *FEAR*. The feeling that hit those who had made it down from the third floor had to work hard to stop their minds from gibbering.

The *fear* caused Harry and everyone around him to struggle to get up and move as parts of the roof collapsed.

Harry made an effort to get on his feet and moved from desk to table to chair to the wall and the switch. It was one of those old-time switches; it looked like a handle with two braces coming down. He grabbed the top and smiled, holding the handle as he turned to the video feed and saw a human in a black coat and hat walk through the hallway into the large outer room which was just on the other side of the wall from where he and his people were making their last stand.

When the dark man walked into the middle of the room, Harry grinned.

"Welcome to my lair, motherfucker!" he said as he yanked down on the switch, sending millions of volts of electricity arcing around the room on the other side of the wall. "Survive *that*, you sonofabitch!"

The *fear* stopped and palpable relief washed through the teams.

That's when the laughing started. All eyes turned toward the door.

Michael felt the ionization in the air before the electricity started arcing throughout the room.

He reached out, dropping his *fear* as he focused everything he had on trying to pull the electricity through his hands. "Don't you dare mess up my coat, and leave my damned hat alone!" he said menacingly to the power surging through him, "or I'll figure out how to ground you in another dimension!"

The power he was shunting wasn't nearly as strong as the many lightning bolts Michael had handled on the ship in the storm. However, it was still enough that he moved some of it to the Etheric before he aimed his left hand at the door to the room and released half the power he was channeling.

He never noticed he was laughing.

The door exploded inward, bouncing over a desk and landing ten feet to Harry's right. His eyes went from the remains of the door to the doorway, and the bright white person who was walking in.

That was when electricity started arcing around the room.

Harry pushed up on the switch. Even *he* could see that giving more ammunition to this monster was a bad idea.

He reached for his pistol.

Michael read the minds of those around him, flitting from head to head and striking those first who had their wits about them.

He casually threw out his left hand, frying the leader in the back of the room who had disconnected the power in an attempt to rob Michael of any more ammunition.

"Fool," Michael said as he ransacked the man's mind for any news of the Duke. "Dammit!"

He was done here. Flinging out his arms, he sent tendrils of electricity through everyone in the room. Twice guns fired, once because one of the mercenary's fingers convulsed and pulled the trigger. "That's bad gun safety," Michael told no one in particular.

The second exploded; due to the electricity, Michael presumed.

In ten more seconds he sent his last bit of electricity out, and silence reigned. He listened for any minds near him and found none that weren't in extreme pain. Over to his left, a light fixture broke off from the ceiling and crashed to the floor.

Michael touched all the minds and walked around the room, nudging a couple to make sure they were dead. Even *his* mind was a little messed up for the moment.

He reached up and took his hat off. He looked it over and smiled. *The few marks that had appeared just gave it more character*, he thought. There had been something silver on the side.

It was melted now.

He wiped his skull and slid the hat back on. He wanted to help those below before... He turned, listening to a comment from Akio.

Walking back toward the front, he sought the minds Akio had found and then nodded.

Come, he sent to the people who were ready to rush the building to honor those who had fallen and those they sought to help.

The police who had been at the end of the road were making their way here.

They never saw the man leave, but they found the results of his fury. In the lower levels, some bodies were so emaciated it made hardened men and women cry.

Why hadn't they done something sooner?

It is enough, a voice told them as they sought to help those they could, *that you are here now.*

Over in the corner, Leo turned from his partner and reached up, drying the tears that had overcome his ability to keep them from falling.

Peckham, England, Two Buildings Down from the Blood-baggers'

Four men held state-of-the-art sniper rifles against their shoulders. Each had an area to cover and was waiting for the vampire to come out of the building, fingers on the triggers.

"Head shots, folks," Liam told his team members. "Might not kill him, but it will mess him up enough we can go take his head."

Some forty feet behind them, a small woman climbed up the fire escape and lifted her leg over the ledge to step softly on the roof. Standing up, she saw the four heads; all had their eyes focused on their scopes.

Fifteen seconds later, Akio waited as Sabine dropped the last few feet from the fire escape. "Four more fuckers who won't be bothering Michael."

"True," Akio agreed as the two walked down the back alley behind the buildings. "And he will be happy to find out these four knew where The Duke is located."

"No shit?" Sabine asked.

"No, I do not shit you," Akio answered as they took a left and saw Michael down at the other end of the alley.

Sabine sniffed. "Akio, you have a ways to go with your cursing."

Akio chuckled. "No shit?"

Overlooking the Kurobe Dam, Toyama Prefecture

Yuko felt a sense of dread flush through her body. She looked up from her computer screen at Eve. "Something is wrong. It's Michael and Akio. I can feel it."

Eve cocked her head. "Michael, Akio, is everything ok?"

There was silence on the line. A moment later they both heard Akio through their implants. "No. It's Michael. He needs our help. How soon can you get here?"

Eve did a quick calculation. "Twenty minutes, give or take?"

Yuko interjected. "We've just put Mark and Jacqueline into a high-risk situation. I'm concerned about leaving them."

Akio was clear. "Then the ArchAngel may die."

Yuko's eyes filled with terror. "We'll sort it out and be right there. Stand by."

"Thank you," Akio responded.

Just then the twin of the Etheric communications device she had given Jacqueline came to life.

"Speak of the devil," Yuko mumbled. Before responding, Yuko shot an instruction to Eve. "Let's get ready to leave."

Eve busied herself packing up the operation as quickly as she could.

"Jacqueline, hi?" Yuko responded. "How are you getting on?"

2 0

London, England

"He's *where?*" Michael asked.

"The Large Hadron Collider area near the old France/Switzerland border," Akio answered. Michael had spirited them away after a quick check of the building one last time in Myst form. They were now far enough away that they didn't expect anyone to put the three of them together with the carnage in Peckham.

Michael pulled his hat off and wiped his head before replacing it. The three of them were under a tree in a park, and he was looking off in the distance. "Why would he want to be near the Hadron Collider?" He turned to Akio. "What exactly is it again?"

"That would be for Eve to explain." Akio pursed his lips. "Effectively, back in the time before the WWDE, a bunch of scientists got funding to build two incredibly large circular rings underground. The purpose was to push atoms together with the intention of smashing them, causing tiny explosions."

"See?" Sabine interrupted. "More boys with their destructive toys."

Akio looked at her. "There were female scientists as well."

"Of course," she replied. "Otherwise the guys wouldn't have gotten anything done." She looked at Michael and then back at Akio. "Ok, I'm talking out my ass. I've no idea what a Hadron, large or small, even is, or why we would want to collide one."

"They were looking for a Higgs boson." Michael's voice was just a bit distant. His eyes unfocused for a moment, then he directed his gaze on the two of them. "Sorry, I remember that much. Like Sabine, I've not a clue what a Higgs boson is."

"It was called the God particle," Akio answered. "And that is about the end of anything I know. The important part is, the Large Hadron Collider was destroyed back near WWDE, so the only thing I can think of is William likes the fact that everything is underground."

"How far?" Michael asked.

"Something like a hundred meters, I think. The important part is that the large ring is something like twenty-seven kilometers in diameter."

Michael whistled. "I bet there are a lot of ways out of that circle." Akio shrugged. "It would make a very large place to stay out of the sun, and yet give him ways to exit if we attack." The three enjoyed the wind for a moment. "How did your guy know where the Duke is?"

"He saw one of the signs that had been damaged in a

battle," Akio answered. "They were flown there without having been told where they were going."

"Well," Michael replied, "it goes to show that no matter how careful you are, you can always make mistakes." He pointed up. "Let's bring our transportation down and go visit William."

Akio murmured into a microphone on his collar. Moments later, the three of them saw the Pod coming down out of the afternoon sky.

"Think we should go now, or tomorrow morning?" Michael asked as they walked toward the Pod.

"If he sleeps during the day, tomorrow, assuming he doesn't know that his team has been killed. If he will find out when he wakes up, then now. We can be there in twenty minutes."

A few in the park noticed the ship dropping out of the sky, then the three figures coming out from underneath the trees. One of the figures was a lady, one an Asian dressed in something resembling a cross between military fatigues and a martial arts outfit, and the final... looked like someone from the old American cowboy films.

Their ship, however, appeared as if it was from the future.

"It is so beautiful!" Sabine spoke in the stillness of space. Akio had taken them all the way up into the mesosphere on their way back toward France. "I don't understand why you don't go up every day to see something this beautiful."

Akio smiled as he confirmed their course. Michael was in Myst form, allowing Sabine to sit in the back seat.

"Wait until you get a chance to see it from a true spaceship. You will be just as impressed, if not more, than you are now," he told her.

"I'll just have to trust you," she said as she turned to look behind them at the little island they had been on not that long ago. "With no clouds, it's amazing."

Akio stayed quiet.

How far away will we land, and do we know if William has anything that can locate us? Michael asked.

Unlikely, and at least five kilometers. I will come in about twenty kilometers away and fly close to the ground. We will land on the other side of a mountain range, Akio replied.

Very good.

The craft started down, the antigrav engines creating a shaft of air ahead of them, cutting through the air and reducing the friction and drag on the Pod.

For all intents and purposes, the craft was in its own bubble as it came out of the sky, keeping the wind from buffeting it and preventing contrails.

Five minutes later the Pod was zipping over the ground, flying nap-of-the-earth as it headed toward the mountains. Within moments, enough time for Sabine to worry that they wouldn't slow down and would just fly straight into the mountain itself, they landed.

Near Saint-Genis-Pouilly, France

Sabine slid out of the Pod and reached back in to grab her gear. She took a few moments to admire the landscape as she locked her belt and made sure her pistols were set on safe.

It was a testament to her weird life that she didn't jump at Michael's appearance as his body blocked her view. "Could you appear somewhere else for a moment?" She waved him to the left. "I'm enjoying the view."

Michael shook his head, but took two steps to his right and spoke to Akio. "Direction?"

Akio picked up a tablet from inside the Pod. "We are here." He pointed to a map displayed on the screen. "We need to go here." Both men looked up at the peaks and Akio pointed again. "Between the second and third there," he explained.

"Looks right to me," Michael agreed as he grabbed his sword out of the Pod. He turned toward Sabine. "Ready?"

She nodded, then turned back to him. "I never want to say I failed to enjoy the view."

The Pod backtracked, following the landscape before it rose into the sky. The Myst went the other direction, heading between the two peaks.

William stood and closed the drawer next to him. Grabbing a set of keys and a remote control, he walked to the office door and stepped out. He nodded to Gerard. "He's coming."

"We've got nothing, sir." Gerard looked back at the screens he could monitor.

"Trust me," William touched his head. "I can feel the bastard. I trust my instincts where he is concerned. Make sure everyone is ready." He continued walking toward the elevator. He had stopped sleeping during the day decades before. He imagined Michael thought that attacking today, after he had killed his team, would be the best choice.

He did rather enjoy outsmarting Michael. It was a shame he wasn't going to have time to gloat once he powered up the LHC. He punched the button for the elevator and waited for it to arrive.

Once in the elevator, he dropped another three floors to the main concourse. This was a large tunnel with a flat floor. Stepping out, he nodded to his first group of protectors and continued walking down the concourse.

He walked a total of a kilometer, passing the multiple doors his people had specially fitted in the large tunnel. The actual channel to run Michael through was a damned pipe. They had to figure out a way to get Michael to slip into the pipe, but once he was in they could fire it up.

He checked on four of the little Michael-traps, making sure they were set appropriately. They had placed another six in the tunnel earlier, in case Michael paid more attention than he remembered.

Even an old dog like Michael might learn a new trick or two…

But he doubted it.

Michael swept through the buildings, registering no minds. He stopped, and the three materialized on a grassy hill.

"Just for the record," Sabine stepped away from the two

and bent over, spitting into the grass, "that's not easy to get used to."

"I'm impressed. Most people who get bothered by traveling in the Myst would have been vocal earlier."

"I'm trying to be a good rider," she said over her shoulder.

"Eve," Akio said, "I need those schematics." A moment later, he pulled out his tablet and started swiping on the top. He stopped and looked to his right, then held the tablet up and rotated it a quarter-turn counterclockwise. His eyes went from the tablet to the buildings and back again. "That way," he said, and pointed toward a building a couple blocks away.

The three moved along, Michael allowing his senses to reach out. "I'm thinking one up here to protect our back door."

Akio turned to Sabine. "Do you want topside or underground?"

"No contest," she told him. "I see plenty of things I can use to make a fort."

The three of them walked into a building and looked around. "That way." He pointed.

Walking past an area that Michael could imagine had been a security station once upon a time, they started to head down a hallway. "Hey!" Sabine called, and the two men turned.

"I'm going to build up my little protection area here," she told the men, then grabbed a wooden bench and started pulling it across the floor. Both men's faces scrunched up as a squeal from the wood hurt their hearing.

"Hey!" she called one more time. "Don't let anyone come up behind me!"

Michael touched the brim of his hat and turned back around. Both walked down the hall.

Sabine watched them go, then turned back to her area. "Well, *merde*," she said, hands on her hips. "Where is a strapping vampire when you need one?"

She walked over to a desk and started pushing it. "Perhaps I let them go a little too quickly. Should have played the 'small, frail female' card there," she grumbled as the desk started moving across the floor.

The two men descended the stairs, their senses alert for any hint of where William might be. They searched two floors before stopping in front of an elevator.

"Good place to get stuck," Michael said, eyeing the elevator.

"Myst down?" Akio asked.

"Should be plenty of space, sure." Michael pulled Akio into his Myst and slid between the closed doors, then headed down the elevator shaft.

Rather deep, Michael commented.

Hai.

At the bottom, the two materialized on top of an elevator car. Akio bent down, grasped the top, and pulled. A door screeched off in his hand, and he tossed it aside. Standing up, he jumped into the car feet-first and hit the button. The door opened and he peeked out.

No one.

Michael Mysted down and appeared next to Akio. Both men looked both ways down the circular tunnel.

"Damn," Michael exhaled. "I can sense people both ways, but not William."

"*Hai.*"

"I'm thinking left is a good direction."

"Splitting up is a very bad idea," Akio said.

"I know." Michael looked to the left. "I'm going this way."

"*Hai*, I'm going the other," Akio replied as the two men parted.

Michael spoke over his shoulder. "Hope we don't meet up thirteen and a half kilometers from here with nothing to show."

Akio's chuckles could be heard for a little while as Michael walked down the tunnel.

Ten minutes later, he received a call from Akio. "Michael?"

"Yes?"

"I've found a bunch of scientists spread out. And, a group of undesirables."

"You mean you found some fun, and a group to put you to sleep afterwards?"

"Which is which?" Akio asked.

"If I have to explain the joke," Michael replied, "it isn't funny." He stopped. "Sonofabitch, Akio. You got me."

"*Hai!*"

"I've got humans ahead." Michael's eyes narrowed. "They've seen William. Looks like we have the right place."

"Be careful," Akio advised.

"'Careful' is my middle name." Michael chuckled.

"Sorry, that is so wrong. It's more like my fifth or sixth name after Maim, Kill, Destroy, and a couple others that I forget."

"Regretful and Repentant?"

"Uhhhhh, no."

Akio's mood sobered. "If you get killed right after we found you, Bethany Anne is going to resurrect you so she can kill you herself." Akio heard Michael's chuckles through the communications device. "Akio out."

He put away the comm and limbered up. Maybe this time he would just use a sword.

Using the pistol wasn't providing him any practice.

"Michael, Michael, Michael…" The voice came from speakers located every thirty feet or so in the tunnel.

"William," Michael answered as he allowed the last guard to slide off his sword. He cleaned the blade on the man's pant leg. "Have you decided what should be on your tombstone?"

"I see you are still annoying."

"I hear you still have a penchant for believing you are somebody in this world," Michael replied. "Your days are numbered. I'd say somewhere between zero and none."

"Cute," William replied. "I believe I'll have to satisfy myself with just how many times you have been wrong in your life when I think about you. Which I'm afraid to admit won't be too many."

"Well," Michael slid his sword back into the sheath, "I

should let you know that Valerie asked me to provide you a chance to repent and change your ways."

"*My* Valerie?" he asked. There was a pause. "I had such hopes for her, but she was too weak."

"Not too weak. I believe you need to assign that attribute to Donovan, since she kicked his ass and then killed him. Mind you, she was horribly hurt at the time."

"I did have such hopes for him," William replied, annoyed. "Perhaps I'll toast you on the anniversary of your death as being a decent adversary."

Huge *BANG*s started occurring, and Michael turned around. His eyes narrowed as he heard them coming from the other way as well. He changed to Myst and flew in the same direction he had been heading. He made it perhaps a few hundred meters when he stopped, blocked.

He reappeared, his eyes blazing red. "I thought you considered me nothing but a pest, yet you seem to not want us to meet, William."

The speakers in this area of the tunnel worked for William as well. "I'm smart, Michael. I'd rather have all the time in the world to kill you."

Michael looked around the room, noticing the two-foot-diameter pipe which went through the wall. He changed to Myst and went up to where the pipe met the wall. He couldn't locate any spots to make it through to the other side.

He reappeared.

"And that is why I think we need to agree."

"What?" Michael responded. "Sorry, I tuned you out there for a moment."

"Tuning me out, or are you losing your focus in your old age, Michael?"

Michael's face twisted in annoyance. His eyes kept flitting back to the pipe, then the door.

A kilometer away, William was in a section of the tunnel which had an exit to the surface. If Michael was able to get out of the trap, he would leave and close the door, giving him more than enough time to get away and work on trapping Michael another time.

He had watched Michael disappear the first time from his hidden camera, then growled internally when he reappeared.

Patience… He just needed to have patience.

Sabine looked around the area, bored. With Michael and Akio, attacks had rarely been boring.

Now she was almost impatient, wanting her turn to do something. Anything. Hell, she was willing to be taken up in his Myst again and swung around so much she felt like throwing up.

This waiting shit sucked.

Akio had just dispatched the third guard when a bullet

pinged two feet from his head. He ducked low and searched ahead of him for whoever had shot. Not seeing anyone, he wondered if it had been a ricochet from farther down.

He started jogging down the tunnel, his eyes red and his lips pressed together. He was in his zone, and he was a happy man.

"You know, William," Michael called, "I don't suppose you had anything in that chalet you wanted?"

Michael smiled when William's voice changed timbre. *He is definitely annoyed now*, Michael thought. He started ranting about the things he, Akio, and Sabine had destroyed.

He disappeared and headed into the pipe.

"You cowardly, useless cretins aren't worth the effort to shoot you." William was spitting now. He breathed in, ready to fire off another vitriolic paragraph when he noticed Michael wasn't in the room anymore.

"Sonofabitch!" he shouted, slamming his thumb on the button. He turned and hit another radio button. "GO!"

The noise was just enough to bring Sabine out of her

daydream. Her hands flashed down and drew her pistols before she understood what was going on. She got off two shots before her fort was attacked, rounds slamming into it as she heard boots arriving through the front of the building.

She thought she saw one person go down before she had to duck. "You bastards!" she shouted. She looked down at her pistol and dialed it up to eight. "I'd better not get a broken hand!"

She started firing through her own fort. "This isn't going to be a good solution in the long term, Sabine," she bitched. "You've simply got to stop destroying your protection from the inside."

That's when life went upside-down for her.

She was violently blown down the hallway when something large and explosive slammed into her fort and blew it apart, sending her rolling over and over. She spat out blood. She couldn't hear anything, but she did notice that her right arm was still aiming down the hallway and pulling the trigger.

Her left was hanging at an odd angle. She returned to looking down the passage, pleased that she had taken the time to admire the landscape earlier that day.

If it was her day to die, it had at least been a pretty one.

A helmeted head came up above what was left of her protective fort just long enough for her to squeeze the trigger, blowing that fucking asshole's brains across whatever friends were behind him.

If she was going to die, she was going to send a shit-ton of enemies in front of her to announce her arrival.

"Miiiichaeeellll." William's voice reverberated through the pipe. "Have a nice death."

Hell opened and started pulling him everywhere and nowhere at once. It was worse than David's device, and in his mind, Michael screamed in pain.

Akio flinched, hearing the scream in his mind and realizing it wasn't himself. He slid his sword back into his sheath and got on the communicator. "Yuko, Eve, I need you here!"

21

Under the Kurobe Dam

Yuko's voice came back to her over the communicator.

"Jacqueline, hi?" Yuko responded. "How are you getting on?"

Jacqueline tried a door on her right. "Mark's in the server room now. He's already powered up the server he needs. I'm just taking a look around." The door opened, and she stepped into a dark room. She found a light switch and realized she was in a control room with more computers than she'd ever seen in one place. "Wow! This place is…" her voice died away.

Yuko prompted, "Jacqueline? Are you still there?"

"Yeah. I've just found a room full of more computers. Like you have in the flying box."

Yuko waited.

Jacqueline remembered something. "Oh yeah, that's the other thing that is strange about this place." She was vaguely aware that Akari and Ichika had wandered in behind her and were now examining the Aladdin's cave of technology they had stumbled upon.

Jacqueline brought her attention back to the conversation over the device. "We've not come across any bodies or skeletons, which is suspicious given that the history buffs are telling us there was an accident."

Yuko's voice sounded curious. "You think that maybe it wasn't the earthquake that caused the base to be shut down?"

Jacqueline could hear Eve in the background as she responded, "It's certainly looking curious." She watched Ichika's eyes light up as she ran her hand over the console she was inspecting.

Yuko's voice returned. "Ok. Eve says to grab the data as quickly as you can and get out of there. Michael is in danger. We're going to have to go help him."

The color drained from Jacqueline's face, and a second later her eyes flared. "What's wrong? Where is he?"

Yuko's voice was even. "It's ok. Nothing we can't help with. But we're going to have to leave you. Will you be ok?"

"Yes, of course. The hard bit is done. We're fine here."

She paused. "What about the Pods?"

Yuko responded quickly. "Eve can control those for you. Just make your way back to them when you're ready, and we'll be notified that you're there and get you out.

"Ok. No problem," Jacqueline agreed. "Now go. Save Michael, please," she added softly, her anger giving way to her vulnerability.

"We will. Speak soon," Yuko confirmed before closing the call.

Suddenly there was a clatter and Jacqueline's attention snapped to where the sound had come from. Akari was standing there, her hair still wet and dripping, scuffling to pick up a microphone-like device that was attached to one of the computers.

Jacqueline raised an eyebrow. "Everything ok?" she asked, bemused by the girl's expression of surprise coupled with that of a child about to be chastised.

Akari nodded, fumbling with the device before replacing it on the top of the console. "Yes. Sorry," she said, her face flushing with embarrassment.

Jacqueline glanced at Ichika, who was a few feet away. Ichika shrugged. "What can I tell you? Ninja training at its best." She smiled.

Jacqueline chuckled quietly, noticing how Ichika certainly didn't fit the mold of the other fighters she'd seen at the dojo. Even her smile was bright and mischievous.

"Come on." Jacqueline grinned. "Let's go find out if the boys are nearly done."

She headed out of the room, followed by the others. "Hit the light—" She stopped, and looked at the light switch. "This place had power?"

Ichika wandered over. "Backup generator?"

Jacqueline rolled her lips inward. "I guess so…" she responded, her Spidey senses tingling even more. "Come on, let's get out of here," she reaffirmed, striding out and back down the corridor.

Ichika followed, and then Akari left, hitting the light switch as she exited the room.

Saint-Genis-Pouilly, France

Sabine ducked when a rocket came over her fort, rushing past her down the hallway to explode fifty feet back. "You missed me." She coughed. "Fuck it." She started shooting down the passage like they had back in England, using up her ammo like it was free.

She barely considered what she would do when she ran out. She didn't have an arm to load another magazine anyway.

She struggled to get up on one knee, shooting the whole time through what was left of the barrier. She used the wall to walk forward, firing and waiting for the bullet with her name on it to find her.

She made it back to her fort. There were at least nine bodies that she could see. An occasional bullet made its way into her area. She sat down, crying out when her arm hit a board and nearly fainting. She leaned back, allowing her eyes to flit from area to area, looking for the next target to shoot.

The pain was horrible, and the desire to just give up and dissipate was intense. Then he remembered who this was all for, and he fought on. He would offset the pull of the magnets with the energy he drew through the Etheric. He could not move into the other dimension, but neither could the collider pull him apart. He wasn't sure if he was moving down the pipe or holding still.

All he could be sure of was the pain. That, and the fact

that he had people depending on him not to give up. For him to be there when they did whatever it was, they would be doing, to save his arrogant ass.

He hoped to God that Bethany Anne couldn't feel what he was going through right now because he was sure it would piss her off so much that she would remember until they met again.

He doubted he would get the toe-curling kiss he was looking for if that happened.

He tried to send extra energy into the device that was pulling him apart, but nothing happened.

He was well and truly fucked.

"Why. Won't. He. Die?" William screamed. He was watching a video from the main operations room. It should have shown a glitch in the system, perhaps an energy anomaly, but instead there was a massive energy flux. Hell, it was in some way driving the damn collider itself.

"You power your own demise." William chuckled. "How ironic."

Under the Kurobe Dam, Server Room

"Eureka!"

Riku heard Mark celebrate his geeky success for the second time in as many minutes. He poked his head around the stack to see him still standing at the console, the light from the screen illuminating the intense concentration on his face.

Haruto came up beside him and watched Mark with him. "And to think he'd never really seen this level of tech before he came here a few days ago."

Riku heard the hint of admiration and respect in Haruto's voice. "I don't know why the Diplomat saw fit to give *him* the task and not us," he commented. "After everything our master has done for her, you would think she would have honored him by entrusting us with the task."

He felt Haruto's eyes on him and turned in the half-light to meet his gaze. "What?"

Haruto's eyes were full of compassion, which only served to irritate him even more. "We're warriors, not tech wizards," he explained. "You hold anger in your heart, brother. In the heat of battle that will cause you to make mistakes. Allow it to leave so you can be free." He put his hand on Riku's shoulder, then wandered into the darkness away from where Mark was working.

Riku seethed as he watched Mark continue his task. He knew Haruto was right. *Sensei* Kashikoi had told him as much many times over the years. He just hadn't figured out how to release this fire that burned in his heart all the time. He clenched his fists, trying to burn off the energy, and disappeared behind the stack again to give himself time to think.

Under the Kurobe Dam, Server Room

"Aw, shit!" Mark exclaimed.

Riku emerged from behind a dead server. "What's up?" he asked with a look of concern.

Mark rubbed the top of his head, having hit it on a shelf as he was looking behind the server. "It's ok. Just not paying attention to my physical dimensions," he responded, turning his attention back to the server he was hooking into.

Riku squatted next to him. "So how does this work?" he asked, peering at what Mark was doing.

Mark readjusted the position of the battery he had just connected. "Well, this is just booting up now," he said, nodding at the server. "Then I need to put this in a port somewhere," he explained, pulling the dongle out of his suit pocket. He leaned forward again, being more careful about the shelf under which the server was positioned. His head disappeared between the server and the wall. "Got it!" he exclaimed triumphantly.

Riku watched carefully as he swapped the dongle into his other hand to fit it into the server port. "Now what?"

Mark started to get up, and Riku stood up and stepped out of the way. "Now I need to find a way of accessing this node," he explained, looking around. He spotted a terminal tucked between more servers with different-looking facades.

He pulled a coil of wire out of his pocket and ran it between the battery and the terminal.

"Anything I can help with?" Riku asked.

Mark didn't even look up as he worked. "Not at the moment," he answered. "Just chill for a bit. We'll need to get moving as soon as we have what we came for. If it works."

Riku frowned. "What do you mean, 'If it works?'"

Mark sighed to himself. "Well, these machines aren't compatible with modern machinery, so Eve had to call in some favors to find a dongle that would work with these old-style ports. I'm just keeping my fingers crossed that this is actually going to work."

Riku nodded, then hesitated. "I'll keep my fingers crossed too." He wandered off.

Mark continued to work, doing a little fist-pump when he got the terminal powered up and another when he successfully uploaded Eve's patch to grant him access. Once that was done, it didn't take him long to locate what they needed and start transferring it to the dongle.

Riku was at his side suddenly. "All done?"

Mark nodded. "Will be in a few minutes. When that bar reaches full, it will be done, and then we just need to retrieve the dongle and get out of here. Wanna see if you can find the girls?"

Riku bowed slightly and disappeared.

Mark watched the bar process. His arms folded, he felt rather pleased with himself. He was enjoying this new world with its technology and coolness. He found himself wondering idly if this might be somewhere he could come back to. Unless what they were talking about with spaceships really was possible, and then maybe he could end up in spa—

"Watch out!" a voice shouted from behind him.

Mark spun around to see a refrigerator-sized server falling on top of him from the second tier. He held his arms up instinctively to cover his head but felt the impact anyway. His legs crumpled underneath him.

Feeling dazed and overwhelmed and hurting all over, he tried to scramble out from under the weight, but his leg didn't work. A second later he felt a jarring pain all the way through his body, like every nerve ending was on fire.

And then nothing.

2 2

Minutes earlier

Riku hadn't heard anything from Mark for a short while. He stood up from the stack he'd been leaning against and in doing so, it rocked a little. Glancing up, he saw it was top-heavy because of a large, encased server.

He pushed it again. It rocked again.

I wonder, he thought as he peered between the shelves of equipment at Mark and his illuminated console.

His method of escape dawned on him.

He looked up once more before turning and heading back around the stack to talk to Mark.

He paused at Mark's elbow, looking at the screen he was working on. "All done?"

Mark nodded. "Will be in a few minutes. When that bar reaches full it will be done, and then we just need to retrieve the dongle and get out of here. Wanna see if you can find the girls?"

Riku bowed slightly and disappeared, only he had no

intention of locating the others. In fact, if they stayed away a little longer, so much the better.

He returned to his spot behind the wobbly stack and checked that it really did line up with Mark's position. Satisfied, he took a deep breath and pushed as hard as he could.

The whole shelf moved slowly at first, but after a moment in what felt like suspended animation it lurched forward. The server he had spotted slipped forward faster, falling off the shelf onto Mark.

"Watch out!" Riku shouted, far too late to be helpful but just soon enough to assuage any suspicion that it might have been a deliberate attempt to hurt him. Insurance, should Mark actually survive the next few attacks he had in mind to layer on top of this one.

Mark spun around just in time to see the fridge-sized server falling onto him. Riku watched with a degree of satisfaction as Mark's leg crumpled underneath him. The rest of the gear and the shelving itself continued to crash down on him, pinning him perfectly in place.

Riku hurried, knowing Haruto would return in a matter of seconds on hearing the crash. Riku pulled out the severed power cables that had been placed ready for him across the aisle against another stack. He tugged, pulling the long cabling out of its hidden place. He touched the ends together and they cracked, discharging an enormous spark. Without waiting, he threw one end down on the metal shelving that had fallen atop Mark, and then the other.

The metal frame buzzed and sparked in cracks and

bangs, and then he heard the *thunk* of a circuit breaker, and it all stopped.

He could smell burning rubber where the frame had been in contact with the floor. He hoped it hadn't grounded before it circuited through Mark, although he had no idea what charred vampire might smell like.

He stepped closer, peering into the half-light. He couldn't see anything. He heard nothing. He pulled his flashlight from his pocket, and then his tiny concealed gun. Flicking the safety off, he turned on the flashlight and swept the area. He spotted Mark's head and torso. His eyes were closed, and already there was a lump forming on his forehead.

Looks nasty, he thought to himself, raising his gun hand over his flashlight hand. Carefully taking aim, he focused on the spot where the bruise was already evident on Mark's head, breathed, and pulled the trigger.

He heard footsteps running in their direction. "Mark, Riku, are you ok?" It was Haruto.

"Over here!" Riku called, trying to make his voice sound as panicked as possible. "Help! It's Mark."

A second later Haruto came running around the shelf at the end and right into Riku's sights. "I heard gunsh—"

Haruto froze.

Still holding his hands and weapon in the same position, Riku squeezed the trigger and delivered a shot straight into the forehead of his colleague and friend.

Haruto's body stood for a moment and then fell backward.

Riku glanced at the vampire, who now had a hole in his head and was still motionless. Picking his way through the rubble of the data servers, Riku headed over to the other side where the dongle had been quietly downloading the information he needed. He scrambled deftly and quietly and pulled the unit around so he could access it. The light that had been flashing was now solid. He pulled the dongle out and made his way back down the aisle.

He walked straight past the body of his former friend without so much as a glance in his direction, his eyes searching the illuminated area in front of him for his exit. Although it was almost obscured by another set of shelves with data storage units, he spotted it and jogged over double-time. This door didn't need unlocking—it had already been left open for him. Without any hesitation he pushed through and disappeared on his escape route.

Under the Kurobe Dam, Server Room

Jacqueline made her way back down the corridor to the server room where they had left Mark and the others. She headed in the direction of the stack where he had been working. "I spoke with Yuko. She and Eve have been called away to help Micha—" She rounded the corner and found Mark only semi-conscious, and an exposed cable a few feet away.

She ran to him. "What happened?" she shrieked, feeling her Were-self losing control in anger and panic. She touched him and got a spark, which quickly discharged into floor of the server room.

Mark looked like his head was swirling. "Riku. Took the data…"

Jacqueline spun, looking for the little maggot. "Where did he go?"

Mark tried to get up before surrendering to his injuries and slumping back to the floor. "He must have left," he said, wincing in pain. "I didn't see, though. I was unconscious."

Jacqueline hesitated a moment, not wanting to leave him.

"*Go!*" he told her, "I'm already starting to heal."

Jacqueline turned and ran out of the server room, taking a route behind the tiers of servers she had walked to the other side of. She saw Haruto lying ahead of her and ran to him. "Haruto!" she shouted. He didn't respond. As she got nearer, she saw a bullet hole in his forehead.

She felt her anger swell inside of her, but thought, *This isn't the place to turn Were*. She needed to keep her wits about her and not be blinded by rage. She breathed, recalling the training she had undergone with Michael. Restraint was necessary for the advantage, he had taught her, even though when she saw him wreak devastation it never really seemed to jive with his worldview.

She headed out of the room to see Akari and Ichika coming down the corridor.

"What is it?" Ichika asked.

"It's Riku," she blurted. "He took the data and killed Haruto. We've got to go after him!" She ran past them to retrace the route to the exit.

Akari shouted after her, "I wouldn't do that if I were you."

Jacqueline wheeled around, annoyed at the distraction, and saw the gun—the gun Akari was pointing at Ichika's head.

Jacqueline stopped, catching on to what was happening. "You?" she accused, confused by the turn of events.

Akari nodded. "I have a duty," she said simply.

Jacqueline scowled as she started pacing toward the two women. "A duty to whom? To what?" she demanded, her eyes flaring werewolf-yellow.

Akari reaffirmed her grip on the gun at Ichika's head. "To maintain the *vallitseva tila*. These relics don't belong with outsiders. They belong with us, the keepers. The protectors of the Sacred Clan."

Jacqueline shook her head. "And who exactly are the keepers?"

Akari looked like she was under pressure. "You don't need to know the details. You just need to know that this is bigger than you and your friends. We've been working far longer than you know about the existence of the relics, and we will prevail long after you're gone. This is what is written."

Jacqueline shook her head. "You've been brainwashed, girl."

Akari adjusted the position of the gun against Ichika's temple, and Jacqueline backed off a touch.

"Protectors!" Ichika scoffed. "You're not protecting anything if you're not in line with Kashikoi."

"You're wrong," Akari shouted back defensively.

"No, *you're* wrong," Ichika insisted, her courage growing despite the gun at her head. "Whatever these people have been telling you, they're not trying to protect the technology. They'll be trying to use it themselves. It has great commercial value. That is the cause you're helping."

Akari's grip on the gun tightened. "You don't know

anything!" she shouted, her agitation growing. "You're blinded by your allegiance to your grandfather and his mysterious teachings."

"No, I'm not," Ichika continued. "Tell me, what have they promised you?"

Akari stopped.

Ichika continued to push. "They've promised you something, haven't they?"

Akari's voice was at a normal level now. "That's none of your business. I'm serving the greater good," she declared angrily.

Ichika managed to wriggle away a little. "If that were true they wouldn't need to incentivize your alliance," Ichika reasoned, knowing she was on the right track with Akari.

Akari opened her mouth to protest and at that moment Ichika saw her opportunity to get free. She spun and grabbed the gun as Jacqueline advanced.

The girls scuffled.

The gun went off and everyone jumped.

Except Jacqueline, who was quite accustomed to gunfire by now.

Jacqueline looked to see who had the gun so she could grab it, and she noticed blood on her hand.

She backed away from the two girls to see Akari's horror as she was left holding up a slumped Ichika. She panicked, laying the girl down and hyperventilating.

A second later, gun still in hand, she was sprinting down the corridor.

Jacqueline watched her and then went to Ichika. "Hey! Hey..." she called, trying to get the girl to revive.

Ichika could barely keep her eyes open. "Tell grandpa I'm sorry..." she said before her eyes closed properly and she slipped away.

Jacqueline wasn't accepting it. "No! You're going to live. Get it together. Eyes open!"

Ichika obeyed, her eyes snapping open.

Jacqueline inspected her quickly. The blood was all coming from her thigh. "You've been shot, but you don't have to die. Mark can help. You just need to stay awake. I'll be right back, I promise. Can you do that for me? Just stay awake?"

Ichika nodded. "Yes," she responded with the quiet passion and determination Jacqueline knew she was capable of.

Jacqueline nodded, scrambling to her feet. "I'll be right back," she repeated before sprinting after Akari.

She charged back down the corridor to the waterlogged cavern where they had come in and saw Akari disappear underwater. Jacqueline dove in after her, her limbs powered by anger at the betrayal. She swam as hard as she could, trying to reach the traitor before she could escape into the lake.

Jacqueline felt her arms and lungs burning from the exertion and lack of oxygen, but she pushed harder and harder. Her eyes stung as she tried to see through the water; Akari had disappeared from her view.

She would not let her escape.

Not with the only lead they had on the ship pieces.

Then her eyes clapped onto Akari just ahead of her.

Akari raised her wrist and hit a button on a device. An

explosion blasted through the water like the gates of hell had been opened on top of her, and then all went black.

She didn't know how long she was out, but it couldn't have been for long because she came to choking for breath. She flailed her arms and felt the water. Opening her eyes, she saw rocks and concrete debris falling all around her. She got her bearings from the direction of the falling debris and pushed her way to the surface, breaking into the air and the aftermath of the explosion that had knocked her out.

She caught a glimpse of Akari's limp body twenty yards away, obviously caught by her own blast. The chamber had been breached, and water was pouring in, the levels rising.

She dove again. She had to make it back to Mark and the others to warn them.

Swimming as hard as she could, coughing up water and swallowing more as she tried to suck in air, she made her way to the steps and pulled herself out.

Once out of the water, she glanced back to see a slab of concrete fall from the collapsing chamber onto Akari's already limp body. She winced, scanning the water for it to resurface before coming to terms with the inevitable. She turned on her heel and scrambled back to Ichika.

"Hey!" she shouted. "How you doing?"

Ichika had dragged herself across the corridor and propped herself up, and was currently trying to stop the bleeding from her leg. She'd managed to remove her t-shirt and was tying it around her thigh as a tourniquet.

She looked up. "What did you do?"

Jacqueline shook her head, jogging toward her and

helping her tie the knot. "I didn't do anything. She blew the entrance so we couldn't get out. The water is pouring in."

Ichika's eyes were filled with fear. "We're all going to die then?"

Jacqueline was already on her feet and helped Ichika to hers. She slipped a little in the blood, putting her hand against the bunker's wall to catch herself, and heaved Ichika up. "Not if I've got anything to do with it. Mark can help you…stop the bleeding. Then we need to find another way out of here."

Ichika cried out in pain as she put weight on her leg.

Jacqueline started her moving down the corridor, holding her around the waist to help support her. "You can do this. We've got to move fast."

The two women hobbled back through the corridors to find Mark.

Saint-Genis-Pouilly, France

Yuko dropped out of their Pod the last twenty feet to the ground, shooting two soldiers in the back on her way down. She stood up and jogged to the building, following the bodies and smell of explosives.

Upon entering the building, she called, "Sabine? Akio? Michael?"

A weak voice replied, "Yuko?"

Moving quickly, Yuko made it to the destroyed furniture and kicked some aside. On the other side she found a bloody Sabine, her right hand gripping a pistol, her left arm useless, broken. Yuko's eyes flared red and she called over the radio, "Eve, bring an injection."

"Which one?"

"Whichever is the best we have," Yuko answered and reached down to lift Sabine's body up. She was whispering as her eyes closed.

"At least I saw the view. Please have that written on my tombstone, I took the time to watch the view…"

Yuko turned and headed back toward the entrance, hurrying to meet Eve as the little EI made her way into the building.

Moments later Eve continued farther into the building, dashing toward Akio down below.

It took her a couple minutes to race down the steps, following the building schematics she had in her memory. She accessed several shortcuts her smaller body could take.

When she met up with Akio, he pointed to the controls. "Stop this machine. Do not kill Michael."

She nodded her understanding. "Routing the communications from this place to my tablet."

She nodded again. "Done."

23

Japan, Below the Kurobe Dam

The two girls stumbled back into the server room. Ichika had left a trail of blood along the corridor and, now pale and fading, slumped in Jacqueline's arms.

"Mark!" she called desperately.

Mark appeared, bedraggled and the worse for wear but alive, albeit with an enormous hole in his forehead. "Yes, dear?"

Jacqueline was in no mood for humor. "She needs some of your blood."

Mark quickly forgot his own woes and hurried over, his eyes anxious at the sight of all the blood. "What happened?" he asked, biting his wrist.

"Akari happened," Jacqueline explained quickly as she laid Ichika down and then held her head up so Mark could feed her from his wrist.

Mark shoved the bloody mess to Ichika's lips and

pressed. "What d'you mean?" he asked, glancing up and then readjusting his position on the floor.

Jacqueline kept her eyes on Ichika to make sure she had started to suck. "She had a gun. Ichika got caught in the struggle. She also blew the entrance."

Mark's eyes filled with horror and his wrist moved, slipping away from Ichika's lips. He suddenly felt hands gripping his arm and looked down to see that Ichika had revived and clamped down on his arm to continue feeding.

Jacqueline pulled the girl's hands off. "Easy! Slow down. You don't want to turn all vampy."

Mark pulled his wrist away, watching Ichika.

Jacqueline looked at him. "I have some good news, and some very bad news."

Mark rubbed his head as he looked at her, his eyes clearly showing that the bullet was giving him a headache. "Tell me the good."

"That traitorous bitch is dead," she said simply.

Mark nodded. "And the bad?"

"The *very* bad," Jacqueline corrected. "The very bad news is she blew the chamber that was holding the water at bay. We can't get out that way because water is filling the entire bunker. We've got to get out of here. *Now*."

Ichika had opened her eyes and was struggling to sit up. Jacqueline and Mark helped her. "Steady, take a moment," Mark told her.

Jacqueline's eyes flashed. "Haven't you been listening? We haven't *got* a moment."

Mark nodded and scurried away. "We might have."

Jacqueline followed him around the mess of destroyed computers and shelving.

"Careful!" Mark warned. "There are some live power cables around there. Well, kinda. The circuit breakers turned off whatever power was running through them, but if there are in capacitors – they could still pack a bite."

Jacqueline trod carefully as she scrambled over to the terminal Mark was using. "What are you doing? Didn't you hear me?"

Mark pulled up another screen. "Well, I was thinking… If Riku was going to escape, he wasn't going to be able to use the Pods, remember. Not without alerting Eve, and Eve wouldn't let him get too far once she knew we weren't with him."

Jacqueline frowned. "So?"

"So," he continued, "I figure he must have found another way out."

Jacqueline was still frustrated, and now confused. "But where?"

Mark had pulled up the schematic Eve had given them earlier. "I'd love to play a game and get you to guess what's out of place, but since we don't have time I'll tell you. There is a door over there that isn't on this map."

He looked from the screen to Jacqueline, stumbling a little over the precarious position with the damage around him.

Jacqueline raised one eyebrow. "What are you thinking?"

Mark smiled despite his dire headache. "Would the Japanese, the most technologically astute people on the planet, really build an underwater bunker with only one way in and out?"

Jacqueline's face relaxed. "Good point!" she agreed. "And where is that schematic from?"

Mark grinned. "Eve pulled it off a government server."

Jacqueline smiled. "So those are the *official* schematics, then. My money's on that door leading us out."

Ichika interjected a comment into the conversation. "Or to something very, very secret!" she exclaimed dryly.

Jacqueline pursed her lips. "That's a good point," she conceded, "but we're running out of options. No way we can hold our breath long enough to get through all those corridors; they'll have filled with water by now. We can't get to the original chamber we came in through."

Jacqueline and Mark started back through the rubble toward Ichika. "Well, you two might be all right," Ichika observed, "but those of us who are human would struggle."

Jacqueline headed straight to her. "We're all getting out of here alive," she said firmly, bending down and placing her hand firmly on the girl's shoulder. "Are you ready to move yet?"

Ichika nodded. "Yeah. Let's do this," she said, putting her weight on her leg. She stumbled a little, her face creased in pain.

"Just one second," Mark told them and dove over the mess to the server he had resurrected.

Jacqueline scowled. "What are you doing now?" she asked in an almost scolding tone.

"Just grabbing the data we came for," he said, a hint of cockiness in his voice. His butt went up in the air as he bent over and retrieved what he'd been working on. Reappearing from behind the stack, he showed them the dongle he'd just pulled out and then placed it into his pocket.

"But…I thought Riku took it?" Jacqueline asked, bewildered.

Mark grinned at her. "And what kind of tech nerd would I be if I came down here with only one dongle that would fit this setup?"

Jacqueline stood and headed over to him. She grinned, pulling him close and giving him a quick but warm kiss on the lips.

Ichika was already making her way toward the door. Jacqueline grinned at Mark again, then quickly followed her. Mark caught up with them and, seeing that Ichika was struggling, put his arm around her waist to help her.

"I've got you," he told her. "And you can always have some more blood."

Ichika screwed up her face and shook her head, then quickly changed her expression. "Oh, I mean, I'm very grateful, but I don't—"

"Want to be like me?" Mark smiled.

Ichika looked sheepish, lowering her eyes and continuing to move toward the inconspicuous door. "I'd like to stay human if at all possible."

Mark squeezed her waist a little tighter for a moment. "It's totally cool. I get it," he told her. "Really," he added reassuringly.

Looking satisfied that she hadn't offended him, Ichika put all her effort into moving as fast as she could to keep pace with Jacqueline. The Were had already gone through the door and was jogging down the corridor with her flashlight jumping all over the place.

Japan, Below the Kurobe Dam

"Just through here," Jacqueline called back two corridors and a narrow passageway later. "Good thing the weasel went out this way before us," she remarked as she pushed open a final door to a tiny room with nothing more than a vertical ladder.

She shined her flashlight up, examining the ascent, and sniffed the air.

Fresh air, she thought. *We're there.*

Just then Mark and Ichika stumbled into the room. The young female warrior looked distraught. "Dead end?"

Jacqueline smiled, a hint of Mark's geeky cockiness rubbing off on her. "No, a climb to safety." She looked up and shined her flashlight upward again. Ichika followed her eyes.

Jacqueline shined the light on Ichika's leg. "How's that leg doing?" she asked seriously.

Ichika looked down. "Painful, but… How far do you think it is?"

Jacqueline shrugged. "Can't be that deep. I think we've been climbing on those last two corridors. That's dry land up there."

Ichika nodded.

Jacqueline pushed her forward to the ladder. "You first."

Ichika looked at her in horror. "But…I'll be the slowest."

"All the more reason," Mark chimed in, giving her another nudge toward the ladder. "No time for arguments. Got to get this done. The water isn't far behind us."

Ichika was in no state to argue. She placed her hands on the cold metal bars of the ladder and started climbing, trying not to telegraph her pain to the others.

Mark and Jacqueline watched like parents when a young child toddled precariously close to a fireplace. When she was a body-length above them, Jacqueline turned to Mark. "Why isn't she healed already?" she hissed urgently, her air of calm having evaporated.

Mark shrugged. "I dunno. I've never done this before, but if I had to guess, she probably needed a bit more blood."

Jacqueline glanced up again before looking back at Mark. "And you didn't think to give her some?"

Mark put a hand on the ladder and pulled Jacqueline toward him. "She didn't want to risk it."

Jacqueline nodded. "Silly girl," she said, still anxious and sensing the water coming through the tunnels.

Mark put Jacqueline's hand onto the ladder. "Up you go. This structure is likely to collapse before the water ever reaches us," he added, hearing the cracking of concrete several hundred meters away.

Jacqueline looked panicked. "You better be right behind me!"

Mark had a glimmer of humor in his eye. "Yes, ma'am. I'll be enjoying the view."

Jacqueline looked annoyed, and then the tension of the situation dispersed. She slapped him gently on his body and started climbing. Mark followed, careful not to catch up too quickly for fear of being kicked in the face with her feet as Jacqueline climbed.

They ascended for a while. Jacqueline slowed down when she caught up to Ichika. Eventually, they reached the surface and found that the grid that had covered over the hole had already been removed. Ichika emerged breathing hard, her face contorted in pain.

She rolled over on the slightly damp grass, catching her breath as Jacqueline and Mark scrambled out.

Jacqueline was on her feet first. "How are you doing?" she asked the little human.

Ichika opened her eyes and looked at Jacqueline's silhouette against the background light of the moon and the nearby town. "I'll live." She smiled weakly. "Thank you for saving me," she said, sitting up and looking in Mark's direction too. "Both of you."

Jacqueline waved her hand. "Don't mention it. We're not out of the woods yet, though. Lemme get in touch with Eve, and then we need to get your leg seen to."

Jacqueline walked away a few paces and retrieved the communicator from her suit.

Tokyo, Undisclosed Alley

There was a chill in the night air, one that Riku was unaccustomed to in this land. Of course, on his travels, he had experienced everything from Siberian winds to tropical climes.

But here in Japan? It seemed a little out of place.

If he didn't know any better he would have thought it was a foreboding that something was coming. Finally, he might fulfill his destiny and play his part in the protection of the Sacred Clan's relics.

He waited patiently in the alley for his master.

It wasn't long before he heard footsteps. He observed

from the shadows, just in case it was an unwitting passerby who had stumbled into the alley by accident.

The stranger moved toward the center of the alley with a confident stride and stepped into a sliver of light from the street. It was indeed Kuro's face.

Riku moved out from behind the big metal box and revealed himself.

Kuro remained motionless. "You have news?" he called in a low, controlled voice.

Riku moved closer. "Yes, sir. I have the data." He produced the dongle and handed it over.

Kuro looked almost impressed despite his attempts at maintaining a formal face. "Thank you. This was good work."

Riku bowed deeply, relieved to have satisfied his master. "The honor is mine, sir. May the *vallitseva tila* be upheld."

Kuro returned the bow, though not as deeply. "Indeed. To the *vallitseva tila!*" He paused, his face now accentuated by deep shadow. "Your funds will be deposited in the morning."

Kuro suddenly saw the whites of Riku's eyes in the half-light. "But sir," Riku protested, "I didn't do it for the money."

Kuro bowed his head briefly. "Yes, but you must understand that by taking the money we indemnify ourselves. You will be more careful about who you inform of our transaction."

Riku's eyes looked pained. "I would never betray you. We are fighting for the cause."

Kuro had slipped the drive into his pocket and now

studied the young ninja's face with compassion. "I believe that," he confirmed, "but still, we do business this way to ensure long-term loyalty."

Riku accepted the explanation, knowing that he had no choice in the matter. "I understand. Sir, there is one more thing," he added quickly.

"What is that?"

"It's Akari," Riku continued. He paused briefly, the words catching in his throat. "She didn't make it."

Kuro's facial expression shifted to surprise, followed by sorrow. Then it returned to his polite expressionless default. "I'm sorry to hear this. I know you and she shared a bond of purpose."

Riku nodded, his eyes glistening with a tear. "Would you…"

"Yes, I'll let him know," Kuro confirmed. "Once again, my sympathies."

Riku bowed deeply before taking his leave of his master. He knew the drill. He was to remain out of sight for several more minutes and then exit via a route other than the alley's entrance—he had a fire escape already picked out that would take him to the roof. He blended into the shadows and listened as his master's footsteps retraced their path out of the alley the same way he had just walked in.

Riku stood alone in the darkness next to the pungent odor of the dumpster he had concealed himself behind.

He allowed his tears to fall, finally permitting himself to mourn the loss of his friends.

24

Ōyama Hospital, Japan, Near Kurobe Dam

Mark and Jacqueline sat in the waiting room talking in whispers and feeling very out of place.

Jacqueline's tone was one he recognized from his sister—gossip. "From what Akari was saying, they were part of some kind of cult."

Mark's eyebrows sprang to the top of his head. "She called it a *cult*?" He was partly amused by the recounting but was careful not to let on. He didn't want to have to explain to Jacqueline how cute she could be when she was doing normal girl stuff like gossiping.

Jacqueline tilted her head to one side. "No," she conceded slowly, "but she sounded like she'd had her brain scrambled by someone. She was spouting all kinds of mumbo-jumbo."

"Hmm," Mark said, contemplatively stroking his chin with his finger. "So what does this mean?"

Jacqueline pursed her lips and settled back in the

waiting room chair. "It means that Akari and Riku weren't working alone. It also means that whoever these people are, they now have the locations."

Mark's eyes took on a distant look. "Yes, but so do we."

Jacqueline nudged his arm, pulling him back to the present moment. "What are you thinking?"

Mark leaned forward over his knees, resting his arms on his legs. "I'm thinking that as soon as Yuko and Eve get in touch we should head to China asap."

"Agreed," Jacqueline said, watching the flow of scrubs-clad medical people move in and out of the double doors at the end of the waiting room area. "And I think there is more we need to understand about this Sacred Clan and why the Chinese want to hold onto their ship pieces."

She paused. "I wonder if Michael will come…"

Mark looked at her, twisting awkwardly to see her face. "Why?" he asked, a little confused. "Wouldn't that be less physical diplomacy for us?"

"True," Jacqueline conceded. She quickly lowered her voice before continuing the conversation, remembering they were in a place of healing. "Not that we've been doing too much physical diplomacy since we've been here, all things being equal."

She watched another doctor deposit a chart at reception and then take off again. "I feel better when he is within striking distance. That way, when he goes and gets himself killed, I'll be close enough to kill him all over again."

Jacqueline's tone was playful on the face of it, but Mark could see that her emotions ran deep. He didn't have any words for her, at least not words that would help the situation. He sat up and slung his arm around her as they waited in the very quiet room.

Eventually, the doctor who had admitted Ichika came back and the pair sprang to their feet. Having changed out of the wetsuits into the overalls they had packed in the Pod's storage compartment, they were looking semi-presentable, if a little out of context.

"How is she?" Jacqueline blurted as he approached them.

Dr. Goto bowed to them briefly before delivering his diagnosis. "She'll be fine. She lost a lot of blood, and we have her on a transfusion. We'll need to keep her on fluids for a little while too. The leg is already partially healed," he added, his eyes narrowing suspiciously. "I suspect this is because one of you lent her some non-conventional assistance?" He gave them a knowing look.

Mark looked sheepish. Jacqueline looked concerned. "You mean…you know?"

Dr. Goto smiled and nodded. "Diplomat Yuko sends you to *my* hospital and tells you to ask for *me* personally. One can only suspect."

Jacqueline caught a little glimmer in his eye. "You're not…"

Dr. Goto chuckled. "Oh goodness, no, although if *I* had been through what your friend had been through, I would be very grateful to have friends like you to heal my injuries."

Mark sighed and scratched the back of his head. "I'm afraid we were too concerned about overdoing it and, you know—transforming her. We maybe didn't give her enough."

The doctor nodded, his face a little more serious. "I think she is glad to be alive, although they have very strict rules in her discipline. She will be able to return to her family with her secret intact. No one will suspect that she was ever healed. The bullet wound will leave a scar and a limp."

Jacqueline frowned. "What do you mean, 'strict rules?'"

Dr. Goto moved them away from the reception desk and prying ears. "Yes. They're not to use substances like vampire blood or artificial healing agents," he explained. "Anyone found to have used them normally ends up being exiled. And as you know, these disciplines are like family." He shook his head. "Terrible business really," he confessed, sadness tainting his eyes.

Jacqueline's eyes flared yellow. "You mean she might be exiled if anyone finds out we healed her?"

Dr. Goto nodded.

Jacqueline stepped back and looked around, frustrated, before snapping her attention back to Mark. "Should have gone the whole way and transformed her!"

Mark lowered his eyes.

Dr. Goto put his hands out, palms flat, trying to contain the situation. "No, no—you don't understand. That would be like death to them. They have very strict beliefs. Ichika herself would likely not want to live like that," he explained, his voice a little agitated, willing Jacqueline to comprehend.

Jacqueline calmed a little. "Really?"

The doctor nodded again.

Jacqueline sighed, still unsatisfied. "Well, I guess there's nothing we can do then."

"May we see her?" Mark asked calmly, trying to smooth things over.

Dr. Goto nodded. "Of course. We'll need her to stay overnight, but by tomorrow afternoon she'll be ready to leave." He motioned in the direction of the corridor. "Room 211."

Jacqueline and Mark thanked the doctor and headed toward Ichika's room, their outside boots squeaking conspicuously and drawing curious looks from the dainty, polite nurses and medical personnel walking around in their covered slippers.

Mark tapped on the door and then pushed it open to reveal a tiny-looking Ichika, who was dwarfed by the hospital bed she was ensconced in.

Jacqueline followed him into the room, her eyes conveying sympathy.

Ichika smiled weakly as they stepped inside and closed the door behind them. "Don't look at me like that," she said to Jacqueline, still smiling.

Jacqueline looked taken aback. "Like what?"

Ichika grinned. "Like I'm some delicate little thing who needs taking care of. I'm a warrior! I knew what I was getting into."

Jacqueline couldn't help but smile at her spirit. She adjusted her attitude to match as she approached the girl's bedside and perched on the bed next to her. She held her hand. "I know that, but I'm still sorry this happened to you." She paused, lowering her eyes to their hands. "If there was anything I could have done—"

Ichika clamped her other hand on top of the hands that held each other. "You did the right thing. I couldn't have asked for a more dedicated and brave team on that mission."

She smiled at Mark, who had perched on the other side of her bed, pulling the blanket a little.

"Both of you," she added sincerely. "Truly. I'm so grateful for what you did to keep me alive and get me out of there. You risked your own lives."

Mark nodded at her leg. "So you're all healed up?"

Ichika tilted her head from side to side. "The doctor said I will recover a little more with time, but there will need to be lots of rehabilitation and it will never be as strong as my other leg." She lowered her eyes, her voice softer now. "Sucks for martial arts and future adventures."

Jacqueline had already started tearing up. "I know. It sounds like it wasn't enough—"

"Shhh…" Ichika told her sternly. "This has worked out well. This way I get to return to my grandfather and my training, *and* I get to live. If I had gone back changed…"

Jacqueline nodded, thinking of how unfair people's prejudices made everything. A tear escaped from her eye. "I know. The doctor explained to us."

"Yes," Ichika continued, her eyes looking brighter now, "but did he explain to you about the power of the mind?"

Jacqueline looked at her, sadness giving way to curiosity. "How do you mean?" she asked, glancing at Mark to see if he understood.

Mark frowned. "You're going to *think* your way healthy?"

Ichika was wearing a fully confident smile now. "Yes. With Grandfather's help, I know I can."

They talked a little more before Jacqueline moved the conversation to tomorrow's itinerary. "Right, so we'll be taking you back to your grandfather then?"

"Yes," Ichika confirmed. "As much as I'd love to continue this journey with you, I think in my current state I'd be more of a hindrance than a help."

Mark pulled out his wrist again. "Well, unless you just want to bite the bullet, so to speak, and join us permanently." His voice was teasing, but for a moment Jacqueline could have sworn she saw Ichika thinking about it.

A split second later Ichika laughed and slapped Mark's exposed wrist playfully. "Thanks," she said, "but my place is with my grandfather. And *our* mission."

The three shared a few more laughs before the nurse came in to usher Jacqueline and Mark out of the room. They made their farewells and returned to the guest house that Eve had booked them into, promising to return for Ichika tomorrow to take her home.

And help her break the news of the recent events to her grandfather and *sensei*.

Kuro's Loft, Somewhere in Tokyo

Raiden jumped to his feet as soon as he heard the footsteps outside the door. "He's back," he announced to an almost disinterested Orochi.

Orochi muttered something inaudible, his eyes never leaving his papers.

Kuro entered the room, quietly closing the door behind him and securing the two locks. He turned to Raiden, his face unreadable.

"Well?" Raiden prompted.

Kuro's face broke into a smile. "I've got it!"

Orochi jumped to his feet and made his way across the large open-plan apartment they used as a lair. Raiden, bursting with excitement, couldn't resist throwing his arms around Kuro. Kuro stiffened and stepped back after a moment, shrugging Raiden off.

Raiden looked embarrassed. "I just... It's just so exciting."

Kuro raised one eyebrow at him. "Yes. I see that your time with the younger generation has made you... *modern*...in your reactions."

Raiden felt sure the use of the word "modern" was an insult. He immediately calmed himself and moved over to his computer terminal.

Kuro shoved his hand into his pocket and held up the dongle for the two men to behold.

Orochi displayed a rare expression that resembled victory. "This is excellent indeed!"

Kuro smiled and looked at his old adversary and new ally. "Twenty years," he said softly.

Orochi nodded. "Twenty years trying to find someone who could retrieve that data, and finally we have it!"

The two men shared a moment of silence and appreciation as Raiden unceremoniously swooped in and took possession of the antiquated storage device. He carried it over to the old computer they had been working on for the last several months and got straight to work.

"Now that we have the map," he muttered partly to himself, "we have a way forward."

Orochi was the first to break the moment of celebration. "Well, if your goons hadn't been so boneheaded about wanting that data destroyed in the first place, we could have had this long ago."

Raiden shook his head. "Look, it was a different time. We can't keep reliving the past. The government had it coming."

Orochi started to say something about never getting into business with a former hacker or anarchist, but Kuro hushed him and pulled him over to the sofa on the other side of the room.

"Orochi," he said solemnly, "there is something you need to know."

Orochi looked up at Kuro, trying to understand the sudden change in mood at a time of such a breakthrough.

"It's Akari," he explained. "She didn't make it."

Orochi's brow creased and lifted in an extreme expression of sorrow. Kuro saw Orochi's body visibly crumple under the news. He helped the middle-aged man to sit.

Orochi recovered his facial expression rapidly, returning a blank polite look now. Kuro could sense the sadness in his colleague's chest, though. "I'm so sorry," he continued. "I just learned from her colleague, who delivered this to us."

He paused. The yellow from the artificial lights made it impossible to see into the blackness beyond the windows, but Orochi's glance was drawn there as if hoping for her to appear.

"She lived and died for something she believed in," Kuro added softly. "She died a good death."

Orochi nodded. "A good death is all we can hope for," he agreed in the tone of one wise to the doom of all life.

The two men sat there for several minutes sharing the silence, but then Orochi got up without another word, bowed absently to his business associate, and picked up the coat he had dropped on the arm of the sofa.

He crossed the floor of the room and left via the front door.

Raiden was surprised to see him leaving when they were on the brink of a revelation. He turned to his screen and continued to fiddle with the setup. Kuro crossed the big open room to join him, looking over his shoulder.

Raiden's thoughts were still on the project. "You know, looking at this, we couldn't have extracted this data without that AI's capabilities. It would have taken a dozen of me several decades to come even close with those servers," he explained, impressed by what he saw on the screen already.

Kuro didn't respond.

Raiden paused. "Where did Orochi go?"

Kuro sighed. "The bar downstairs, I suspect," he told the former government whiz kid-turned-anarchist.

Raiden frowned, not taking his eyes from the code that flickered across his antique screen. "Why?"

Kuro's voice was quiet when he answered. "I just had to tell him his girlfriend was killed acquiring this data for us."

There was a pause between the two men.

Finally, Raiden responded as empathetically as he could. "That bites."

Kuro agreed, placing his hand gently on the back of Raiden's wooden chair. "It does. How long until we have the map?"

Raiden shrugged. "Not long. We should also keep tabs on which site they hit first."

"Ok," agreed Kuro. "Keep me posted." Still wearing his coat, he headed over to the door and opened it.

Raiden's eyes finally left his screen. "Where are *you* going?" he asked, surprised.

"To console an old friend," Kuro responded, stepping out the door and closing it gently behind him.

Saint-Genis-Pouilly, France

"You are going to fail, William," A new voice interrupted William's thoughts. "The ArchAngel is not going to die in this trap."

"Ahhh, is this Akio?" William said to the speaker. "Even if he isn't dead, I don't think even the vaunted Michael is going to be the same man as the one who had the energies of the universe trying to rip him apart. I will be surprised if he can still tie his shoes."

"You might be surprised by just how much pain the Dark Messiah has been through," Akio replied. "Even a nuclear bomb was insufficient to kill him."

"Bah!" William snorted. "I'm sure it wasn't a real bomb, or even he would not be here." William looked at the pipes. "Well, not exactly here, more like there, there, and over there. Hopefully soon, I'll have him spread apart around a…"

The lights flickered and died. William's eyes glowed in the darkness when the temporary lights came on. His voice was calm, deadly. "You despicable dilettantes!" He gave another scream and looked down at his tablet, but it still didn't show him the flag that would confirm he had killed Michael.

He flung the tablet across the room. "I will not forget, nor will I forgive you, Akio." William walked over to where he had draped his jacket. He picked it up and slid his arm into the right sleeve. "I have a long memory, and I will be certain to take care of you." He slid his other into the left sleeve and shot his cuffs.

"You will have to do it without your teams. It seems they met with a deadly case of sword infection."

William sniffed in annoyance. "I will find more. Mercs are a dime a dozen." He walked to his escape door and put a hand on it, then turned toward the speaker. "Look for me, Akio. When you least expect me, I'll be there."

William yanked on the door, and his eyes opened in shock and pain when both his kneecaps were blown off. His body collapsed to the floor, his mind screaming as he dragged himself back from the opening.

Akio walked in, his face impassive. He waved a tablet in William's direction before placing it on a shelf. Akio smiled. "When you least expect me, William, I'll be there."

Akio pulled the trigger twice more, taking William's hands off at the wrists.

"You dare to hurt me," William spit the blood out of his mouth. "I was centuries old before you were even born."

"And I," another voice was heard in the room, William turned to see a man in a long coat and black leather cowboy hat, "deem you but a sniveling child I failed to punish correctly the first time."

"ArchAngel." Akio bowed.

"Dear friend." Michael bowed slightly lower than Akio. "I owe all of you my life." Michael walked over to William. His stumps had stopped bleeding. Michael took off his hat and reached down to run a finger through some of the blood on the floor. "I made a promise, William," Michael said conversationally. "That I would baptize this hat in your blood to commemorate your death. It honors a father, and the mother and daughter whose lives you destroyed."

"Who?" William spat. "Some cattle? Some plebeian humans who aren't—" William stopped talking when Michael put up his hand. A solid ball of white energy had started to form in it. William brought his handless arm up to block the light from blinding him.

"The problem with using the power of the cosmos, William," Michael looked down at him, "is that the cosmos can teach new tricks."

William screamed when Michael dropped the ball of energy on his chest. It started melting his body, consuming it and causing it to disappear as the energy globe shrunk.

Michael stood, and the two of them watched. The body stopped disappearing when the only things left were his legs from the knees down.

Michael looked at Akio. "I owe you all an apology." He put up a hand to forestall anything Akio might say. "I am arrogant, I know that. However, in my arrogance, I figured I was more than enough for one such as William. I was wrong, and without your support and the others', I would have failed in my task of honor to return to Bethany Anne."

Akio nodded his understanding.

The two of them walked toward the door that led to the surface. Michael turned and opened his palm, a red ball of energy shot out, consuming the remains of the legs in the fiery explosion.

Not that Michael or Akio knew that though, as they had closed the door quickly to protect from themselves any backsplash.

25

Sabine's eyes opened, and she looked up into a face she recognized. "Yuko?"

"Yes, little one."

"I'm not dead?" she asked and looked around.

"No, unless I'm dead with you, and I do not think that I am."

"But," Sabine stopped and lifted her left arm. "Now, I know this was broken."

"Yes, it was." Yuko agreed.

Sabine's eyes narrowed and she looked back up at Yuko, who was making sure Sabine's head was comfortable. "Am I a Vampire?"

Yuko started laughing and shook her head. "No!"

"Then how?" Sabine asked.

"Consider it a gift from us, to you." Yuko pursed her lips. "You have had a special dose of Bethany Anne's nanocytes."

"Michael's Bethany Anne?" Yuko nodded. "Does that mean I can fly?"

"No," Yuko told her. "It just means you will be more than you were, before." She put a hand on Sabine's head, "Now sleep, the nanocytes aren't done helping you, yet."

"But I'm not," Sabine started, but never finished her comment.

Five minutes later, Eve joined her. Yuko had heard the android's footsteps walking through the broken glass, then across the street and into the park area where Yuko and Sabine were.

"It's an amazing amount of technology," Eve commented. "Michael's own energy was fueling it. Which is why the scientists couldn't make it stop, even with Akio threatening to run them through with a sword."

Yuko shook her head. "I don't believe scientists think best with the end of a sword pointed at them."

"Well, to his credit, I understand he wasn't using it to point at them, and it was sheathed. But since he was bloody..." Eve let her sentence die off and changed the subject. "Mark and Jacqueline are at the hospital. Dr. Goto checked in their patient."

"He is a good man," Yuko looked to her left. Eve followed her glance and saw Michael and Akio coming down the street, about a half mile away. Yuko adjusted Sabine's head. "Speaking of men."

"Not good men?" Eve asked.

Yuko snorted, "Jacqueline was ready to come all the way here and kick Michael's ass, or at least try she was so mad at how close he came to dying."

"Yet, she fails to see the truth of how close she and Mark came." Eve pointed out.

"The young do not care to have the hypocrisy of their actions pointed out to them." She nodded down the street, "Or the prideful."

"You would think he would learn."

"Or the stubborn."

"How stubborn can a human be?"

"Let's just leave it at men." Yuko finished. "Their heads are as hard as granite, and yet just as brittle as sandstone. Should you give them their vaulted logic, their world view can explode."

"You act as if females are any different, except insert emotions instead of logic."

"Eve," Yuko turned back to look at her friend. "I love you, but you can be such a logical *bitch* sometimes."

Eve chuckled, "Just pointing out the hypocrisy of the old and aged."

Yuko sighed. "Let me change that to logical bitch *frequently*."

The two friends stayed in a peaceable quiet while the two men walked down the street. Yuko enjoyed the look of one, a man from the East, his clothes those of her country, his sheathed sword the physical manifestation of an exclamation point for anything he said.

The other a man from the West, his coat one of the most technically advanced clothes on this world, his hat the product of human hands, yet the manufacturing techniques from centuries before the World's Worst Day Ever.

East and West, calm and fiery. Yet, she admitted, both a bit arrogant in the belief of their abilities.

Eve spoke first as they walked under the tree, Michael checking out Sabine. "The scientists are still below, but they cannot start up the LHC anymore."

"Why is that?" Michael asked, half of his attention on Sabine.

"I shut down their systems, and put a crypto-lock they have to bypass to get it up and running again."

Michael stood up, "Thank you." He spoke a bit louder as he looked from person to person, "I need to thank you all. Without you, I would not be standing here and William would have accomplished tearing me apart." He smiled, "Normally, my stubbornness, nurtured in the millennia plus I've been alive, has been enough in these trials. This time, it was enough that I trusted you four to get me out, I just had to stay together and wait."

"Didn't it hurt?" Eve asked.

Michael turned to the short android, "It hurt like a Gott Verdammt sonofabitch."

Akio spoke up, "William believed you would come out of the effort mentally unhinged."

"I never know why people presume I'm hinged in the first place," Michael admitted. "I'm so damned old all of my give up, got up and left my body already. I move forward because of honor, of love," he smirked when Yuko grinned like a young school girl, "and the knowledge that I had the best people working to get me out of the cocked-up place I got myself in. Whatever the pain I was feeling," Michael grunted, "and it was a lot." He looked over to Akio, "Didn't hold a candle to being ripped apart and burned in a nuclear explosion where you slowly mend for a hundred and fifty years."

He exhaled heavily, "So," he reached up with his right hand and pulled off his hat, pulling it down to hold it with both hands as he stood there. "I am promising to do my best to let my team in on my plans. To let each of you shoulder the responsibilities and to perhaps learn how to effectively lead, not just tell you what I expect, but rather to seek your advice in the process." He looked to Yuko, "Not that I expect to always do what you logically suggest, but that I'll consider it and reflect rather than dismiss it out of hand."

He ignored her blush as she realized he had heard her and Eve talking earlier.

Michael held his hat in his left hand, reaching out with his right to Akio, "Thank you Akio, I'm proud to call you my friend."

Michael watched as Akio fought to bow in service and smiled when he held out his hand, and the two men shook. "Forever will you be my brother."

"Hai, mine as well, Michael."

Michael released his handshake with Akio and turned to Eve and stepped forward, then he took a knee, his head and hers almost equal height. "Eve, without you I would not be here. Your intelligence and abilities are beyond mine in ways I cannot fathom. You are my daughter, for whom I will give up my life to protect."

Eve's face dropped, her body losing emotions for a minute. Michael turned to Yuko, "What's happening?"

Yuko reached up and wiped a tear, "You have overwhelmed her ability to comprehend this reality. She will be back."

Michael turned back, waiting for Yuko's pronouncement to come true. After about two minutes of silence, Eve came back around. The little human body stepped forward and reached around Michael's neck to hug him. The little head turned and set its ear against his chest. "Father."

Michael reached around and hugged the little android back. "You may call me Michael, or Father. Whatever works best for you." Eve nodded her understanding and stepped back.

Michael stood up and walked over to Yuko, turning around and sitting next to her and Sabine. "Yuko, I personally owe you for all of your service. For protecting and saving Sabine. I cannot possibly repay you, but I would offer you whatever I can. You have but to ask."

Yuko stared at Michael, wondering what she might ask of this man. "Michael, since I was drafted by ADAM almost two centuries ago, I've never had an Uncle."

Michael chuckled, reached around and grabbed Yuko around her shoulders and pulled her in close. "I'd be honored to call you my family, Yuko. Just know that it comes with a negative or two."

Her voice was muffled as she spoke into his coat, "Like what?"

"Like I'll be checking out your boyfriends, to make sure they are worthy of you."

Akio, Eve and Michael chuckled as she swore into his chest. She reached up and wiped her eyes and they all heard a muffled, "I accept." from her.

"And Sabine?" Eve asked.

All eyes turned to the young woman sleeping on Yuko's lap.

"She will see the stars; her name will be spread to galaxies in stories for generations to come."

"I heard that," Sabine said, sleepily.

"On my honor," Michael told her and put his hand on her head. "We will get up there one day."

"Just not today," Sabine told him. "Goodnight."

"Goodnight little one," Michael told her. He reached up and started to wipe his head off to put his hat back on, then stopped.

His mouth was open, his face in shock.

"What is it?" Akio asked, concerned.

Michael looked up to Akio, his voice incredulous…

"I feel hair!" he told him, rubbing his hand all over his head.

The scream could be heard for hundreds of yards in all directions.

"I FEEL HAIR!" The voice reverberated through the buildings in the night.

EPILOGUE

Nagoya, Japan, Hirano Residence

"Dear Diary,

I am writing this down in case I should ever forget. And by "forget" I mean not in the memories fading because they were unimportant or without significance, but in case they are ever taken from me the way they were from my father and his father before him.

This weekend the one they call the Diplomat showed up on my doorstep. And though I refer to her as the Diplomat, I have come to know her as a person. Her name is Yuko. It seems that my feelings for her weren't unrequited or unwarranted. Alas, I fear her world and her mission has ripped her from me for good.

It all started on Saturday morning when there was a ring at the door. I hadn't seen her since my last entry when I helped her out at the docks..."

Hirano continued writing far into the night, hoping

that if he kept expressing his feelings, they would neither die in his chest nor consume him with longing.

When he was finally done, he glanced out his apartment window into the night sky where he had only hours before seen Yuko's Pod disappear to her next destination.

He closed the large leather-bound diary and carried it over to the living room carpet. Pulling the rug up, he exposed the floor safe. He placed the diary into the safe, locking it again and quickly replacing the rug. He rearranged the coffee table and then sat for a moment staring at the spot where the diary rested.

FINIS

AUTHOR NOTES - MICHAEL ANDERLE

I know that Ell Leigh Clarke's Author Notes are next, so I don't want to steal any of her thunder...

But I will, anyway.

Just not yet.

Before I do that, I'd like to say 'thank you!' to Ellie for picking up the Yuko / Eve / Jacqueline / Mark side of this story. I will admit that I've been fighting burn-out pretty bad. Ellie offered to help one time and I had pushed her back because…

IT WAS MICHAEL!

He was one of my first characters, and I wasn't comfortable letting go (empty nest syndrome…kinda?) until after I wrote another two more Bethany Anne books. When it was time to come back to Michael, I was up against a wall pushing on the business and it was very tough to get up and get myself in front of the computer to write.

I decided to reach back out and ask her if the offer to help collaborate on the book was still open.

A bit of a background

When Ellie decided to write, she had two books under her belt that were unpublished. She started reading The Kurtherian Gambit (no, she isn't finished with the series regardless whether she owns a Kindle, or not.) We had many, many story discussions for her series (The Ascension Myth - TAM) and then wrote and gave me her book.

Ummmm.... I gently pushed it back, with comments.

She re-wrote her first book...and gave it back.

With much (read MUCH) trepidation, I had to push it back to her again. Wondering (worrying) that I would really hurt her professional feelings having her change stuff...again. This was an 80,000 word book, so it wasn't *pleasant*.

<<Ellie edit. 85, 000! >>

She did it *and* she was easy to work with even though I was thinking she must HATE me by this time.

Now, I had previous experience working with her on something when the feedback wasn't 'YEAH!' and I'm comfortable that if I had to push her back on her parts of this story, we could work through it. We started working on the beats for the story, and recognized that the way for us to collaborate would be to split the story into two groups.

I would take the Michael and Akio story (remember,

my baby so to speak) and Ellie took Jacqueline and Mark (she will tell you 'less killy-killy.') We worked out the time lines and what was going on (the beats.)

Then, we started.

I had a couple of thousand words early, and she had nothing. Then, a few days later I finally came back and did a few thousand as well. A few days after that, I put a bunch of hours together and hit about 15k. Ellie tells me (she doesn't remember, I don't think) that she was at like, 16 k. Later, she realizes she was actually thousands of words short of what she remembered.

So, I was WAAAY ahead.

Now, she did ask about plot beats, but I seem to remember that she was working on things and finally, we needed to meet because she was finished with her stuff, and I was 'finally' holding her back.

<< Ellie Edit: You're kidding me! I was just working on the next Molly book! >>

We spoke the next day.

During this time, she was having some CRAP experiences and pain with dentists. So, she wasn't behind me due to me crushing it, but rather out of it due to painkillers and stuff.

<< Ellie edit: soooo not true! >>

Eventually, I hit words complete, and so does Ellie one day later. I had already sent my work to Stephen Russel for editing, and I now had Ellie's work to go through. I went through it, and the next day or so, I worked to move the two sets of stories together in a timeline (according to the beats) and delivered it all to Stephen, Steve and Lynne.

They then worked it with the wonderful JIT team to fix the broken stuff.

(Like, "Reputation" not "Rep"!)

<< Ellie edit: was that me? That wrote rep? Was it in dialogue? Coz if it was dialogue, you know I have a rule with my editors that it should stay... in NON-Michael books at least! >>

FUN STUFF - IT'S ABOUT A CAT

In the TAM series, there are always stories. Usually, stories about how Ellie and I have argued over something.

I'm here to share a cat story (and being *right*...but, you know... that's not the important part.)

<< Ellie edit: Pha! That's the ONLY important part to MA!! >>

Ellie shares a few weeks ago she is going to Austin (she lives in California.) So I ask her why and she explains she is going to housesit for a friend.).

Sounds ok. Austin is a great place, she can have fun if she cares to get out.

Then, she mentions the horror part of the horror story.

Her friend has CATS.

I tell her immediately that she is going to travel 1,500 miles to become a slave.

She laughs it off.

A couple of more times, I mention it and by the third time, she is rolling her eyes (since she doesn't believe me.) Then, last Wednesday she flies from California to Austin.

Thursday morning at some unGODly time, I get a Slack message that says:

"4am ellie feels a weight on her leg. She wakes up. It's a kittie.

Kittie demands to be pet. Ellie pets kittie. Kittie wanders off.

4.20 am. Ellie still awake. Gets up. Makes tea. Kittie nowhere to be seen.

It has begun."

HAHAHAHAHAHAHA....

(Here's the culprit according to the pic she slacked me...)

Yes, I was right.

(Cue cat lover responses – please go to https://www.facebook.com/ellleighclarke/ and type away!)

Thank you ALL for reading these Kurtherian Stories. We are coming to the end of the journey for The Kurtherian Gambit (we have 3 books to go) and Michael (we have 1 book to go.)

For those waiting patiently, they meet in book 04 and book 21 … Which I will probably / possibly release on the same day.

February 14th seems appropriate.

<< Ellie edit: because that's the day before my birthday?

Or because it's a romantic time for Michael and Bethany Anne to reunite? >>

What do you think?
It's just FOUR MORE BOOKS to write in time.

Ad Aeternitatem,
Michael

(No, I'm not thinking about the challenge Emily Beresford has expressed about being all caught up with the Bethany Anne books for Audible by the time I finish book 21…
Not at all.)

Ad Aeternitatem,
Michael Anderle

AUTHOR NOTES - ELL LEIGH CLARK

MA, Michael and Trust

As you may have figured by now, it wasn't a typo on the cover. MA and I actually wrote this episode of Michael together.

The reason that this came about was probably around Molly Book 3 when MA made a few unrelated comments during one of our conversations.

comment 1: "I like your writing. It's probably the most like mine out of anything I've read." Or words to that effect.

comment 2: "I'm so behind on my writing. I wish there was a way to catch up."

Meanwhile I was writing something like 2000 words per hour.

MA comment 3: "*bitch!*"... or words to that effect.

So of course the natural thought that came to mind was: "Hey, why don't I write with you on the Michael series."

MA liked the idea of not having to write as many words. But then hated the idea of someone else writing his characters.

And I could understand that.

So I dropped it. And wrote a bunch more Molly.

Then about two months later MA brings up this idea about writing Michael together again. One thing led to another and we agreed to do it. The result is what you hold in your hand.

Writing with MA has been super fun. I've been a total pain in the arse asking him if I can do xyz, and would Eve be able to eat (the answer was no!), but all in all I think we got there pretty efficiently - although I have very little to do in the editing process, so for all I know it was a total bitch for MA!

But what I'm really trying to get to is to say Thank You Michael. Thank you for trusting me with your series, and for giving me the honor of being the only collaborator to have my name UNDER yours!

I hope this was as fun for you as it was for me.

(Aside from the fact you only had half the number of words to write, I mean.)

MA and competition

At the risk of being repeato girl (for those who have been following The Ascension Myth Author Notes) MA has a **thing** about competition.

While most people can see it as a potentially fatal flaw, he sees it only as a driving force. Something to thrive on.

Little did I realize how he was banking on this to motivate him to get through the word count on the rest of this series. I thought this was just going to be a fun story to tell. Together.

Na ah.

This was a trap, to give him a "sparring buddy" to push him to get ahead on the word count!

And when he feels like he is winning... wow, he goes for it.

After our second story meeting we had enough pinned down to start writing scenes. So off we went. By the next time we spoke I had about 15k words down, and he had... well, a lot less.

Then it got to the point where I had done everything I could do until we made some big story decisions. I heard nothing from him for DAYS. (Well we talked about other things, but when it came to the Michael books, he hadn't "got into it" yet.)

Eventually, (probably about a week and half later) he's announcing he's about 10k from finishing!

WTF?

And what about our story line?

So eventually he got around to reading what I'd written and some time after that (when he had 2k left to write) he got around to talking to me about the next beats to tie all the threads together.

It quickly became apparent that when he was ahead in terms of word count, he liked being out ahead. Even if it meant I was going to hold up the editing process by needing another week to catch up. Sigh.

Now I'm sure he'll feed y'all the same story he was feeding me at the time. "I've been on calls. I've been traveling. I was going to read it last night but we've had releases that needed to go out..."

Don't get me wrong. He does a *fuck tonne* of stuff in each day. But I see now this collab thing was (probably) a (smart) psychological hack to spur him through the writing process.

So there we go. MA and competition.

MA and man-bashing.

The morning I was (finally) due to finish writing, MA called me. He wanted to tell me about a scene he'd just written. (This is one of the *most* fun things about having a writing partner!)

So he read it out to me. It was the scene where Yuko was talking about how the young don't like the hypocrisy of their actions being pointed out to them. Which quickly turned into a man-bashing statement:

"The young do not care to have the hypocrisy of their actions pointed out to them." She nodded down the street, "Or the prideful."
"You would think he would learn."
"Or the stubborn."
"How stubborn can a human be?"
"Let's just leave it at men." Yuko finished. "Their heads are as hard as granite, and yet just as brittle as sandstone. Should you give them their vaulted logic, their world view can explode."

<MICHAEL EDIT - ELLIE IS LAUGHING HER ASS OFF AT THIS POINT.>

Ellie: Dude, you don't half give guys a hard time.

MA: yeah well, they're an easy target.

Ellie: still.

MA: hang on, let me finish this reading this to you.

MA kept reading.

Yuko: "You act as if females are any different, except insert emotions instead of logic."

<MICHAEL EDIT: Ellie is NOT as happy at this point.>

Ellie: ah. So you balance it out!

MA: you have to. Else the guys give you a hard time.

Ellie: but you have a **whole paragraph** on the failings of 'men' and one line on women. That's hardly fair.

MA: (shrugs awkwardly)

Ellie's conclusion: MA has waaay too much genuine respect for women to really give us too much shit.

Despite our failings. #Awww... :)

Ellie and Editing

Ok, so I realise that a lot of these notes focus on the Ellie:MA banter. But since Steve started taking over the publishing process, he's been sharing his humor with us. (See Author Notes for The Ascension Myth Book 7, which resulted in him being nicknamed George Clooney.)

Now, Steve has always handled the JIT team and process. And Ellie is not keen on the editing process. When she was brought on board by MA a serious conversation was had about her not having to faff with stuff, like edits and rewrites. (Unless it really needed it from a quality control perspective.)

So over the months we've put in place various processes which have meant that Steve and his team of badass JITers and editors handle *all* of it - except where it's a story consideration. In which case it get's bounced back to the author in a quick slack message.

It's become a highly honed, polished process to minimize frustration and drama. (For Ellie, at least!) <MICHAEL EDIT – You will realize in time that minimizing frustration is ALL about Ellie.>

So imagine my surprise when for *this* book Steve writes me:

steve: Oh, by the way, Michael said I should work directly with you for any changes to the new Michael book.

Ellie: *(in her head: Hang on, did I read that right? He's got to be kidding me. No way is that happenin-)*

<STEVE EDIT - One of the things you learn in dealing with Ellie is that you can say the most outrageous things and she will, at least briefly, believe you. Hey - you take your fun while you can when dealing with *eccentric* authors.>

steve: HAHAHAHA
[3:57]
JK
ellleighclarke [3:58 PM]
lmfao -- you had me!!!!
[3:58]
you *totally* had me then
steve [3:58 PM]
I should have let it hang a little longer :)
LOL

ellleighclarke [3:58 PM]
yeah, given me time to REALLY freak out'
[3:59]
you have an evil streak Mr. Clooney
steve [3:59 PM]
It's what keeps me sane ...

MA and Magic

I have a pet theory.

One that when I talk about it MA takes on that super-skeptical look. It's like the opposite look to when I'm explaining something logical or sciency to him.

Here's the theory: that magic happens when we work on stuff together.

Historically MA has just put most of this down to my being a genius. Or an AI. But that leaves no room for magic. And heck this existence would suck if there was no magic. I don't know how Muggles can stand the boredom quite honestly.

So anyway - there we were on one of our calls, chin wagging about something or other, and MA mentions that he's been having trouble with the fb banner. It wouldn't let him update it. We talked through some reasons why it might be the case, but it turned out that three different people on three different machines had tried to update it.

Ellie: try it now.

MA: No. It doesn't work. I've been trying it before we got on.

Ellie: yeah, but it might now that we're both on the line. Try it.

MA: (goes ferreting for the image and the fb page.)

Ellie: (watches his screen light up his face in the darkened room, and his eyes dart about effecting the upload.)

MA: I'll laugh if it works just because you're on.

Ellie: How many times do I have to tell you that magic happens when we do this stuff together?

MA: (ignores comment, continues watching screen). Shit. It's working!

Ellie: Told you so.

MA: (coggs turning). Yeah. That's... That's funny!

Now, I know he's still skeptical about my pet theory, and I don't blame him.

BUT - this is the same guy who's last words to me before I headed out to New Orleans was "be careful. There's a lot of magic out there."

Ellie: how do you mean?

MA: Just be careful.

Ellie: ok.... *Mom*.

Tee hee.

<MICHAEL EDIT- She got DEATHLY sick out in New Orleans...just saying.>

So, my secondary hypothesis to this theory is that he doesn't **not** believe in magic.

He just doesn't believe in a particular magic that might be close to home. Happening every day. All around him.

And I'm sure he's not alone. And that's cool.

This author just chooses to see things in terms of multi-dimensional, multi-coloured, magical terms. And I know some of the folks who read our words often do too.

Anyway, regardless of my pet ideas about MA and magic... I hope you've found at least some magic to the story we wrote together for Michael: The Darkness Before the Dawn.

Thanks for reading, and for your continued and awesome support on the reviews and Facebook pages.

You rock!
Ellie x

CONNECT WITH THE AUTHORS

ELL LEIGH CLARKE

Facebook: www.facebook.com/ellleighclarke

MICHAEL ANDERLE

Website: http://kurtherianbooks.com/
Email List: http://kurtherianbooks.com/email-list/
Facebook Here:
https://www.facebook.com/TheKurtherianGambitBooks/

The email list is changing to something…New. I don't have enough details but suffice to say there is so much going on in The Kurtherian Gambit Universe, it needs to go out more often than "when the next book hits."

I hope you enjoy this story!

BOOKS BY ELL LEIGH CLARKE

~KURTHERIAN GAMBIT UNIVERSE~
* With Michael Anderle *

THE ASCENSION MYTH
Awakened (01) - Activated (02) - Called (03) - Sanctioned (04) - Rebirth (05) - Retribution (06) - Cloaked (07) - Rogue Operator (07.5)

CONFESSIONS OF A SPACE ANTHROPOLOGIST
Giles Kurns: Rogue Operator (01)

THE SECOND DARK AGES
The Dark Messiah (01) - The Darkest Night (02) - Darkest Before The Dawn (03)

BOOKS BY MICHAEL ANDERLE

KURTHERIAN GAMBIT SERIES TITLES INCLUDE:

FIRST ARC
Death Becomes Her (01) - Queen Bitch (02) - Love Lost (03) - Bite This (04) - Never Forsaken (05) - Under My Heel (06) - Kneel Or Die (07)

SECOND ARC
We Will Build (08) - It's Hell To Choose (09) - Release The Dogs of War (10) - Sued For Peace (11) - We Have Contact (12) - My Ride is a Bitch (13) - Don't Cross This Line (14)

THIRD ARC
Never Submit (15) - Never Surrender (16) - Forever Defend (17) Might Makes Right (18) - Ahead Full (19) - Capture Death (20) - Life Goes On (21)

THE SECOND DARK AGES
* with Ell Leigh Clarke *
The Dark Messiah (01) - The Darkest Night (02) - Darkest Before The Dawn (03)

THE BORIS CHRONICLES
* with Paul C. Middleton *

Evacuation (1) - Retaliation (2) - Revelations (3) - Redemption (04) *Coming soon*

RECLAIMING HONOR
* with Justin Sloan *

Justice Is Calling (01) - Claimed By Honor (02) - Judgement Has Fallen (03) - Angel of Reckoning (04) - Born Into Flames (05) - Defending The Lost (06) - Saved By Valor (07) - Return of Victory (08)

THE ETHERIC ACADEMY
* with TS PAUL *

Alpha Class (01) - ALPHA CLASS - Engineering (02)

TERRY HENRY "TH" WALTON CHRONICLES
* with Craig Martelle *

Nomad Found (01) - Nomad Redeemed (02) - Nomad Unleashed (03) - Nomad Supreme (04) - Nomad's Fury (05) - Nomad's Justice (06) - Nomad Avenged (07) - Nomad Mortis (08) - Nomad's Force (09) - Nomad's Galaxy (10)

TRIALS AND TRIBULATIONS
* with Natalie Grey *
Risk Be Damned (01) - Damned to Hell (02)

~THE AGE OF MAGIC~

THE RISE OF MAGIC
* with CM Raymond and LE Barbant *
Restriction (01) - Reawakening (02) - Rebellion (03) - Revolution (04) - Unlawful Passage (05) - Darkness Rises (06) - The Gods Beneath (07) - Reborn (08)

THE HIDDEN MAGIC CHRONICLES
* with Justin Sloan *
Shades of Light (01) - Shades of Dark (02) - Shades of Glory (03) - Shades of Justice (04)

STORMS OF MAGIC
* with PT Hylton *
Storm Raiders (01) - Storm Callers (02) - Storm Breakers (03) - Storm Warrior (04)

TALES OF THE FEISTY DRUID
* with Candy Crum *
The Arcadian Druid (01) - The Undying Illusionist (02) - The Frozen Wasteland (03) - The Deceiver (04) - The Lost (05) - The Damned (06)

PATH OF HEROES
* with Brandon Barr *
Rogue Mage (01)

A NEW DAWN
* with Amy Hopkins *
Dawn of Destiny (01) - Dawn of Darkness (02) -
Dawn of Deliverance (03) - Dawn of Days (04)

~THE AGE OF EXPANSION~

THE ASCENSION MYTH
* with Ell Leigh Clarke *
Awakened (01) - Activated (02) - Called (03) - Sanctioned (04) -
Rebirth (05) - Retribution (06) - Cloaked (07) -
Bourne (08)

CONFESSIONS OF A SPACE ANTHROPOLOGIST
* with Ell Leigh Clarke *
Giles Kurns: Rogue Operator (01)

THE UPRISE SAGE
* with Amy Duboff *
Covert Talents (01) - Endless Advance (02) - Veiled Designs (03)

BAD COMPANY
* with Craig Martelle *
The Bad Company (01) - Blockade (02)

THE GHOST SQUADRON
* with Sarah Noffke and J.N. Chaney *
Formation (01) - Exploration (02) - Evolution (03)

VALERIE'S ELITES
* with Justin Sloan and PT Hylton *
Valerie's Elites (01) - Death Defied (02)

ETHERIC ADVENTURES: ANNE AND JINX
* with S.R. Russell *
Etheric Recruit (01) - Etheric Researcher (02)

OTHER BOOKS

* with Craig Martelle & Justin Sloan *
Gateway to the Universe

~THE REVELATIONS OF ORICERAN~
THE LEIRA CHRONICLES
* with Martha Carr *
Waking Magic (1) - Release of Magic (2) - Protection of Magic (3) - Rule of Magic (4) - Dealing in Magic (05)

SHORT STORIES

You Don't Touch John's Cousin

Frank Kurns Stories of the UnknownWorld 01 (7.5)

Bitch's Night Out

Frank Kurns Stories of the UnknownWorld 02 (9.5)

* With Natalie Grey *

Bellatrix

Frank Kurns Stories of the Unknownworld 03 (13.25)

AUDIOBOOKS

Available at Amazon, Audible.com and iTunes

Made in the USA
Middletown, DE
07 October 2020